Praise for *Season's Revenge*

"There are many pleasures on display in this excellent new mystery: Characters leap from the page and lodge instantly into your mind, a plot that manages to be outrageous and logical at the same time, a brisk and pungent writing style that suits the story perfectly. But it's the sharply evocative sense of place that will probably grip readers hardest and hold them the longest."
—*Chicago Tribune*

"A satisfying mystery with a clever plot, engaging protagonist, and believable dialogue. And Kisor doesn't stop there. He adds a nice love story and even tosses in a little homespun Christmas cheer. An impressive debut."
—*Booklist*

"A solid mystery debut."
—*Publishers Weekly*

"Kisor effectively evokes his setting and the attractive pave of life there."
—*Kirkus Reviews*

"Kisor has written a book that one imagines will please his colleagues in the literary community, as well as a good number of mystery fans. Season's Revenge is a light, enjoyable mystery, with a deft use of setting, realistic and intriguing characters, and a plot that is interesting and direct."
—*Associated Press*

"The plot of *Season's Revenge* presents some unique elements. . . . Great attention to detail."
—*The Mystery Reader* (4 stars)

"As compelling and intriguing a mystery as I've read in as long as I can remember. . . . It is a wonderful book that exists on a number of levels. It takes me to a place—the Upper Peninsula of Michigan—that Henry evokes in a way that I feel like I have been there." —Rich Kogan, *WGN Radio* (Chicago)

"A winner . . . Kisor has crafted a compelling mystery, braiding many strands of plot into a satisfying story."
—reviewingtheevidence.com

"The plot is taut and the characters very well drawn."
—*Kaw Valley Senior Monthly*

SEASON'S REVENGE

* * * *

HENRY KISOR

A TOM DOHERTY ASSOCIATES BOOK

New York

SEASON'S REVENGE: A CHRISTMAS STORY

Copyright © 2003 by Henry Kisor

A Forge Book
Published by Tom Doherty Associates, LLC
175 Fifth Avenue
New York, NY 10010

www.tor.com

Forge® is a registered trademark of Tom Doherty Associates, LLC.

ISBN 0-765-34587-0
EAN 976-0765-034587-5

First edition: October 2003
First mass market edition: November 2004

Printed in the United States of America

0 9 8 7 6 5 4 3 2 1

For Vicki

SEASON'S REVENGE

The people to whom I was born had lived here before fiercer tribes from the East chased them onto the Great Plains. From time to time they, too, must have stopped to take in the view. Framed in oak, it would have rivaled the photographic landscapes sold in the hopeful little gift shops that crop up in every dying small town in the Upper Peninsula of Michigan. This one was a panoramic shot of a stand of tall virgin white pine that crowned a rocky escarpment submarining upward from a deep green sea of pine and hemlock, birch and aspen. Just below the escarpment, a lily pond sparkled in the freshening sun. At dawn a light rain had misted the forest, raising the loamy aroma of damp woods. It was a still, cloudless morning in August, the loveliest time of the year.

Blood stained the foreground. Deep claw marks raked the victim's grizzled chest and bearded face, twisted in the rictus of sudden and painful death. His right arm jutted rigidly from the torn sleeping bag in the tatters of his tent, the shoulder deeply punctured, shreds of muscle and sinew dangling from the bone. Under the ruined ripstop nylon, blood puddled in a grisly pudding. Dozens of bear tracks—some of them streaked with crimson, bits of tissue clinging to grooves dug by claws—crisscrossed the moist ground around the campsite.

I looked up and sighed, trying to make sense of what I saw. From the bow of the escarpment jutted a lone wolf pine a hundred feet tall, its windward side limbless from decades of tacking into winter storms howling off Lake Superior. In the second-growth forests of western-most Upper Michigan, wolf pines—aged, once-lordly white pines that escaped the logger's ax because they were just out of easy reach—are symbols of flinty endurance to the people who hang on in this rugged wilderness country where livings are hard to make. The Finns who set-tled here a century ago called that quality *"sisu"*—perseverance, forti-tude, steadfastness. That morning I didn't know I was going to need it in the weeks to come.

Far from the well-trod hiking paths, Big Trees is a favorite retreat of veteran woodsmen who know the most remote crannies of Porcupine County. I'd been there once myself, as the companion of a local hunter. The place lay a rugged three-hour trek through clouds of mosquitoes and biting flies along a rocky, barely visible footpath—little more than a deer trail—branching southwest from an axle-snapping old loggers' track. The latter led into the Ottawa National Forest from a narrow paved road serving as the southern boundary of Wolverine Mountain Wilderness State Park, largest of its kind in all Michigan.

Still sweating from the hike, I stepped back from the tent, squashed a mosquito, and hitched up my gun belt, from which hung a .357 Combat Magnum in a tooled leather holster. No yuppie 9-millimeter Berettas for me, I had vowed when I took the job with the sheriff's department. In the woods, I had reasoned, a man wants a heavy slug carrying lots of foot-pounds of energy. Large animals, especially charg-ing ones, are harder to stop than gangbangers carrying Glocks. Aren't they?

It was not long until I discovered people don't need firearms of any kind in the woods, not unless they're hunting, either for game or for a dangerous felon. The people who live here walk in the forest all the time without weapons, except maybe a four-inch Buck knife, the woods-man's favorite tool, far handier than a cell phone is to a stockbroker. They feel comfortable in their surroundings, and they know the woods intimately. If one should encounter a large animal, both parties to the meeting usually take their respective leaves with as much dignity and alacrity as they can muster. And felons? They're in short supply here in the north woods. There's little to kill for, and less to steal. People here don't have a lot of cash.

In the seven years I'd been a Porcupine County deputy, I hadn't had to draw my weapon except to dispatch an injured deer or wounded dog after a highway encounter. But I hung on to the heavy, old-fashioned .357 anyway, out of either fondness or sheer stubbornness, maybe, or just to be different. Nobody else in the sheriff's department carries a revolver.

Normally a deputy wouldn't be called in for ordinary bear incidents in either the park or the national forest—local rangers and conservation officers take care of matters—but this was a human death, the first bear-related fatality in the county in more than a decade. And the bloodied victim was no hapless tourist but a wealthy eminence of Porcupine County and one of its most celebrated woodsmen.

2 When I was a brand-new deputy, a big-bellied and elderly but strong and rangy man in sportsman's khakis and old-fashioned high-laced boots had paid a visit to my boss, Eli Garrow, the epitome of the good-old-boy country sheriff, more politician than peace officer. As I watched from my desk in the squad room, they met behind closed doors, and when they emerged half an hour later, Garrow looked as if he had swallowed something unpleasant.

I shot a quizzical glance at Joe Koski, the chubby, deceptively cherubic head dispatcher, chief corrections officer, and foremost gossip of the Porcupine County Sheriff's Department. Joe nodded and put a finger to his lips.

"Who's that?" I asked when the principals had disappeared.

"Paul Passoja," Joe said. "He is *the* big cheese of Porcupine County, bigger even than the sheriff or the prosecutor or all the county commissioners rolled together—and, Steve, don't you ever forget it, if you want to keep your job."

Passoja, Joe continued, was the retired founder and president of a big Minnesota paper company who had grown up in Porcupine City, son and heir of Einar Passoja, the county's biggest lumberman and landowner. Like so many who call themselves Porkies, Paul had left his birthplace to make his fortune, adding a large pile of his own to his considerable inheritance. When he retired, he built a huge, showy summer home just east of Porcupine City on prime lakefront land that had been in the family for generations. In it he had installed a succession of young trophy wives—four or five, Joe wasn't sure how many.

Unlike most Upper Michigan timber barons, Einar had not abandoned all the forest land he owned to the taxman once it had been clear-cut, but hung on to prime acreage, including some along the lakeshore. In their monumental log mansion on one of the lots, the Passojas had long spent May through November, wintering at an equally luxurious pile in La Jolla.

Paul Passoja's public face was that of an amiable, unpretentious old-timer. Everybody liked him instantly on first meeting, and so did I. The teenage boys of the county loved him, because for decades he generously taught them the skills of survival in the woods, often taking half-a-dozen hikers at a time deep into the forest for several days' camping. In the last quarter century he had included members of the local Girl Scout troop as well, for he could change with the times.

But beneath that Santa Claus avuncularity, Joe had warned me, lay an iron will that brooked no impudence, especially in the affairs of Porcupine County. Paul Passoja was the wealthiest man in the county, maybe even the whole U.P., and held strong and conservative opinions about its welfare. No politician, not even the U.S. congressman who represented the entire Upper Peninsula, made a move that might affect Porcupine County in the smallest way without first consulting Passoja.

Often deals were struck during one of the all-male retreats he hosted during deer season at Nonesuch, his hunting camp just south of the Wolverine State Park in the western end of the county, close to Big Trees. An invitation to Nonesuch meant you were a man of parts, that you had arrived, for the most powerful person in the county had noticed you. It was a kind of rite of passage in Porcupine County and one I had never undergone, being a lowly deputy sheriff as well as a relative newcomer.

Passoja's campaign contributions were just too hefty for politicians to ignore, and while he exercised his power in an unseen and largely benevolent manner, he also had a way of subtly turning people against those who had offended him with either their actions or their ideas. One soft word and a county commissioner too adventurous with his opinions would find himself isolated, the lamest of lame ducks until the next election turned him out.

Once a year Passoja would hike alone into the most remote corners of the forest and camp, often under the Big Trees he had loved so much in his youth, just to keep up his celebrated forest skills. Out of these trips came captivating stories and pictures of his adventures with wildlife, both as a hunter and as an accomplished amateur photographer. It seemed that he had met just about every inquisitive bear in the park and national forest. Only one man in the county, it seemed, knew more about bears than Paul Passoja did. That was Stan Maki, the Michigan Department of Natural Resources conservation officer who had arrived on the scene shortly after the hikers who discovered the body radioed their grisly discovery to him on their truck's CB.

3   Though he had been officially retired for years—he was in his late seventies, like Passoja—Stan was an unofficial part-timer who almost always was called in whenever a bear became a nuisance. Nobody in the Upper Peninsula was better at handling them than this small, bald, leathery, whipcord-strong and ageless man, so tanned by years in the outdoors that his skin never faded, even in the winter.

He was accompanied by a tall—six-seven, at least—and broad-shouldered lad of nineteen or so, also clad in DNR uniform. "Garrett Morton," Stan said by way of introduction. "Summer ranger. Plays basketball for Kalamazoo."

I shook hands with the blond giant. I'm not a small man, but Garrett towered over me by nearly a head. "Nice to meet you, Garrett," I said. He grinned, his dewy cheeks dimpling, and bobbed his head like an oversized puppy, cheerful and eager to please despite the grim circumstances of the morning. Still a kid, and probably not overly well-upholstered with brains.

Neither of the two middle-aged brothers who had found the body were strangers to me. Like the victim, Frank Metrovich and his younger brother, Bill, both short, squat, solid, hard-working, and public-spirited paper-mill hands, were "good men in the woods," the quiet and rare accolade Upper Peninsula natives give those who know the wilderness intimately. They stood uncertainly to the side of the small clearing, drawn and white, looking ready to part with their breakfasts.

"How'd you come to find him?" I asked the brothers.

"Paul told us in Merle's Café yesterday ago that he was going to Big

Trees," Frank said. "The weather's so great we thought we'd hike in and say hello."

Bill nodded in assent, then sighed. "You know, Steve," he said, "Paul had seemed a little out of it lately. He's getting on to his eighties now and sometimes he gets forgetful. In the space of half an hour he told us three times he was going to Big Trees. Frankly, we were a little worried and wanted to check up on him."

By this time another hiker had trudged up the trail to join the scene. The place was becoming a regular Grand Central.

The newcomer was Hank Heikkila, a slight but immensely strong hermit in his fifties with a long, flowing, untrimmed beard like a Lubavitch Hasid rabbi and the same sour, untrusting view of his fellow man that a Lubavitcher has for the *goyim*. Hank lived in a rude shack deep in the forest on land he sometimes claimed was handed down from his grandfather and sometimes said belonged to a private party who let him live there in exchange for watching the place.

Many of us suspect the shack illegally lay on state forest land, but because Hank led a tough life—a manic-depressive, an off-again, on-again mental patient, from time to time he washed up at a halfway house in Porcupine City—we let him be to make his meager living among the "voices" he said he heard. He called himself a trapper, but—legal fur-bearing mammals being rare in this country and the trapping season quite short—he really scratched a few dollars together now and then as a woodsy jack-of-all-trades, as did so many people in this land of high unemployment. Now and then Hank cut a little aspen pulpwood from the national forest to sell to the mill. Once in a while he carpentered a shed for a landowner. I suspected he grew a little pot, too, mainly for himself.

In his cups he often claimed to be descended not only from Finns but also *voyageurs* from Quebec who in the seventeenth century left their long canoes on the beach, settled in this country and intermarried with the local Ojibwa. He spoke only when spoken to, and always in an almost inaudible growl. His neighbors, however, did not fear him. Frightening as he seemed to the uninitiated, he never turned violent. Though we suspected him of poaching, he took a deer quite legally every season—the resident license fee is only thirteen dollars—with a

.45–70 Springfield, a heavy, long, cumbersome single-shot Army rifle with a trapdoor breech that was obsolete before the Spanish-American War. His transportation was a 1960s-vintage Ford pickup so rusty the only place solid enough to hold the license plate was the rear window.

"Hi, Hank," I said.

Grunt.

"How'd you hear about this?"

Mutter.

"Hank, I'm talking to you!"

"Scanner," he said finally.

Yes—the rural jungle telegraph. Porcupine County lay way too far out in the boonies for reliable cell-phone coverage. Some people owned CBs, but everybody had a radio scanner. I did, too. We listened to the road commission, especially in winter, when we wondered where the plows were and when they'd arrive to free us from our snowy prisons. We eavesdropped on PorTran, the state-subsidized commission that sent buses all over the county to pick up riders on demand. We listened to ambulance runs, to lake freighters and pleasure boats calling the Porcupine River swing-bridge tender, and to the operations at the sprawling paper mill. Everybody listened in as Joe Koski dispatched deputies everywhere. Hank, I suspected, owned a scanner just to keep one ear on the doings of the law while he performed the duties of the lawless.

Stan broke the mood. "This campsite is set up good and proper," he observed in a crisply professional tone that drew us all back to earth. "Tent well away from the cook site. Food pack hanging in the air."

Passoja had pitched his nylon backpacker's tent a good twenty yards from the bare flat rock where he had prepared his last meal. His food cache dangled fifteen feet in the air, suspended on a rope between two tall aspens. But tracks and claw marks from a large black bear—"a mature one, at least four hundred pounds," Stan estimated—lay scattered around the tent, not the cooking area or under the food pack.

"Why'd the bear go after the tent instead?" Stan asked, echoing the thoughts of everyone present. "That's not how they behave. They go for the food."

"No weapon?" I asked, already knowing the answer. Like most

people in these parts, Passoja never carried a firearm—unless he was hunting.

"None," Stan said.

It didn't look like a crime scene, but I am a cop, and cops always process scenes of violent death as if they were homicides. Nobody knows what really happened until all the facts are in.

So I did what cops do. I donned latex gloves and scanned the scene for clues. Dozens of them—platter-sized and claw-tipped—stared back at me.

Stan beckoned. "Look here, Steve," he said, crouching over the damp loam. "See those? The slash across them?" A faint raised diagonal line crossed the indentations made by the bear's left front paw. "An old scar, probably from a trap. That'll identify the bear when we catch him."

With a Polaroid camera I snapped pictures of the tracks, the body, and the tent, carefully peeling back the nylon shreds after taking each photo, until Passoja's ruined corpse lay fully exposed. Then I saw a few dark quarter-sized spots on the nylon, one a splatter, near a corner of the tent by the entry flap. I sniffed. Bacon grease.

"Hey, Stan," I said. He squatted and nodded as he saw the spots. I photographed them.

A tiny gray lump lay almost hidden in the dust by the tent entry. I picked it up. A shred of bacon.

It figured. "Nothing like coffee and bacon on a cold evening in the woods," Passoja often had said. He was an old-fashioned woodsman—none of that high-tech freeze-dried adventure-backpackers' stuff for him, although, out of respect for the danger of forest fires, he carried a modern one-burner butane stove. He always packed a small iron skillet and a rasher into the woods, and anybody fortunate enough to camp with him would spend the evening wreathed in the world's most delicious aroma.

I placed the scrap of bacon into a tiny flat-lidded tin that had once held a dozen cough drops—I save little containers like Sucrets tins and photo film cans, intending to use them to hold small things like fishhooks and screws, but never seem to get around to it. They pile up on my workbench, in my glove compartment, in my kitchen drawer, the detritus of good intentions and poor follow-through. I slid the tin into my shirt pocket.

"Looks like Paul might have carried his supper to the tent while he got something else and accidentally spilled some," Stan said soberly. "Maybe he wasn't even aware of it. But the odor would have attracted the bear during the night, and it would have tried to rip into the tent after more food. Probably Paul woke up and struggled to escape from his sleeping bag, and the surprised bear did what comes natural, defending itself. This isn't the first time something like this has happened."

I nodded. I am a great believer in Occam's razor, the adage that the simplest explanation for an event is most likely the true one.

By then another deputy had arrived with a litter. She was Mary Larch, the department's sole female sworn officer, a rookie with less than a year's experience behind a star. She and I worked the same eight-to-five shift. I covered the north and west of the county while she patrolled the east and south. We encountered each other frequently, both in the office and on patrol, especially when one of us needed backup.

Mary was a native of Porcupine County, a determined late bloomer in her mid-thirties, and studied criminal justice part-time at the university in Hancock. She was small but rugged, pretty, and very ambitious, and I was sure she'd go on to bigger and better things in larger departments. I admired her.

"Need help, Steve?" she asked brightly, always ready to pitch in in whatever way she could. "Joe thought you might. I brought a four-wheeler, but it's about a mile from here—I couldn't get it any farther in than Mills Creek."

The sheriff's department kept a powerful four-wheel-drive all-terrain vehicle in the bed of a pickup truck to get around in the boonies, but the faint track from the creek to Big Trees was too steep and rocky even for it.

"Nope, we're done here," I said. "We're ready to zip him up."

Stan and Garrett rolled Passoja into a body bag and levered him onto the litter. Even with Mary and Hank helping the big basketball player, it would be a laborious hike through the forest to the four-wheeler for the half hour's ride to Porcupine County Memorial Hospital. There Fred Miller, one of the county's two physicians and its elected coroner, would pronounce the death.

"I'll take the tent," Stan said, "for the dogs."

I nodded. He'd hire a local farmer and his brace of bloodhounds to hunt down the bear, and he needed the tent to establish a working scent of both bear aura—those animals stink mightily—and Passoja's blood.

Stan gathered the gory mess into a large wad and stuffed it inside a plastic supermarket bag. When he returned to headquarters, he'd arrange transport of the dogs and their handler to Big Trees to start the search.

"You'll come?" Stan asked.

"Sure thing," I said. It was my case, after all, and I always enjoyed hikes in the woods for any reason, any reason at all. Wilderness is a purgative. Every time I return from a walk in the woods I feel clean, all the poison scoured out of my system.

When I finally emerged from the rocky brush and returned to the department's Explorer, I radioed ahead to Joe Koski, asking him to tell the hospital that the body was on its way.

4 At noon I left the sheriff's department and drove down to the DNR office near Lake Gogebic in Gogebic County, well outside my jurisdiction, to meet Stan and the rest of the search party. Though I was still in uniform, I was now technically a volunteer civilian, not a law officer. Mary Larch had driven back to Porcupine City to break the news to Marjorie Passoja, Paul's gorgeous young wife, that she was a widow. I knew Mary would be gentle and caring. She and Marj were good friends.

As I pulled into the parking lot, I saw that the news of Passoja's death had spread rapidly across the western Upper Peninsula. Fifty or sixty men of all ages milled about, their faces shining with eagerness, some sprawled on the benches in front of the office and some lounging in the beds of their pickup trucks. All were armed with high-velocity rifles, some of them with huge scopes. Clearly they were out after big game.

Stan whistled from the office doorway. "Your attention, please, guys!" he shouted. After the men had swiftly gathered about him like kindergartners around a teacher, he laid down the law in softly reasonable but firm tones.

"Thank you for coming here to volunteer," he said, "but the truth is everything is under control. The dogs have found the trail and the rangers are closing in. A crowd's not a good idea during a rogue-bear hunt. We appreciate your concern, but please go home."

Actually, Stan told me after the disappointed volunteers had pulled out of the lot, only two men—the dogs' handler and an armed park ranger—were in hot pursuit of the bear, or at least as hot a pursuit as can be mounted after a swift quarry in thick woods. They had started from Big Trees late in the morning and, reporting their positions by radio, were moving swiftly southwestward in the direction of Match-wood, a small town nine miles from the wild place where Paul Passoja had died. The trail, they said, was hot and the dogs spirited.

"You don't want all those untrained fellows with rifles crashing through brush scaring the bear and maybe shooting each other," he said. I nodded. Pounding the woods after dangerous quarry is not a job for people without experience at it.

"All we need is four who know what they're doing to help the trackers once they locate the bear and to take it down. And that's you, me, Garrett, and that Commando for Christ over there." Stan pointed across the parking lot at a short, muscular blond fellow, dressed in faded desert fatigues and bearing a heavy scoped rifle.

"Ah." In southern Porcupine County lay a large training camp for missionaries operated by a religious organization that was nondenomi-national but so fundamentalist that mainstream evangelicals raised their eyebrows at it. It trained young men (women need not apply) in the arts of wilderness survival, using rigorous techniques borrowed from the Army Rangers and Navy SEALs, even teaching the campers to fly and to fix their own aircraft at the jet-capable concrete airstrip in the middle of the camp. Graduates could go anywhere in the world, win souls for Christ, and emerge alive. I had no doubt that they could break Satan's neck if they had to. We called them "Commandos for Christ" behind their backs, and the sobriquet wasn't far wrong.

I'd met a few of the polite, well-scrubbed missionary cadets, who asked almost immediately whether my soul had been saved but did not press the issue when I changed the subject. They impressed me. If any-body had the physical and emotional endurance needed to run down a rogue bear, they did. Single-mindedness can be an asset. No wonder Stan had called the camp and asked for its best man with a rifle.

I introduced myself. "Gary Keefe," he said, his sky-blue eyes gazing directly into my dark brown ones. He shook my hand with a grasp as gentle as his smile. I was grateful for that. His palm felt like boulders. He looked to be in his late twenties and carried himself with ramrod military bearing, his blond hair clipped into a brush cut with whitewalls.

"Let's saddle up," said Stan. "Get your weapons."

From the Explorer I fished not a rifle but a police riot gun—a short-barreled 12-gauge pump shotgun—and a box of deer slugs. The power-ful rifle Keefe carried would be deadly at a distance, but a riot gun with its slow but heavy slug was unbeatable at close-in work. You could knock down a wall with it. Stan and Garrett both were armed with tran-quilizer dart rifles and huge .44 Magnum revolvers on their hips. We bundled our arsenal into the back of a wrinkled green DNR Suburban, and departed the parking lot, Stan and Garrett in front, Keefe and I in the back.

"Do we know anything about the bear besides it's a big one and has a scar on its paw?" I asked Stan as we pulled onto the highway.

"There's a fair possibility it's one of the dozens of adult bears in the Wolverines and that it drifted outside the park," Stan said, "although it could also have wandered in from elsewhere. If we can, we'll try to put it down with a dart and look over its fur and claws. 'Course, if it comes at us, we'll have to kill it. We will anyway if we find human blood or tis-sue. Can't relocate a bear that has tasted human blood."

The radio on the Suburban's dash came alive. "Fred to Stan," said the disembodied voice of Fred Mitchell, the chief DNR ranger at Gogebic. "We're on M-28 four miles west of Matchwood. The bear's crossed the highway and gone into the state forest. Trail's still hot. We're not far behind, but he's moving fast."

Stan stopped the Suburban, pulled out a topographical map from the glove compartment, and spread it on the dash. At the point on the state highway where the trackers had reported in, I saw, the state forest is only half a mile wide before it ends in a vast expanse of scrubland, huge stump fields denuded of their trees nearly a century ago. Old log-ging roads crissrcross the scrub.

"We'll cut around here on that track and park at that clearing south of that copse, get out, and wait for them to come to us," Stan said, pointing to a spot on the map just a mile and a half south of the high-way. "If the bear changes its bearing"—if he noticed the inadvertent pun, he didn't show it—"we can move quickly in either direction."

Stan would have made a great tactical general, I thought as the Sub-urban turned off the road and bounced down a barely passable logging track. The Patton at the wheel drove hell-for-leather after the enemy as if the Suburban were an armored personnel carrier, his vehicle creaking and groaning as it jounced and jolted. Actually we were doing less than twenty miles an hour, probably ten too fast for sensibility. The Suburban wasn't built for that kind of abuse, but Stan was retired and didn't have to answer to DNR headquarters in Lansing for damage to official equipment.

"Jesus!" I said as the Suburban jarred across a deep rut, the seat belt saving me from bashing my head on the roof.

That was Gary's cue. "Have you met Christ?" he asked solicitously, as if we were sitting in a parsonage drinking tea instead of bouncing around the backwoods. I almost laughed, but won the fight with my face.

"Gary, this isn't the time or place!" Stan said, chuckling, as he wrestled the wheel, the Suburban's right front wheel scraping a boulder by the side of the track. Had the vehicle had any hubcaps at the start of this hunt, it would have lost them long ago.

Keefe did not press the question but stared ahead serenely.

"Jesus comes to all who seek," he said. "We'll talk about it later, okay?"

I ducked instinctively as the Suburban crashed through a thick tangle of alder branches hanging across the track.

"What's a man of the cloth doing bearing arms?" I asked, just to be provocative. Keefe's question had irked me a little. I don't care for religiosity displayed on the sleeve in public. One's faith, I felt, ought to be practiced privately, like sex, or at least in church where it wouldn't offend nonbelievers.

"God gave us dominion," Keefe said, fervent certainty edging his quiet voice with steel. Passion like that scares me sometimes.

"Stan to Fred," the old bear ranger said into the mike. "Where are you?"

The tracker gave his map coordinates.

"You're just half a mile north of us," Stan said. "What's the bear's heading?"

"Directly at you, it looks like," Fred said.

"We'll be ready. Keep your heads down." Stan didn't want the trackers caught in a cross fire. "Out."

Stan stopped the truck at the edge of a large clearing and opened the door. "Let's roll!"

"Isn't that what we've been doing since Gogebic?" I asked as I stepped out,

"You know what I mean. Move over there, please."

We spread out just off the track in the waist-high brush in a skirmish line not more than twenty yards wide, Stan and Garrett at the edges with their dart rifles, Keefe and I in the middle, directly across from a wide promontory of trees jutting from the woods about fifty yards away. I crouched slightly in front of Keefe, ready to fire down the bear's throat if it came out of the tree line directly ahead. Keefe stood erect, rifle at his shoulder, arm through the sling, ready to pivot in either direction.

Not five minutes passed before we heard the bloodhounds, their faint baying masked by the forest. "Stan to Fred," the ranger said quietly into his handheld radio. "We hear you now."

"Fred to Stan. If you're where we think you are, the bear's gonna be upon you in less than a minute."

Now we could hear it crashing through the brush, the crackling of branches growing louder with each passing second. I stared straight ahead, the shotgun held loosely in my hands. Where would the bear emerge? The promontory of trees that jutted from the forest was about two hundred yards long from edge to edge. If it came out of the woods directly in front of me, I'd have a clear shot, but not much time to get it off. A bear can cover a lot of ground in a second or two.

I could feel Keefe behind me, breathing softly but regularly, coiled like a rattler ready to strike. At the left end of the skirmish line Stan crouched in tall grass, his dart gun poised, his holster unbuckled. To the right Garrett stood nervously behind a small aspen, dart rifle in his left hand, revolver in his right, its muzzle pointing forward. He was taking no chances.

"There it is!" Stan cried.

The bear erupted from the woods far to the left at the base of the promontory a good seventy-five yards distant, well out of dart-gun and deer-slug range, heading slightly away from us, aiming at full gallop for another patch of woods to our left. In the space of a tenth of a second I took in these things: First, the bear was big, almost grizzly-sized. Second, it was half hidden by brush and tall grass. Third, even for an expert rifleman it was going to be an almost impossible full-deflection shot, through patches of saplings and brush that would knock any bullet from its path.

"Stay down!" Keefe shouted just above me, rifle butt in his shoulder and eye at the scope as he swiveled smoothly from the waist, leading the bear with his crosshairs. The crack of the heavy cartridge stunned me, but not so much that I could not see the bear leap, then tumble end over end through the grass, fetching up in a twitching heap.

Stan, Garrett, and I stood up and plunged through the brush to the bear. It lay motionless. After a sensible interval, no more than two minutes, Stan approached the animal, revolver trained upon its massive head. "Dead," he said, just as the bloodhounds emerged at full bay from the tree line, Fred Mitchell and the farmer who owned the dogs close behind. The latter yanked back the hounds and spoke sharply to them. They sat, quivering with excitement, their eyes fixed on the carcass.

Stan picked up the bear's left front paw and turned it over. "It's our boy, sure enough," he said. "Look at that scar."

The dirty scarlet sheen on the bear's jaws and chest, I thought, doubtless would prove to be Paul Passoja's blood.

For a moment we all contemplated the bear. Then I said, "Keefe, where did you learn to shoot like that?"

"Marines," he said. "Discharged last winter."

"Afghanistan?" I asked.

"Yeah. First Marine Expeditionary Force. Recon."

I whistled. Gary Keefe had been one of the elite, a highly trained killer, probably a sniper. I wondered how this man had come to discover Christ and become a missionary.

"Semper Fi," said Stan quietly, extending his hand to Keefe. Stan had been a Marine in Korea.

"Semper Fi," Keefe replied.

After a moment Stan said, "This bear has to be a known bear. It wore a radio collar some time ago—see this groove in the fur? They often rub the collars off after a while. No ear tags, though. This bear's never worn any. Feel the ears."

I rubbed an ear between thumb and finger, searching for ridges of scar tissue left by staples.

"Weird," said Stan. "Researchers almost always tag the bears for easier ID when they collar them."

"Where could it have come from?"

"Wisconsin, probably, or even Minnesota. Rogues often travel long distances."

Garrett, who had barely been heard from during the entire operation, stood slack-jawed, gazing alternately at the bear and at Keefe. A mixture of terror and elation crossed his face, enlivening the dull expression he had worn all day. Still a boy, I thought.

Nobody said anything more as we dragged the smelly carcass to the Suburban, and hoisted it in with the help of a block and tackle.

Just before getting into the truck I spotted a small bear sitting on its butt like a little Buddha in the middle of a thimbleberry patch, unconcernedly munching the sweet fruit while watching us intently. The cinnamon fur that marked the typical black bear's muzzle extended over his face past his eyes and almost to his ears, giving him the look of a wise and worldly chimpanzee. The bear gazed at me steadily, not at all frightened or wary, as if it were the most natural thing in the world to share this small space in the forest with human beings. I nudged Stan and pointed.

He chuckled. "About sixteen months old. Momma probably kicked him out of the nest last week. Not too bright, is he? That shot should have scared him all the way into Ironwood County."

The little bear watched steadily as we climbed into the Suburban. As Stan wheeled the truck, clanking under its new burden, around the ruts and headed back to headquarters, I looked back. The bear had disappeared into the woods.

Later, on my way back to Porcupine City in the Explorer, the radio crackled.

"Steve?" said Koski. "We just heard from Doc Miller. He says he doesn't think Passoja's wounds killed him. He's sending the body to Baraga for an autopsy." Dr. Miller was an internist, and questionable deaths were sent fifty-three miles east to be investigated by Dr. John Oakes, a certified pathologist and the medical examiner of Baraga County.

The shadows were growing long when I arrived at my cabin on the lakeshore. I patted my shirt pocket and found the tin with the bacon shard. I had forgotten to turn it in at the sheriff's office with the photographs of the scene that morning, but I could do that the next day. I popped it into the freezer between a couple of frozen trout I had caught in a mountain stream a few weeks before, and fell wearily into bed.

5 The next morning Dr. Oakes faxed his report to the sheriff's office. A massive heart attack had killed Paul Passoja. His seventy-nine-year-old arteries had been clogged from a lifetime of steak and potatoes. It had just been a matter of time before sudden stress did him in. He probably was dead before the bear's teeth and claws ripped into him.

What's more, Dr. Oakes said, he had found in Passoja's brain scattered gray plaques that were unmistakable evidence of encroaching Alzheimer's disease. This aging man definitely had not been in full ownership of his faculties. The Metrovich brothers had been right.

Eli Garrow nodded expressionlessly as he slipped the fax into the Passoja case file, salting away the whole in a cabinet. Without a doubt, I thought, Passoja's death had relieved him of a huge political pain in the ass.

Eli, the second most powerful politician in Porcupine County—only Garner Armstrong, the county prosecutor, outranks him—is a short, bald, and bullet-headed man with a luxurious iron-gray handlebar mustache, so broad-shouldered and big-bellied that two of him could span a barn door with room to spare. While all his deputies wear solid brown uniforms, Eli stands out in a blindingly white shirt and gold braid as befits the boss. "The Target," we call him behind his back, for he'd be the first one the bad guys would try to take out during a firefight—if we were ever to have one.

Still, as country officeholders go, Eli is popular with the voters—so popular that he barely has to break a sweat running for reelection. He is surprisingly honest and upright for a career politician, though over the years what passes for scandal in the Upper Peninsula has slightly tarnished his reputation. When Eli hired his own wife as jail matron and took on a nephew as a deputy, the Republican candidate gave him a run for his money in the next election. Another time Eli used a brand-new departmental four-wheeler for deer hunting, thinking it was a perk of the job, but the county board roasted him over the coals for that. As a deputy in his forties, he had been a notorious womanizer, but now, close to retirement, he rested on the laurels of that reputation, even poking fun at it.

A born campaigner with a folksy manner, he calls women of all ages "young lady" and greets men with "my fine man" or "young man" as he pumps their hands, one meaty paw on their shoulders. But nobody mistakes his cheeriness for insincerity. For all his commodious ego, Eli loves being a politician. Most people can't help liking a man who enjoys his job so. Small children and dogs adore him.

As for me, he is sometimes irritating, but I feel benign tolerance toward him as long as he stays out of my way, which he does, mostly. He's rarely in the office, preferring to cruise the county pressing flesh, and he believes in the chain of command, dealing with his troops mainly through Gil O'Brien, the undersheriff.

Gil is the real boss of the department. Tall and rangy, he is a former Army drill instructor and a dour martinet who, unlike his hail-fellow-well-met boss, thinks the department should be run like the military. He is very good at his job and is highly respected by fellow law enforcement officers all over the state. He is also brilliant at writing grants to wrest funds out of state coffers for departmental equipment—grants Eli, ever the beamish pol, tends to claim credit for. And Gil is a by-the-book stickler. Thanks to his meticulousness, judges and juries rarely found fault with the Porcupine County Sheriff's Department. I'm very careful around him.

"There you go," Gil said. "It's cut and dried—Passoja had a heart attack during the struggle with the bear, which happened because he got old and demented, and Doc Miller's going to rule it death by misadventure. Case closed."

I nodded. Anyone with an ounce of sense would agree with that conclusion. Not being of sound mind, the victim forgot his own teachings, carried his dinner to his tent and spilled bacon on it. Bear smelled the grease, bear came to get it, there was a confrontation, and a man died. Very simple.

Or too simple? A small cloud began to shadow my thoughts.

"At least Passoja died doing something he loved," Gil suddenly added. "Be nice if that happened to us, too."

I forgot my doubt and winced inwardly. This banal sentiment always turns my stomach. How can anyone declare what goes through another man's mind when he meets violent death? Did Passoja feel joy at struggling against the sharp claws and teeth of a huge animal with halitosis? Did he exult when pain tore through his heart? I kept this thought to myself. For all his brisk competence the stern undersheriff was not an empathetic man, and my observation would have been lost on him.

Not for many days would my reservation about Passoja's death again work its way into the sunlight.

6 At two o'clock in the afternoon on the fifth day after Paul Passoja was found dead, Porcupine City buried him. It seemed that not only the entire county but also the whole Upper Peninsula turned out for the funeral, and the full complement of the sheriff's department was called in to handle the hundreds of cars from in and out of town that arrived at Holy Redeemer Lutheran Church, the county's largest and wealthiest place of worship. I pulled duty at the entry to the parking lot.

When Eli Garrow arrived in his chief's cruiser—the department's newest, never used on patrol and kept shiny and waxed by the deputy with the least seniority—I waved him to a VIP slot close to the lot's entrance. Though the lot was nearly as large as the asphalt meadow in front of the town's supermarket, it was filling up fast and we'd have to direct cars to the city's Little League field next to the church.

He emerged puffing from the cruiser resplendent in dress uniform and all the decorations he had gathered in a lifetime. I could have sworn he wore his Boy Scout medals among the gaudy ribbons and brass gongs bestowed upon him by sovereign bodies ranging from the Chamber of Commerce to the Elks. He clanked when he walked.

"Look at all these cars," Eli marveled. "Bet half the people have come to say good-bye to Paul and the other half just to make sure he's dead."

I chuckled dutifully at the boss's joke.

Then I had to hasten as two long black limos pulled in, full of politicians from Lansing as well as the Upper Peninsula congressman, Geoffrey Armstrong. A cynical thought fleeted across my mind: they were there to make sure Paul Passoja stayed buried.

In a few minutes Marjorie Passoja arrived in her gray Mercedes sedan—no ride in a common undertaker's limo for her—with Mary Larch at the wheel. I saluted respectfully and directed the Mercedes to the place of honor in front of the pathway to the church. I opened the curbside door for Marjorie and whispered, "My condolences, ma'am," as she emerged.

"Thank you, deputy," she said in a tiny voice, dry-eyed, her face composed, touching my sleeve gently. She looked straight ahead, almost rigidly, as if trying to control her emotions.

She wore a tailored black jacket and sheath that could not subdue her exuberant curves. Marjorie Keenan Passoja was a classic Southern California beauty in her mid-thirties, and she always dressed like one, in smart designer clothes that would not have looked out of place in a Maryland mall. For this reason alone she stood out in Porcupine County like a swan among mallards. For this reason, too, people in these parts were a little wary of her, just as they watched themselves around her husband.

But she never struck me as putting on airs among the peasants. Unlike many of the wealthy women who summered on Lake Superior—especially the tanned and wrinkled matrons who had married money and who couldn't go out of the house unless they were decorated with at least ten pounds of gold and diamonds—she never wore jewelry, not even a wedding ring. Nor was she wreathed in clouds of expensive but cloying perfume; up close, I am sure, she would have smelled simply of soap.

Whenever I encountered her, either during official duties or not, she often just seemed painfully shy. At social events, I noticed, the Passojas arrived as a couple but did not mix as one. Marjorie gravitated toward the women while her husband peeled off to talk to the men. Only at the end of the evening would they get together again—to depart. That certainly was not unusual, of course, in a social milieu that still believed in old-fashioned gender roles. Porcupine County is nothing if not conservative.

As she walked into the church Mary supported Marjorie's left elbow gently, and nodded to me as they passed. I didn't think it odd, as some did, that a local working-class girl like Mary would mix with out-of-town gentry like Marjorie.

Marjorie was Porcupine County's Lady Bountiful. It seemed that her main task as Paul Passoja's consort was to bestow their charity on the most deserving institutions in the county. And that they did. But a string came with each boon: A large brass plaque bearing the legend GIFT OF PAUL AND MARJORIE PASSOJA—Paul's name always preceded hers—had to be affixed somewhere visible. Sometimes the thing had to be named for them: The new wing on the county's nursing home. The MRI scanner room in the county hospital. The gorgeous stained-glass window bearing the image of Christ on the cross in the nave of the church. Their gifts had to be large, imposing, and enduring. They were generous people and they wanted everyone to know it.

I knew, however, that one of Marjorie's pet projects was the Andie Davis Home, the county's only battered women's shelter. She had given a considerable pile of money—I suspected it was her own, not her husband's—to buy and fix up an old motel in a hamlet in the eastern part of the county, but had not insisted that it carry the Passoja name. Indeed, Marjorie had not mentioned that at all, according to Mary, who volunteered there during her off hours and had befriended the reticent Californian.

Soon the flood of arriving cars slowed to a trickle, then stopped. While another deputy kept watch upon the lot, I sneaked into the sanctuary of the crowded church just in time for the eulogy. Geoffrey Armstrong, Paul Passoja's man in Washington, did the honors, and he pulled out all the stops. Passoja's generosity was prominently mentioned, and so was his probity, his courage, his saintliness, and so on. It was a nauseating performance even for a beholden politician, and the congregation stirred restlessly.

So did I, standing in the doorway of an anteroom just off the sanctuary. As Armstrong droned on, filling the air with a fog of insincerity, I looked about the room and directly into Joseph's eyes. This was a wooden Joseph, a full-sized effigy hewn from white pine a century ago by an immigrant Finnish logger who had created the figures for the Christmas crèche placed out front in the snow every December since then. The flat, oblique planes of Joseph's face, stained a deep walnut, bespoke a folk artist of genuine talent who had carved it as a labor of love. So did the faces of the Magi, whose gentle expressions, molded by the dim shadows inside the anteroom, appeared sour and nauseated as Armstrong phumphered away. I took comfort in their rustic honesty as I sneaked a look at Marjorie and Mary, sitting alone in a front pew before the casket, all of the elect occupying rows behind them. They gazed stonily, unmoving, at the altar.

It was almost with simultaneous sighs of relief that the pastor launched the crowd into a hymn and I slipped out the door to take up my station.

An hour later, one of the last vehicles in the departing trickle was a newish but muddy brown Ford van, PORCUPINE COUNTY HISTORICAL SOCIETY emblazoned on its front doors.

"Hi, Ginny!" I said as the driver paused on the way out.

"Steve," Ginny Fitzgerald replied with a brilliant smile.

I couldn't think of a thing to say.

"See you tomorrow night," Ginny said. "Bring a good appetite."

I nodded dumbly, a silly grin on my face. She drove away.

"You bet," I finally said as the van turned at the corner and disappeared.

7

Virginia Antala Fitzgerald is a sturdy, striking green-eyed redhead in her late thirties, all legs and bosom in snug jeans and loose flannel lumberjack shirts, with the kind of scrubbed, freckled beauty that is insulted by makeup. She is almost a ringer for Maureen O'Hara, the gorgeous film star of the 1940s and 1950s, and every time *Miracle on 34th Street* airs on late-night TV during the holidays, I am startled by the resemblance.

Ginny is by profession a historian and the director—indeed, the only paid employee—of the Porcupine County Historical Society. She had grown up in Porcupine City, a third-generation Finnish-American, daughter of a mining engineer. In her early teens the Lone Pine Mine, the last working copper mine and smelter in Michigan, suffered one of its periodic shutdowns, and she moved with her family to Arizona. When she turned eighteen, her father sent her east to college, and there she met her husband. Not long after she was widowed in her early thirties, she returned childless to the county of her birth to start life again.

These scant facts I had heard from Joe Koski. "She hasn't been home but a year, Steve, and she already knows everything about everybody in Porcupine County," said Joe when I inquired about the pretty redhead in charge of the benefit supper I had attended at the Historical Society. "Tell her your name, and if you're from here, she'll rattle off your family tree all the way back to Adam. But I hear she's a grieving widow still and a hard nut to crack—a lot of local men have asked her out, but she always says no. Don't break your back trying to get to first base."

That exchange had occurred when I had been a Porcupine County deputy only three months. I had spoken briefly with Ginny at the supper, attendance at which seemed a good way for a greenhorn law-enforcement officer to learn something about his jurisdiction. I was fresh out of the army and starting a new life myself.

From time to time I had run into her at official functions as well as the society's museum, a cavernous former supermarket in Porcupine City whose donated purple paint, slathered on by volunteers, made it leap out from the weathered, whitewashed wood of the rest of downtown. Later, when I had at last sunk formal roots into the county by buying a little four-room cabin on the lakeshore eight miles west of Porcupine City, she plucked its history out of the air one afternoon.

"Built in 1946 by August Kokkanen, a first-generation Finn, out of the last cedars logged from what is now the state park," she said briskly, unconsciously curling a loose strand of hair behind her right ear. That habit, I would soon learn, meant she wanted to change the subject, to be sharp and businesslike. But at that moment the gesture was immediately endearing, and it caused my heart to do a somersault.

"Kokkanen floated the logs down the shore to the property and let them season for two years before constructing the cabin for Milton Browne, a businessman from Stevens Point, Wisconsin. Browne summered there on the lakeshore with his family for half a century. The cabin was originally rustic, with no running water and only an outhouse, but over the years he improved the place, putting in a well, plumbing, and electricity. When Browne died, having outlived his wife, the family put the cabin up for sale, and it was vacant for a year before you bought it.

"You've got a good place—they don't build them like that anymore, especially that beautiful stone fireplace. It'll last at least another fifty years."

"How did you know all that?" I marveled.

"It's my job," she said, with a brilliant eye-crinkling smile that reduced me to awkward shyness. At that moment I vowed to break through her reserve if I could.

Hers was a subtle aloofness. Ginny really was a friendly, generous soul, openhearted with everybody who came to her cluttered office at the Historical Society. But whenever I—or anyone else—tried to get her to talk about herself, let alone ask for a date, she changed the subject with a warm smile, a gentle but firm hand and a quick tuck of hair behind her ear.

But I had all the time in the world. After carefully managing just to happen upon Ginny at Merle's Café at the same hour half a dozen Sunday mornings in a row and having breakfast at her table, ostensibly to absorb a few more details about Porcupine County history, I suggested that the following Friday evening we try the venison at a new restaurant specializing in wild game that had just opened outside town. "Why not?" she had said after hesitating only a moment. "It'll be good research for me."

That was the camel's nose under the tent, and slowly I had shoved it farther in. Our "dates"—if you can call them that—had been both informal and impromptu, little more than two people agreeing to share the same space at the same time—but at last she had invited me home for dinner.

8

After the funeral I returned to the sheriff's department to attack my never-ending paperwork, then after quitting time stopped at Hobbs' Bar, Grill and Northwoods Museum for a six-pack.

Hobbs' is a cavernous two-story Main Street storefront right across the parking lot from the Historical Society. Its splintery pine walls are festooned with old skis, snowshoes, beaver hides, and rusty nineteenth-century firearms, none of which seems to have much value except to yuppie lounge designers in Chicago, who always are trying—unsuccessfully—to buy them. Nonetheless, Hobbs' is a favorite of the townsfolk, primarily because of its two pool tables and skeeball range. They provide amusement during the long Lake Superior winters when there is nothing else to do except move snow from one place to another, tear through woods and across fields on snowmobiles and four-wheelers, drink, and make love.

Like all such places, Hobbs' has seen its share of barroom disputes. Few escalate to the point where deputies need to be summoned. For the most part the joint is downright peaceable, thanks to its proprietor and barkeep, Ted Lindsay, a Porcupine County native who had spent his professional life downstate as a Detroit patrolman. Though graying and long retired in his seventies, Ted was still burly, agile, and skilled at the uses of a police baton and kept one behind the bar instead of a baseball bat.

On the way home from the sheriff's department after work I passed Hobbs' almost every day and often stopped in for a six-pack and because I liked talking to Ted, not just because he used to be on the job but also because he judges a man by what he does in life, not where he's from or what he looks like.

Three big Harleys squatted in the parking lot as I swung through the doors, dressed in after-work denims, police gear locked away in the Explorer. That was neither surprising nor dismaying—bikers from Wisconsin and Minnesota often passed through Porcupine City on the way to camp in the Wolverines. For the most part they belonged to respectable cycle clubs and, though they sometimes liked to frighten the timid by mimicking Marlon Brando in *The Wild One* with leathers and red bandannas, they usually minded their own business and said "Yessir" and "Ma'am" to old folks. Once in a while, however, an outlaw biker—or a wannabe outlaw—caused trouble.

"A six-pack of Heineken," I told Ted, "and pop a Pepsi, will you? I'm driving."

Ted opened a bottle and placed it on the counter. I took a stool while Ted disappeared into the back for my six-pack.

"Hey, chief?" came a damp voice from nearby.

I blinked but didn't respond.

"I'm talking to ya, Injun!" the same voice said in a slur that suggested a long afternoon with the bottle. I *hate* gratuitous references to my biological ethnicity. I am tall for an Indian—six feet three, two hundred ten pounds—but the color of my skin is reddish-brown, almost mahogany in the summer sun, and I have high cheekbones and a hook nose, the very stereotype of the warrior on the old buffalo nickel.

Sheriff Garrow sometimes calls me "Tonto" when he wants to be funny. "You look like Crazy Horse!" well-meaning people often exclaim, unaware that no likeness of that great war chief ever was made during his lifetime. How would they know what Crazy Horse looked like? The odd thing is that he could have been my great-grandfather, but that's another story.

"Ain't drinkin', are ya?" I shook my head slightly, without looking back.

"Whoever heard of a sober Injun?"

This time I glanced behind me. At one of the pool tables glared a man mountain in cycle leathers and studded fingerless gloves. Burly, sweating, red-faced, and rheumy-eyed, he stood at least six-six and carried an overhanging belly, a heavily creased neck wider than his close-cropped head, and forearms like sixteen-pound hams. At least three hundred pounds, maybe more. Two almost equally large leather-clad comrades flanked him in truculent support.

Ted refuses to serve obvious drunks, so the biker must have concealed a snootful when he rolled in the door.

I picked up the Pepsi and moved down the bar. Sometimes ignoring a challenge will make it go away. Not this time.

"I said I'm talkin' to ya, chief!"

I could smell him as he stepped up close behind me. He reeked of days-old sweat as well as booze.

"What can I do for you?" I said politely as I turned. I took a step back, enlarging the personal space the biker had invaded.

"Bet you know where I can find some squaw pussy around here!" he hissed. "Bet you got a sister! Ten bucks for a blow job?" He leaned menacingly toward me.

By this time Ted had returned. He refuses to allow race-baiting in his establishment, and if people who voice ugly sentiments ignore his invitation to depart, he will encourage them with an expert display of his nightstick. If, however, actual physical force is required, he will call the sheriff's department just three blocks away. "It's their job," he says simply, and he's absolutely correct.

"That's it, asshole!" Ted growled, pure cop in his voice. "Take your attitude outside—right now!"

"Fuck you!" bellowed the biker, kicking a stool aside.

I shook my head slightly, throwing Ted a subtle let's-do-this-by-the-book glance. "Now please calm down, sir," I said to the biker, showing him my palms in peace. "There's really no need for that." Gentle methods first. Especially since my antagonist outweighed me by nearly a hundred pounds.

"Bet you like white pussy!" the biker snarled, clamping an enormous fist on my left forearm, the one toward him. He had reached the point of no return. He was spoiling for a fight, trying to provoke me into throwing the first punch. He was wide open for a short and sweet right to the solar plexus, and I was tempted.

Instead I whispered, without moving, "That's assault."

Ted reached under the beer taps, fished out his baton and slid it down the bar toward my right hand. Now was the time for me to announce that I was a deputy and take matters from there, perhaps with an expert application of the nightstick. But I did not want to allow a racial taunt to result in the use of force. That, I felt, would diminish me in the eyes of the dozen citizens of Porcupine County who looked on in dead silence, their eyes glittering with the prurience of country boys at a gentlemen's club.

Briefly I weighed the scales of justice. An arrest for simple assault and disorderly conduct would result in a night in jail, a couple of meals paid for by the county, more paperwork for Joe Koski, and extra court time for me. If I could just get the oaf out of the county, the hassle would be over.

Besides, the biker had the advantage not only of weight but also a foot of reach, and I was not sure the nightstick would equalize the difference. I wished I had the .357, but it was locked in the Explorer.

The biker hesitated. I quickly took the advantage it presented. "Come over here and let's talk," I said in a reasonable tone, stepping away from the bar and around it, away from the rest of the patrons. He followed stumbling, clumsily knocking aside another stool.

In the corner I took out my star and gave the biker a long eyeful. "I am a police officer," I said slowly and carefully, making sure he understood. "We can do this the easy way or we can do this the hard way." That's a hackneyed but eternally useful offer for a cop to make. "I can either take you down right now for assault and disorderly conduct, or you can step back from me and walk out that door, take your friends with you, and never show your face in here again. Your call."

The biker swayed, considering the unexpected choice. Enough function remained in his sodden brain cells for a simple thought to take root. But just as his piggish eyes began to show a glimmer of intelligence, four grimy hands appeared on his shoulders and made the decision for him.

"We're outta here," said the other two bikers simultaneously, hustling their comrade toward the door. "C'mon."

The air suddenly went out of the oaf with scarcely a hiss.

"Very sensible of you," I said to the smaller bikers.

But I wasn't through.

"Friends don't let friends drive drunk," I said, keeping my voice prim. "There's a motel across the street. Rent a room, let him sleep it off tonight, then get on your bikes and be on your way."

I watched as the two bikers carefully placed one foot in front of the other across the pavement, delicately steering their big comrade between them, and disappeared into the motel. They left their bikes in Hobbs' parking lot.

I turned back to the tavern. The citizens had resumed their chatter, the nightstick had disappeared, and Ted stood by the bar, unconcernedly scrubbing beer glasses.

He looked up at me. "One on the house?" That was a rare show of generosity for this tightfisted barkeep, and I knew I had earned his approval.

"Nope, Ted," I said. "Your backup was enough. Thanks for that."

As I made my way out the door, six-pack under my arm, a grizzled old woman turned from her table, smiled toothlessly and gave me a thumbs-up.

I was grinning as I drove away. "Happy trails," I told the world at large. Sometimes Tonto was worth a quote.

The next morning, as I peered outside the bathroom window of my snug little cabin tucked under a thick stand of birch and balsam just yards from the beach, a family of loons cut the mirror-smooth surface of the water. A golden coin on the eastern horizon heralded sunrise. Before long a small flotilla of Canada geese slowly paddled by in line astern, a feathered naval squadron on maneuvers from its anchorage up nearby Quarterline Creek. Just down the shore a doe and her fawn drank daintily from the lake.

The air tinkled with muffled calls from the geese and loons, with accompaniment from lovesick frogs in the nearby swamp. In the lulls, soft winds sighed through the leaves.

Who could have asked for more?

I loved that little cabin, bare and rustic as she was, furnished in what my mother once called Hopeless Bachelor. She would have been right about the four bare pine planks, separated by unpainted bricks liberated from a demolition site, that made up my overflowing bookcase, and she would have been right about the badly cracked but still comfortable mahogany leather sofa I'd bought for a song at the estate sale of a deceased lawyer. I preferred to think of the decor as Country Eclectic, and I was even proud of some of the pieces, like the brass double bedstead I'd found in a junkyard and restored to shiny newness with Brasso and elbow grease. Someday I was going to brush a dozen coats of finish, carefully polishing them between each application, on a maple rolltop desk I'd built from plans during long lonely weekends. The place was simple, it was comfortable, and it was all mine. I paid no installments and owed no mortgage.

I felt even more benevolence toward the world when, driving into

Porcupine City, I timed the bikers at fifty miles per hour, five under the limit, as they rode their Harleys carefully out of town—heading west, I hoped, for Hurley in Wisconsin, a rough town full of gentlemen's clubs and biker's bars that is well out of my jurisdiction. Identical pairs of green Ray-Bans shaded their eyes, doubtlessly yellowed and bloodshot, like egg yolks kept too long. Not too smugly, I hoped, I congratulated myself on serving as the engine of their departure.

It was a promising start to a day that ended the same way. As the sun lowered into the horizon, I dined with Virginia Fitzgerald at her home on the shore in the woods a few miles east of mine on the highway to Porcupine City. It was the first real evening we had spent together in our slowly—*very* slowly—unfolding relationship.

When she opened the heavy oak door, its leaded glass glinting in the firelight, was that a touch of blush and a dab of eyeliner I saw? Was that very slight scent a hint of Vol de Nuit? Were her jeans a little snugger, her lumberjack shirt slightly smaller?

"My one extravagance," Ginny said as I admired the interior of her efficiently designed log home. She had had it built the previous year by a local craftsman on property her family had owned for generations. Outside, it looked like one of the many small vacation homes owned by modestly well-to-do summer people who came up from Chicago and Milwaukee. These homes dotted the shoreline twelve miles west from Porcupine City to the mountainous, heavily forested state park that anchored the county's western end.

Inside, Ginny's furniture was understated but expensive, I saw with my cop's eye, a mixture of antique Arts and Crafts pieces and contemporary items well-constructed from solid quarter-sawn oak in mission style. Brightly colored cushions helped the oak pieces stand out from the logs of the exterior walls, and other decorations were not the customary rows of bleached driftwood and ranks of kitschy-fussy gift-shop figurines found in most Upper Midwest log homes, but rich tapestries, platters, vases, and urns from the Middle East. This was a woman who had traveled and who knew what to collect.

"Yemeni silver?" I asked.

Her eyes widened in surprise. "How would a north woods cop know that?" she demanded. Then she colored as she realized what she had said. "I'm sorry," she added quickly. "It just seems so unlikely that anyone else up here would know where those things came from."

"I spent time in the Middle East myself," I replied, "as a military policeman in the army. And in college I took a little art history. But I've never seen anything like this."

I peered down at a foot-high balsam fir, seemingly spun from pure silver, gracing a low oaken cabinet. A simple cross crowned its top and garlands wreathed its lacy branches. "Look at that exquisite tracery. That's obviously Yemeni. But a Christmas tree's not the sort of thing you find in a Middle Eastern tourist market full of Jewish artisans from Muslim countries. Where did it come from?"

"Jerusalem," Ginny replied. "My late husband had it specially made by a Yemeni and gave it to me one Christmas. It's so beautiful I never put it away after the holidays. It reminds me of my husband, and it provides me a little bit of Christmas all year."

She blushed, as if embarrassed at being caught in an unguarded expression of sentimentality. But I thought it was a lovely thing to say.

Suddenly she pulled out a chair from the massive oak dining table. "Sit down, Steve Martinez," she said. "I want to hear all about you. Where are you from and how did you arrive in this wild and lonely corner of Upper Michigan?"

"There isn't that much to tell," I said, opening a pricey California merlot I had been saving for just such an occasion. "I'm from Troy, a small city in upper New York State. I went to Cornell on an army ROTC scholarship, then studied criminal justice at CUNY, and when I got out of the service, I wanted to start my career in a place I'd never been. Porcupine County was hiring, and so here I am." That was accurate enough, but incomplete. Some details, I had long thought, were best left unvolunteered.

"New York?" she said. "With your name, your black hair, and your brown skin I'd have pegged you for border Texas, but you don't sound like a Texan at all. You do speak Spanish, don't you?"

"No. I'm not Tex-Mex," I said. "I'm Indian . . . er, Native American." I dislike using the politically correct term. Indians did not invent it. Well-meaning white academics did. Most American Indians call themselves Indian, or use the names of their tribes. Creation myths notwithstanding, the ancestors of Indians probably were no more native to this hemisphere than the Europeans who followed them, most likely having emigrated from Asia via the Bering Strait.

Not knowing how Ginny felt about the issue, and being the kind of fellow who doesn't like to offend needlessly, I employed both terms. If we had been north of the border, I'd used the Canadians' clever and inoffensive "first citizens."

She drew her chair closer, her eyes sparkling with interest. "What tribe? Oneida? Seneca?" It surprised me that she'd know about the Iroquoian tribes of New York State.

My origins were something I rarely talked about, but I could not resist this woman's unsettling directness.

"Neither of those, but Lakota, I was told, or Sioux as most people say. Full-blooded as far as I know."

"From Pine Ridge?" she asked. Many Lakota—especially the Oglala band to which I was born—live on that infamous reservation. I nodded.

"How'd you get from there to New York State?"

I sighed, and opened up. "I was adopted as a baby from the reservation orphanage. My adoptive parents are Caucasian. Or, rather, were—they died long ago in an auto accident. They were evangelical missionaries. My adoptive father was descended from Spanish settlers in Florida, and that's where the family name came from. All the Hispanic tradition had been leached out of them over generations of intermarriage.

"When they went back East after the adoption, they brought me up the best way they knew how, as a good white Christian they'd saved from the Indian witch doctors. In those days that was the thing to do with poor Indian kids—the idea was they were better off in white communities than with their own tribes. The only part of my Lakota heritage they kept for me was the name the orphanage gave to me when I was born, Stevie Two Crow. That's my middle name now, Two Crow.

"I was only ten when they died, too young to start asking questions about my birth parents. I don't know a thing about the Lakota other than what I've read."

"That can't have been easy," she said with a suddenly soft voice. "You're Indian outside, but white inside."

"For some of us it was pretty tough, but not so much for me," I said with a laugh. "Well . . ." And suddenly the rusty floodgates creaked open.

"Look, when you don't fit people's ideas of what you should be, they get confused and disappointed. It's not their fault, they think—it's yours for not being the person they had in their minds. Sometimes it makes them hostile, sometimes it makes them afraid. It's human nature."

Ginny nodded. "What can you do about it?"

"Not a hell of a lot," I said, adding a rueful chuckle. "It takes effort to reach some of these folks. Sometimes you have to meet them more than halfway. Sometimes I'll work real hard to win people over—and sometimes they turn out not to be worth the sweat."

Ginny lifted an eyebrow wickedly. "And am I worth the trouble to get to know?" she said.

"Oh, absolutely not," I said, trying to keep a poker face.

She giggled, then did the thing with her hair.

"Tell me about your childhood," she said.

"My adoptive parents loved me," I said. "They were good people who thought they were doing the right thing, and, really, they grounded me pretty well in their sense of values, and so did the uncle who raised me after their deaths. They truly believed in Christian brotherhood, in people being decent to each other. I have no complaints about that."

Troy was a largely white but in some neighborhoods a fairly diverse small city, I added, spotted with blacks, Asians, and Hispanics, and as a kid I was just another brown face in a multicolored working-class school crowd. Quite a few of the youngsters were deaf kids who spoke sign language, and they gave me the name sign that all my friends, hearing ones included, used when they spoke of me—hand held to the back of the head, palm facing forward, like a single eagle feather.

The odd thing was that all my white friends nevertheless considered me white because my parents were white. To them I just had a very good tan. But my black friends knew better. They thought of me as a minority just like them, casually using the word *honkies* when chatting with me about our white friends. At that preadolescent age we didn't take racial matters seriously.

But when early teenage insecurities brought out cruelty, some of the white kids made fun of my appearance.

"Once a kid called me a 'dirty Indian,'" I said. "I called him back 'a fat white four-eyed slob' because that's what he was, and he burst into tears. I didn't feel very good about that.

"But I was good at sports, and that more than anything else gets a kid accepted despite looking different from the others. Football, basketball, baseball—I was on all the teams in high school.

"When I started dating, some parents weren't too happy about their daughters seeing a boy with dark skin, but they weren't openly hostile about it, at least in front of me. There weren't a lot of incidents, but I remember all of them."

"Is it too painful to talk about them?" Ginny asked softly.

"Not really," I said. "Some of them are kind of funny in a pitiful sort of way."

Once, in college, I had gone home for Thanksgiving with a well-to-do Virginia girl who lived just outside Richmond. Her parents at first treated me with the elaborate politeness of southern gentry uncomfortable with onrushing social change. But they asked me if I'd take dinner in the kitchen to spare two unreconstructed elderly maiden aunts who, they said, "are not kindly disposed to people who are not like them. We know you understand."

I did. I thanked them as graciously as I could for their hospitality, and on the spot left for Cornell.

The very next weekend, I continued, I was the unofficial guest of honor at a faculty cocktail party. The school was just beginning a drive for scholarship funds to diversify its student body, and it paraded me before a host of wealthy alumni like a football team mascot. "Did I ever feel like the Indian in a cigar-store window!" I laughed.

"What was most annoying about that party were the well-meaning people who learned my story and thought I should 'discover my Native American self.'"

"And did you?" Ginny said.

"One summer I did visit Pine Ridge. But I had no more in common with anyone there than you would have. I asked at the orphanage about my natural parents, but the records had been poorly kept, and anyway, they told me, I was probably better off not knowing. Many of those Lakota led pretty dismal lives, full of alcohol and poverty. They often died young. I'm sure my natural parents did, too."

Ginny looked directly into my eyes. "Upper Michigan is a strange place to find a college-educated white Sioux cop named Martinez. Why, really, did you come here?"

"I ran away," I admitted. "Not from the law but from—from—oh, hell, a broken romance. It sounds so stupid now. Before I went to Saudi Arabia, I was going to marry my high school sweetheart. She was such a darling, Scots-Irish and perky, an All-American sort of girl. She was six months pregnant when I shipped out, but we weren't in a hurry to get married. We were going to tie the knot properly, with a big wedding, when I got back."

Her letter had arrived during the height of Desert Storm, when my MP unit was herding freshly captured Iraqi prisoners of war into barbed-wire enclosures. No barb could have been sharper than the news that the baby was blond and blue-eyed, and that the father was not me but my best friend. She had married him in a quiet little ceremony and hoped I could find it in my heart to forgive.

"I was devastated," I said, carefully maintaining an expressionless face. Ginny rested a cool and sympathetic palm lightly on my forearm. "All I could think about was that I couldn't go home. I thought I had to escape somewhere far away, completely different from the place where I had grown up. When I got back to the States, I jumped at the first law enforcement job offered me, and the one in Porcupine County was it."

Ginny patted my hand. "I am so very sorry," she said. After a discreet beat, she added, "In a way, though, I'm glad."

My heart did a small jig. "No regrets either," I said. "The pay is low but my needs are few. This country suits me."

10.

Suits me? "Don't go to work in a small town," my army comrades had warned. The pinched narrowness of outlook and experience these city slickers saw as typical of both cops and civilians in rural America, they said, would have me in no time at all pounding hungrily on the front door of a big-city police station looking for a job.

In some ways they were right. Many natives of Upper Michigan, like the rest of backwoods America, vote Democratic but think Republican; they rely on government handouts for their survival but see that same government as also threatening their right to bear arms and teaching science that challenges the biblical account of creation. The same people also tend to display a neighborly solicitousness nearly unheard of in the cities. They may recoil at your ideas, but they care about your humanity. They're the ones who show up on your doorstep with casseroles when there's a death in the family. They're the ones who drop by to make sure you're okay when illness has kept you out of circulation for more than a few days. They're the ones who bring Christmas to shut-ins.

Many of them harbor surprising secrets, most old and even obscure, but some percolating dangerously just under the surface, like hidden sulphur springs looking for a crack in the rock to burst through. If and when they emerge, things often become interesting for law enforcement officers. People are not always what they seem, and that keeps things lively. That's true in the cities, too, but out here in the wilderness where folks are few and far between, you notice it more.

In other ways the naysayers had no idea, absolutely no idea. There's nothing tiresome about police work in a rural Upper Michigan sheriff's department. Sure, much of it is routine—property theft and damage investigations, bar brawls, assaults, drug offenses, domestic abuse, process serving, and every once in a very long while a homicide. Plus, of course, traffic stops upon traffic stops. In twenty years there had been only three murders in Porcupine County. In the last one, seven years before, a farmer who wanted to get rid of his domineering wife dispatched her with a revolver—but forgot to lose the murder weapon, with which even a little boonies cop shop and a local prosecutor could win an easy conviction.

The Porcupine County department numbers only a dozen employees—besides Eli Garrow and Gil O'Brien, five sworn regular deputies, including me, and five dispatchers who also serve as jailers. All of us have taken the three-month law enforcement officer's course at the Michigan Police Academy in Lansing.

I'm the only outsider. The rest are homegrown Porkies who know every nook and cranny of the county, as well as just about everyone who lives there. I'd been hired because at the time of the vacancy no natives of the county had applied.

In the beginning my Indian features raised some of the residents' hackles. Porkies are 99 percent white—only three residents are African American and a handful Hispanic—and are largely descended from the Irish, Cornish, and Croatian miners and trappers who settled the county in the last half of the nineteenth century as well as the Finnish farmers and woodsmen who flooded in during the first decades of the twentieth.

They are no more and no less bigoted toward people who look different from them than the eastern urban whites I had grown up among, but some particularly resent the Ojibwa who live on the reservation in Baraga County to the east. The Indians, they growl, have things both ways while the whites have to struggle to make a living. Rents on the reservation are low, Bureau of Indian Affairs handouts plentiful. The Ojibwa, they say, love to torment the whites by exercising their treaty rights to take fish with nets and spears—something the whites can't do—while at the same time raking in dough from their gambling casinos. I doubt that the casinos do a Las Vegas sort of business, though—they are too far off the beaten path to attract high rollers from Chicago, Minneapolis, and Detroit.

Even though my Lakota ancestors had been driven out onto the Plains centuries ago by the invading Ojibwa, themselves under pressure from white expansion in the East, I don't begrudge casino Indians their success at double-dipping, if that is what it is—God knows the white man screwed them for three hundred years. And they almost never complain. Indians hate complaining, a fatal trait in a nation in which the squeakiest wheels get the most grease.

But once they heard my name the Porkies figured me for Hispanic, as Ginny had, and except for a few louts the reserve they showed toward me was the same they display toward any unfamiliar outsider—and toward any law enforcement officer.

We keep the peace with just five official road vehicles, only two of which are the usual expensively beefed-up, specially manufactured Ford police cruisers with powerful engines that can chase and capture anything on the highway. They are getting long in the tooth, with more than two hundred thousand miles on their much-patched chassis.

Two of the cars are retrofitted Crown Victoria sedans from a local dealer, used mostly for local investigations. One is a four-wheel-drive Explorer, my usual mount—and one I keep at home with the department's blessing because of all the deputies I live closest to the Wolverines and often find myself representing the law deep in the woods on rough gravel tracks. Off-duty I drive a rusty old Jeep Wrangler.

Sometimes I fly the department's thirty-year-old Cessna 172, a high-winged four-seater kept in a ramshackle hangar at the Porcupine County Airport hard by the lake. It's one of the undersheriff's grant-writing trophies, purchased with state funds when he discovered I had earned a pilot's certificate in the army during the weekends. We don't use the airplane very often, except for occasional low-level sweeps looking for missing elderly people, some of them suffering from Alzheimer's, or boats in distress on Lake Superior. We also use the plane to hunt drug shacks and marijuana fields in the woods or on cutover land, and now and then we'll transport a prisoner to a penitentiary in Lower Michigan.

For the rare forays into the lake or up the Porcupine River, the department also keeps a sixteen-foot outboard boat on a trailer next to the lockup, which consists of eight cells. Four are for general-population cons doing short sentences for minor felonies, one is a detox cell for drunks and would-be suicides, one is for females, one is a max security cell for dangerous prisoners, and one is a holding tank for fresh arrestees. Few cells are occupied at any one time. Porcupine County is not a hotbed of felony, and we deputies are not overworked crime fighters.

Every fall, however, we stomp around in the woods for a few days in the annual permutation of Operation HEMP (Help Eradicate Marijuana Planting), in which local deputies, village constables, state cops, and Drug Enforcement Agency zealots play Green Berets in the jungle, sniffing out and destroying marijuana patches planted on fallow farms and in forests, often by locals but sometimes out-of-staters.

More often we serve not as antidrug commandos but impromptu social workers, refereeing domestic disputes and rescuing people from themselves. Life in Porcupine County is too rugged for most eccentrics to survive, but we do have a few.

Just a few days before, I had had to help the county authorities find an institution to take a mentally disturbed old man who lived in terrible squalor in the woods in a filthy shack with more than three hundred cats. He shared their bulk cat food and, when found, had not changed his clothes in six months. The place stank to high heaven, and I did not envy the county's animal control officer his job dealing with all those orphaned and semi-feral cats.

The job all of us hated the most was dealing with child sexual abuse. There wasn't a lot of it, but we remembered every case. In July there had been one involving a predatory Minneapolis high school teacher who had hooked up in an Internet chat room the year before with a thirteen-year-old girl from Chicago. She and her parents spent a month every year at a lakeside resort just outside Porcupine City, and the previous summer the creep had rented a cabin half a mile down the lakeshore. The parents had thought their daughter spent hours every sunny day walking the beach searching for agates.

During the spring the girl had boasted to her classmates about her special friend, and one of them told her own parents, who contacted the authorities, who tipped Eli Garrow and Garner Armstrong. When the Chicago family and the Minneapolis predator arrived on almost the same day, almost the entire department was ready and waiting in the bushes outside the creep's cabin.

He was short and balding, doughy and almost apologetic, protesting gently as we recited his Miranda rights that he was not a criminal but suffered from a sickness. I could not understand how a precocious thirteen-year-old girl out for a lark could find him attractive at all.

Mary Larch in particular was so enraged that she clapped her cuffs on the guy much too hard, and when we thrust him, whimpering, into the lockup cage his hands had turned blue.

"Easy, Mary," I told her. "Even sons of bitches have rights. What's gotten into you?"

"I've been there," she replied, and that is all she would say.

11

"Now," I told Ginny, "you know everything there is to know about me. Your turn. You haven't told me a scrap about yourself."

In answer she tucked back a strand of hair and stood up from her chair. "All in good time," she said with that crinkly smile, at once endearing and irritating because it was so effective at deflecting questions. "Tomorrow is a working day for both of us. It's time for you to head for your cabin and a good night's sleep."

At the door I said hopefully, "Next Friday, maybe?"

"Sure thing," she replied. And just before she closed the door, she stood on the tips of her toes and graced my cheek with a feathery kiss. "Good night, Steve."

At home, reaching into the freezer for a pint of ice cream, I saw the little tin again. A vague feeling that something was not quite right with the Passoja case had been building up in me ever since the day the medical examiner called in his report. Alzheimer's or no Alzheimer's, would a man who had spent all his life in the woods really have fallen out of ingrained habit so easily? Did Passoja really spill his supper on his tent? And if not, how did that bacon grease get on it?

12

For the next three days, as Labor Day came and went, the more mundane tasks of an Upper Peninsula sheriff's deputy pushed the matter of Paul Passoja to the back of my mind. Most of them had to do with—surprise!—traffic stops. Tourists in Expeditions and Grand Cherokees from Chicago casually did eighty on U.S. 45 from the south and on M-64, the state highway bordering the lake, as is their habit on the interstates in northern Illinois. They are genuinely surprised when I tell them that twenty-five miles per hour over the limit is not a "gimme" in these parts.

Frequently they aren't wearing their seat belts, an automatic forty-dollar fine on top of the speeding citation, when I approach their cars.

"But I took it off to get my wallet and driver's license out of my back pocket!" many of them protest.

"Sorry, sir," I say politely. "I didn't see you do that. All I can see is that you're not wearing your belt."

Sometimes, if a driver seems genuinely contrite over having broken the limit, I'll give him a break and issue just a warning on the speeding violation—but not for the seat-belt violation. Paying that forty bucks ensures that he won't forget to keep his belt fastened, not if his brain has more than two memory cells.

Summer residents who study the sheriff's reports in the local weekly newspaper often observe that few Porcupine County residents are ever fined for traffic offenses. Almost all the convictions are of out-of-staters. More than once I've been asked if we cut breaks for locals.

Though I'd never officially admit it, we do. When we see the people we stop on the highway every weekend in the hardware store, the supermarket, or in neighboring church pews, when our children go to the same schools as theirs do, when we know they barely make enough money to survive, let alone pay traffic fines, we will give them a pass. Rather than hand them a citation, we will administer a thorough roadside chewing out. Indeed, repeated offenses will result in an expensive ticket, but most Porkies have too much sense to risk that.

But there is one violation for which I will never be lenient: driving while intoxicated. That morning I stopped a Caddy that had been weaving in its lane, and when I smelled the bourbon on the driver's breath, I immediately radioed Mary Larch, asking her to drive over from her patrol area for backup. If sexual abuse brought out Mary's dark side, drunken drivers bring out the worst in me, for one had killed my adoptive parents.

Mary's presence kept me from stepping over the line into rough justice. I stood aside, smoldering, as she administered the simple tests—asking the driver to walk a straight line heel to toe, stand on one foot, followed by a request to touch his nose with a finger with his eyes closed. When he nearly poked himself in the eye, she made a face and helped the staggering driver into the backseat of her cruiser for the trip to the department and the breath test.

But I tried hard to be gentle when I informed a summer visitor that there wasn't much the department could do about the bite she had suffered from a German shepherd that attacked her as she waded on the beach past its owner's lakeshore cabin. No, the dog was neither registered nor immunized—we were keeping an eye on it for signs of rabies, uncommon in this part of the state—but legally the visitor had been trespassing, even though everybody walks along the beach for miles without encountering a NO TRESPASSING sign. What's more, no country judge would find for a well-to-do outsider against a resident who was an impoverished old woman whose dog was her only protection. Sometimes the victims have no rights, I agreed soberly. Best to let the matter drop.

Twice that summer I rousted high school kids partying in boarded-up hunting camps, ignoring the sweet smell of marijuana while looking for harder drugs and checking ages. Young people in Porcupine County haven't much to do on weekends except drink, smoke dope, and have sex. The county does provide a teen hangout for them in town, but few use the Ping-Pong tables simply because, in the way of young people everywhere, they refuse to let adults tell them what to do.

But we deputies are sworn to uphold the law, so uphold the law we do—we chase them out of the camps, first checking to see if they've trashed the place, then making sure someone's sober enough to drive home. If a girl is below the age of consent, we'll take her home and tell her parents where she has been. Such matters ordinarily are decided in the family—exactly how varies from family to family, but it's rarely gentle.

With teenagers we're sometimes faced with a dilemma. We might pick up a youngster for a minor misdemeanor, but if the kid's father is an abusive one—many desperately poor men brutally take out their frustrations on their families—we have to decide whether to book the kid, inform the parents, or just let the kid go after a lecture. Once you've seen a pretty teenage girl with new bruises on her face a day or two after you've turned her in to her folks, you're not likely to rat on her to Daddy again.

Only on prom night do we let the youngsters mostly alone—it's better that at the most booze- and hormone-ridden time of the year we keep them within manageable bounds—but we'll bust anybody dumb enough to drink and drive. Judge Kolehmainen always hands first-time DWIs a day in jail and a $340 fine, a lot of money up here where jobs are few and unemployment is high. He believes in early intervention, even if he wouldn't use such a social worker's term—he calls it "nipping sin in the bud," like the conservative Christian evangelical he is. To the judge, the greatest sin in the world is carelessly endangering someone else's life. I'll go along with that.

As the sun reached its apex, I put aside these thoughts and backed the Explorer into a disused gravel driveway, just out of sight of M-64 but within radar range, and focused the beam on the highway. Time to catch some speeders, but first a little lunch. I fished a sandwich and a Pepsi from my cooler and flicked on the radar.

I ignored the traffic doing sixty and sixty-five miles per hour, five and ten miles per hour over the limit, and winced at the elderly men nursing their decrepit pickups down the highway at forty and forty-five—they were accidents waiting to happen at the hands of aggressive drivers. The fines for doing five and ten over the fifty-five-miles-per-hour limit did bring the county some revenue, but breaking the law at seventy or better meant real money. I decided to wait for bigger fish while I finished my sandwich.

The radar readout flashed *60, 66, 64*. At *69* I was tempted, but kept chewing. Four bites in, a large black sport-ute sped by. Seventy-four! A big one! I tossed the remainder of the sandwich to unseen critters in the brush, flicked on the flashers and siren, and fishtailed out onto the highway, the Explorer's tires throwing gravel. Though the sport-ute was more than three hundred yards ahead, almost immediately its brake lights blinked on and it pulled off the road onto the verge. Knows he's caught red-handed, I thought as I maneuvered the Explorer close behind.

Almost immediately I recognized the vehicle. It was Paul Passoja's Navigator. And the driver, I saw, was Marjorie Passoja. I radioed Joe Koski to inform him of the stop and its location and ask for information on the Navigator's license plate. My Explorer didn't have the wireless computer linked into the State of Michigan vehicle registry that the department's cruisers boasted. "It's Marjorie," I told Joe.

"I'm sorry," she said, contrition coloring her voice, as I approached the driver's door. She was wearing her seat belt. "How fast was I going?"

"Seventy-four."

"Damn," she said quietly. "I've been distracted, but that's no excuse."

"I know, Mrs. Passoja," I said, trying to be gentle. My heart went out to her. But I was still a cop with a job to do. "May I have your registration and license, please?"

She fished in her purse and gave them to me, her beautiful face barely suppressing an expression of anguish.

"Wait here," I said. "I'll be right back."

"Joe?" I said into the radio. "Anything for me?"

"Nothing on the plates except it's Passoja's Navigator, all right. License is current."

I gave him Marjorie's driver's license number. The click of computer keys, then Joe's voice again. "No priors," he said. "She's clean."

"Okay," I said. "That's all."

I made a decision.

"Mrs. Passoja," I said, "nineteen miles an hour over the speed limit could cost you several hundred dollars. But considering all that's happened, as well as your clean driving record, and the fact that you admit you made a mistake, I'm just going to give you a warning."

She slumped in relief and sighed. "Thank you, deputy. I promise to be more careful."

"Thank you for that, Mrs. Passoja," I said. "Please take it easy."

"I will," she said.

At that moment I looked up as Mary Larch's cruiser, its lights flashing but siren silent, sped toward us. Swiftly she U-turned, pulled up behind my Explorer, and got out. Striding right past me to the Navigator, she peered in at Marjorie, and said, "You all right?"

"Yes," Marjorie replied in a wavering voice. "Deputy Martinez just gave me a warning for speeding. My mind was elsewhere." The two locked gazes for a moment, then both glanced back at me.

"Marj, why don't you go home and take it easy?" Mary said, patting her on the arm. Marjorie nodded.

"Off with you, then." The Navigator drove away.

"Thanks, Steve," Mary said. "I worry about her, you know."

"I guess you do," I said. "But I think she'll be all right. She didn't give me any crap but owned up to the violation right away. No point in lumbering her with a citation."

"You're a good guy, Steve," Mary said.

I thought about asking her why she was so concerned about Marjorie, but figured it was none of my business. One doesn't casually intrude on relationships in Porcupine County.

With a brisk nod and a thin smile Mary returned east to her patrol area, I west to mine, wishing I hadn't tossed that sandwich away. For the rest of the afternoon I pinched speeders, even those doing only sixty-one miles per hour, figuring that a bunch of small fish would make up for the big one I had thrown back.

13 Before I went home there was one more task that day: taking the sheriff's Cessna into the sky for a maintenance flight: At least once a week I flew the airplane for an hour or so, just to exercise the engine. Disused airplane engines rust inside, shortening their lives, and that is why you see so many weekend pilots going nowhere, just lollygagging around their airports and boring expensive holes in the sky. They're keeping their engines limber and lubricated for the times when they really have to go somewhere.

I could use official departmental time for this job, but the sheriff pays for it anyway, and flying on somebody else's dime is a rare treat. So I perform the task on off-hours, usually in the early evenings when the rising thermals have settled down and the air is at its smoothest and most velvety. Flying low and slow at times like that gives a small-plane pilot a ringside seat on the glories of creation.

The airport lies three miles west of Porcupine City and is almost always deserted, except for the dispatcher and the director of the PorTran bus service, headquartered in the little three-room airport office building. Often I see Doc Miller in his hangar working on his little "warbird," a Korean War–era Bird Dog spotter plane he keeps in pristine condition, looking as if it had just been delivered to the army. He looked old enough to have flown her over Inchon, but I knew that he had served in Vietnam as a navy doctor.

Next to the Bird Dog the faded paint on the sheriff's Cessna looks sadly tattered, like an ancient movie queen who doesn't realize that the ton of makeup she puts on every morning cannot hide the ravages of age. But the decades-old airplane is in excellent mechanical condition, stoutly airworthy, its engine freshly overhauled.

I patted her flank as I began the preflight tasks, checking the hinges on the ailerons, flaps, elevator and rudder, wiggling the control surfaces, draining a sample of fuel from both tanks to make sure water had not gotten into them, marking the oil level, examining the propeller for nicks, the nosewheel strut, the tires, the brakes. This pilot's ritual, I sometimes thought, was little different from that of a Lakota war chief, a shaman who spread out and read the contents of his medicine bag before going into battle. The ceremony comforted both of us, for it meant that we were leaving nothing to chance, that we were preparing ourselves to the last detail for what lay ahead.

Yes, I often think about being an Indian. How can I not? It's what I am, even though any Indian-ness I have comes from occasional reading forays into Indian history, not from living it.

When the Cessna lifted off the runway and I banked east over the lake, a bald eagle suddenly joined me in formation, fifty yards off my left wingtip. Up, up up we rose together in a sweeping circle, soaring wing to wing.

To the Lakota the bald eagle symbolized the spirit of war and hunting, and was a messenger from God. For a brief moment the adrenaline rush coursing through my veins filled me with the powerful medicine of invincibility, as if I were riding with Crazy Horse. *"Hoka hey!"* I yelled, as the Lakota had when they fell upon their enemies. "It's a good day to die!"

At a thousand feet the eagle suddenly folded its wings and stooped. As I banked the Cessna to watch, he plummeted downward, a feathered heat-seeking missile, and slammed into a passing mallard in a cloud of down. Leveling off, he headed inland below me, quarry clamped in his talons.

It was a violent spectacle, but I rejoiced nevertheless. I felt as if the sight—a rare one—had been a gift. Eagles usually snatch fish feeding near the surface of the water, only occasionally going after waterfowl, large and elusive therefore more difficult targets, but always taking whatever fate proffers them. This eagle had lived up to what nature had designed him to do—indeed, it was as if by taking a duck he was counting coup with all creation as his audience—and I felt rapture in his victory.

A Lakota mystic probably would have patted me on the back and informed me that I had just had a vision. Having grown up as I did, however, I hardheadedly realized that my wool-gathering was just a fantasy, the product of an imagination overwhelmed by the joy of flight. *Hoka hey*, indeed. "A good day to die!" is hardly the sentiment of a thoughtful and careful pilot. I was glad nobody had heard me shout it.

I pointed the Cessna's nose inland also, peering down at the land below. As long as I was up here doing an official job, I might as well stretch the sheriff's dollars and search for wrongdoing.

Every year during Operation HEMP I had dipped low over the tailings, looking for one of the DEA's Official (and somewhat redundant) Warning Signs of Illegal Marijuana Growing: "Unusual amounts of traffic on and off the property (usually at night), use of tents, campers, or other recreational vehicles on wooded property with no evidence of recreational activity taking place; unusual purchases of fertilizer, garden hose, plastic PVC pipe, chicken wire, lumber, machetes, camouflage netting, and clothing; large amount of PVC pipe or irrigation hose in heavily wooded areas; and heavily patrolled or guarded woods, swamps, and other remote areas."

I think druggie-hunting is a waste of time and effort—booze, in my view, is far more dangerous than pot—but cops in the north woods sometimes like to play Green Berets just for something else to do besides pinch speeders, even though we know that the American antidrug army has about as much effect on the trade as King Canute had on the ocean. And I go along, usually in the Cessna. I have to; it's my job, and the law is the law.

For miles and miles I flew along searching, the engine thrumming smoothly five hundred feet above the forest canopy and the clear-cut, stump-strewn open lands, from time to time circling rustic shacks used by the locals as deer camps and sometimes as cat labs.

Cat, short for methcathinone, was first made and peddled in the Upper Peninsula in the early 1990s, later spreading all over the Midwest. It's a designer drug closely related to khat, the mildly narcotic weed chewed all day long in Yemen, and is a cheap substitute for methamphetamine. Cat is sold as a white crystalline powder made from easily obtainable ephedrine or pseudoephedrine—common over-the-counter nasal remedies—mixed with a witches' brew of battery acid, Drano, lye, and paint thinner.

Cat, also called goob, Jeff, bathtub speed, and Cadillac Express, is highly toxic and highly addictive. Abusers suffer paranoia, delusions, and hallucinations, sometimes a complete psychotic crash.

It's bad shit, all right. When we bust a cat lab—they still crop up in Porcupine County from time to time—we have to call in the state haz-mat people to haul away the dangerous evidence.

This time I saw nothing, nor did I expect to see anything. Most drug entrepreneurs are smart enough to camouflage their paraphernalia from air searches, though once in a while a large crop of marijuana will stand out from the surrounding vegetation, inviting later investigation on foot.

I checked my watch. Nearly sixty minutes had passed since takeoff, and it was time to get the airplane back on the ground. I wanted to soar on eagle's wings until the sun went down, but aviation fuel is expensive and Gil O'Brien, that tightfisted undersheriff, would demand I justify wasting the department's money.

As I closed the hangar door I felt relaxed and mellow, as I always do after a good flight. One of these days I was going to ask Ginny if she would like to go for a ride in a rental aircraft from Ironwood or Land o' Lakes—I wasn't about to use departmental equipment for pleasure flights with civilians. I hadn't yet asked her, because I didn't yet know how she felt about flying in small airplanes.

The only person who had gone up with me in that Cessna was Mary Larch, as an extra pair of eyes during an official search for a missing boat and once during an Operation HEMP flight. She had no fear of flying, but neither did she take much joy in it. To her it was just part of the job, not a particularly noteworthy event. Not liking to fly certainly does not mean a character defect, but I was disappointed nonetheless.

14

I was not, however, displeased with Mary either as a person or as a colleague. Late in September I learned something new about her, a rare occurrence indeed, for her armor was nearly impossible to breach.

None of us knew what had happened in her youth that would have explained why she was so hard-nosed toward child molesters. I asked once, and she replied with quiet steeliness, "Let's not go there."

That was her answer whenever anybody asked her anything about herself. She was as private a person as Ginny. But unlike Ginny, who was a master at subtly and painlessly deflecting unwanted questions, Mary simply threw up a brick wall. She wasn't rude about it. She didn't say, "None of your business!" but we all knew what she meant. Sometimes, when someone became insistent, she'd level a granite gaze at her interlocutor and say, "Please back off. I don't want to talk about that."

But there was nothing sullen about Mary. She was not terminally bright and bubbly, as are so many impossibly perky small women, but strode into the office every day with a simple smile, wave, and quiet hello for everyone. In the sheriff's department we all had grown fond of her, and as she gained experience as a cop we came to respect her as well, even though we all expected she'd outrank us someday, so determined was she to earn an advanced degree in criminal justice.

Her parents had died when she was still in her late teens and she had struggled to get where she was, waiting tables and digging ditches with the road commission while going to college. On her off-hours she not only volunteered at the Andie Davis Home, the shelter she and Marjorie Passoja had together turned into a sanctuary for abused wives, but also coached the peewee hockey team. She had an easy sense of humor, calling herself "Ms. Bulletproof Boobs" whenever she wore a Kevlar vest on duty.

Best of all, she believed in the same law enforcement philosophy I did: Whenever possible, solve problems with patient reason, not swift force. Unlike many young and inexperienced female cops, she never voiced any kind of macho toughness in a misguided attempt to get along with her male counterparts. I admire calm reticence in both sexes and have never subscribed to the idea that a cop should automatically carry an intimidating presence. There are times to be tough and times to be gentle, and the good cop knows the difference. Most of the time, anyway.

Mary was getting very good at talking overwrought subjects down from the limbs of rage they had climbed out upon, and her relaxed curbside demeanor in a traffic stop was actually a pleasure for a fellow cop to behold. So gentle and polite was she with speeders that they almost took their citations with gratitude.

Except for one thing—her sexuality—Mary was not an off-duty mystery, but a familiar part of the community. She was a regular at civic functions, often flipping pancakes at the annual firemen's open house breakfast. Her powerful throwing arm won her the left field spot on the Hobbs' Tavern softball team. She was as good with the bat as she was with the glove.

And, though she hated drawing her pistol on duty, she was a crack shot. I'm skilled enough with firearms, though no world-beater, but at departmental target practice Mary always outscored me and often beat Joe Koski, a former army weapons instructor and an expert with all kinds of firearms, short and long.

Her petite blue-eyed brunette beauty—she had sharp but delicate features accentuated by the ponytail she always wore, and her male-cut uniform could not conceal a shapely figure—caused plenty of local men, even a couple of deputies, to ask her out. I would have gotten in line myself, had I not already set my hat for Ginny. And, I am sure, I would have been politely but firmly refused, just as everyone else had been.

Out of uniform Mary looked like a typical "Yooper woman." Up here in the Upper Peninsula where the seasons are "winter, winter, winter and blackflies," as the droll U.P.er saying goes, everybody, male or female, wears sensible jeans and flannel or woolen shirts, often with a well-worn, comfortable pair of hiking boots. Dress up is a new sweatshirt with flowers on the front. Ginny dressed similarly, too, but always wore something bright and colorful—a scarf, a headband, a kaleidoscopic ski parka. Mary never did that—I could not imagine her in hose and heels, let alone blush and lipstick. "I wish I could give her a complete makeover," Ginny once said. She recognized quality raw material when she saw it.

Because of Mary's sexual aloofness as well as athletic skills, some men thought she must be a lesbian. I didn't—I thought she was simply asexual, perhaps because of what must have happened to her as a child. But it was none of my business.

Mary and I were sitting in Merle's Café on a coffee break near quitting time when the radio call came from Joe Koski. "Nancy Houlihan needs a deputy out at the airport," he said. "You decide who goes."

"On my way," I said. The airport, just west of town, is properly in my patrol territory.

Nancy is the director of PorTran, and my first thought was that there might have been a fender bender of some kind, but Joe hadn't said why Nancy wanted us. That meant she had asked him to be discreet so that every Tom, Dick, and Einar eavesdropping on the sheriff's frequency wouldn't know about it.

The call piqued Mary's curiosity, too. "I'll go along," she said.

When we arrived, Nancy and the driver stood by the door of his bus with sober and concerned expressions. The bus stood empty except for a teenaged girl sitting in the back.

"Problem kid," Nancy said. "I didn't want to call her parents. She needs a talking-to from someone in authority." That was a familiar role for us deputies.

Jennie Brady was a troubled youngster who on her way home from her part-time job bagging groceries had started acting out, cursing the driver and passengers, kicking the backs of the seats and refusing to get off. The driver had dropped off his other passengers and returned to base at the airport to deal with his young problem.

I knew Jennie. I'd picked her up a couple of times at beer parties and delivered her home. I knew, as Nancy did, that she had a father who in his cups disciplined his children with his fists. She was a good kid, but sometimes a difficult one, as teenagers with family grievances can be.

"Steve, let me handle this?" Mary said.

"Okay," I said, standing back. I had worked with her long enough to know that she had a soft and reassuring touch with youngsters, and they responded to her big-sister approach more readily than they did to my clumsy pseudo-avuncularity. Like most male deputies, I had little finesse with teenagers.

She climbed aboard the bus, where Jennie huddled in back, clasping her knees to her chest, head down, motionless. I stood in the door as Mary sat down next to her.

"What happened, Jennie?" Mary said gently.

The girl did not answer.

"Jennie, we're not arresting you. You didn't break anything. We just want to know why you did this. Maybe we can do something."

Jennie snuffled, then began weeping softly. "It's Daddy. He's drinking. He hit me." She looked up and I saw the fresh welt on her cheekbone.

"Jennie, I'm sorry," Mary said, putting her arm around the girl's shoulders. "But you can't let that make you strike out at other people. The people on the bus didn't do anything to you, did they?"

"I'm sorry," Jennie said. "I won't do it again."

"I know," Mary said. "Come on down off the bus now."

"Please don't take me home," Jennie said.

Nancy and I looked at each other. We both knew what would happen if Jennie went home to her drunken father.

"Jennie, you're coming home with me," Mary said firmly. "We'll have hamburgers and potato chips and watch TV. You can sleep over and go home tomorrow."

The girl looked up. "You sure?"

"I'm sure," Mary said, taking Jennie's hand. "I'll call your mom. Just a sec."

Mary had spotted the glance of uncertainty on my face. We walked around behind my Explorer out of earshot.

"Not the Andie Davis Home?" I asked quietly.

"No. She's underage. My house."

"Is this a good thing to do, Mary? You're a cop, not a social worker. You shouldn't get this involved with a subject."

"You got a better idea?" she countered. It would take days, maybe weeks, before the child protection agencies could act, unless the child was in clear and present danger. Harsh discipline is a gray area.

"Not really," I said after a beat or two.

"Before I take Jennie home tomorrow," she said, "Brady will have slept off the drunk. I'm going to go there and tell him that if he raises a hand to her again I'll beat the shit out of him." In her voice I could hear the sickening thunk of a nightstick against a skull.

I blinked. That was the first time I had ever heard Mary speak in favor of rough justice. I had no doubt she could do what she threatened, too. Small as she was, she had the strength and the skills. Of course, administering impromptu justice is unprofessional and illegal and properly called police brutality. In Porcupine County we never "tune up" bad guys the way cops do in the big cities. Not very often, anyway.

"All right," I said.

"One more thing, Steve."

"Yes?"

"Don't tell Gil." She wasn't going to put her humanitarian act on her report, for the undersheriff would take out his official disapproval at the top of his lungs.

"My lips are sealed."

"Thanks."

Then she did a most uncharacteristic thing. She stood on tiptoe, raised her palm and touched me on the cheek. So surprised was I that I almost forgot the fists and knuckles in her threat against Brady.

15 On patrol at the beginning of October I saw a large knot of cars and tourists outside a fried-chicken-and-soft-ice-cream emporium that had been a constant source of worry to the authorities of the Upper Peninsula, and not just because of the cholesterol bombs it served to hordes of grease-loving campers so obese I often suspected their rusty vans and pickups strained the state gross vehicle weight limits. The Cackle Shack was one of several roadside restaurants struggling for the skimpy tourist business, and its biggest attraction was not fatty drumsticks but garbage bears.

Most restaurants' Dumpsters lay behind high cyclone fences topped by barbed wire, but this one stood unprotected out in the trash-strewn open. Two small bears, little more than yearlings, nosed through plastic bags while the rump of a full-grown sow, its fur stained with mayonnaise, protruded from inside the open Dumpster. Scores of goggling tourists huddled worrisomely close to the scene, snapping photographs and scooting laughingly back to their cars or into the restaurant whenever one of the bears took a step toward them.

The scene was not illegal—backwoods cafés are not required by local law to protect their Dumpsters in enclosures, and many of them encourage the bears with careless storage of their garbage.

"I can't afford no fence," the Cackle Shack operator often said, tongue firmly in cheek. "I clean up the place every morning but the bears just won't stay away."

Not that he cared—clearly the bears were good for business, and more than once I'd seen him toss garbage from the kitchen right into the lap of a begging bear—but they were also an invitation to trouble.

Someday somebody was going to get hurt, especially one of the unwashed trailer-park yahoos seeking to impress his buddies by getting close to a bear. Repeatedly the proprietor had been warned about liability and a lawsuit, but he scoffed, "Who's gonna sue *me?* I ain't got nothin' but this restaurant, and it's worthless without a little attraction out back, if you know what I mean. Besides, I allus call in the bear wranglers before things go too far."

But the problem was getting worse. In past years one and sometimes two bears had taken up residence in the woods just behind the Cackle Shack, but now as many as half a dozen came to supper every evening, some of the bolder ones appearing under the bright sun of mid-afternoon. The population explosion of black bears in Upper Michigan had intensified during the last few years, and the wilderness could sustain only a limited number. The pressure to find food was turning more and more of them into garbage bears, venturing out of the woods and down the shore looking for goodies.

I had seen more than one outside my cabin window snuffling around the heavy lumber enclosure that once sheltered my garbage can. After it had been smashed to flinders once too often—those animals are incredibly powerful and single-minded—I had taken to keeping the garbage can in my kitchen and putting it out on the highway once a week for the scavenger service.

In the middle of the restaurant tableau I spotted a familiar green DNR Suburban, trailing a long, cylindrical bear transporter on wheels. I parked the Explorer and hailed Stan and Garrett. Both stood by the transporter.

"Seems to me I'm seeing a lot of you guys lately," I said. "What's the problem here?"

"That bear in the Dumpster has been charging the crowd," Stan replied. "Time to knock her out and relocate her to another part of the forest before she gets up too close and personal."

Garrett nodded eagerly, as if Stan's words were an enormous revelation.

"What are the chances she'll be able to make it in the wild?" I said, knowing the answer but asking the question to educate the goggling tourists.

"Not good. Once a bear learns about garbage, it's unlikely ever to forage in the wild again. Chances are it'll find its way back in a few weeks. Then we'll probably have to shoot it before it hurts somebody stupid enough to get in its way."

Garrett nodded again.

"The young ones?" I asked.

"They're old enough to fend for themselves," Stan said. "We'll just chase them into the woods."

Nuisance bears, I had learned early in my Porcupine County apprenticeship, came in several varieties. Most were harmless, even amusing, especially those in the Wolverines. Black bears are not ordinarily potential killers, like the much bigger grizzlies of the West. Only about thirty-five deaths from black bear maulings were reported in the United States during the entire twentieth century, and the last bear-related death in Upper Michigan—before Paul Passoja's—occurred in the 1980s when a hiker in the Wolverines climbed a tree, pack on his back, to get away from a persistent sow. He slipped on a mossy branch and fell out of the tree to his death on the rocks below. Statistically, one is ninety thousand times likelier to die in a homicide than from the teeth and claws of bears.

Everybody in bear country will tell you that the animals are always unpredictable. Mothers will protect their cubs, but most will flee from human contact. When cornered a bear will often charge, but stop at the last minute, whoofing loudly and stamping aggressively, then disappear into the forest. Sometimes it'll take a quick swipe at the air with its sharp claws, like a shadowboxing heavyweight, before skedaddling.

Some bears learn that suddenly popping up from a bush next to a trail causes passing hikers to drop their backpacks and slowly withdraw—as the rangers suggest is the safest course whenever a bear is encountered—allowing the bears to sample the contents at their leisure. These bears aim for food, not people.

One that took up residence near the Wolverine Park's drive-in campground would simply amble into a campsite and squat patiently on its haunches, softly huffing like a furry teakettle, a few yards away from a family at a picnic table. Sooner or later the diners would uneasily rise and move away from the table, and the bear would lumber in for the feast.

Bears like these often can be relocated, if not reeducated. But bears that make a habit of gorging on garbage are almost always hopeless cases, and sometimes they get mean. Those have to be destroyed before they hurt somebody. The trick is determining when to relocate and when to destroy.

"Garrett!" Stan growled. "Stop thinking with your dick! Did you shut your head in the truck door?"

The blond giant, who had been gaping with wet lips at an overendowed teenage girl in a tight T-shirt, blinked and turned to us.

"Get the popgun," Stan said. "Be quick about it."

As Garrett strode to the truck Stan said to me, "He's missing a few slats under his mattress, he is. Hard worker, though."

When Garrett returned with the air rifle, Stan slipped a tranquilizer dart into its muzzle.

"Back me up?" he asked. "I could use some crowd control."

I nodded and shooed the gawkers well back from the clearing. With a heavy rifle held loosely in his hands Garrett rode shotgun beside Stan as the older man crept up toward the Dumpster, squatted and waited patiently for the sow to emerge. In a few moments, sated, she threw herself over the edge of the Dumpster and waddled slowly toward the crowd. She bore a large spot on her chest, a slash of cinnamon-colored fur. Stan sidled behind her with the rifle.

"Thut!" The dart struck the bear in one large haunch. Irritatedly she peered back at Stan. She took a step toward the forest, then sat down to consider the new development. Soon she began to sway, then slowly toppled in a stupor. Quickly Stan slipped a muzzle over her massive head, then with Garrett's help dragged her to the transporter and shoved her inside. It was not an easy job—she weighed a good three hundred pounds or more.

"She'll be released in the forest on the other side of Lake Gogebic," Stan said. "That's a good twenty miles away, well past a bear's usual range. Let's hope she won't be back." The dour expression on his face suggested that he believed otherwise.

16 Afterward, on my way into town to drop off some daily reports, I saw Mary sitting in her cruiser on a side road off the highway, head back, eyes closed, taking a break from chasing speeders. I slid the Explorer next to her vehicle and rolled down my window as she awoke sleepily.

"How's it going?" she said.

I told her about the events at the Cackle Shack.

Quickly she sat up. "Hmm," she said. "Where'd they take the bear?"

"Out beyond Gogebic, they said. It'll be back."

"Ya think?"

We fell silent for a moment. "How'd it go with Brady?" I asked.

"All right," she said. "He had a big head this morning and said he was very sorry. He said he wouldn't do it again. I believed him when he said he was sorry, but I also believe he'll do it again sooner or later. They always do."

"Did you tell him you'd beat the shit out of him?"

"Yes."

"What'd he say?"

"He said he'd complain to the sheriff."

"And?"

"I said, 'Do you think the sheriff will believe a woman half your size could wipe up your backyard with you?'"

"And?"

"He didn't respond. He knows I can."

"But will you?"

"If I have to."

"Let's hope not."

She nodded slowly.

"Jenny?"

"I took her there later. She was glad to get home. She loves her father. When he isn't drinking, he's good to her and to her mom. I hope it lasts for a while."

For a moment we sat silently, door to door. I couldn't speak for Mary, but I couldn't help thinking that rogue humans aren't much different from rogue bears. They're unable to stop the behavior that gets them in trouble in the first place.

17

It had been nearly two months since Paul Passoja was found dead when I went to Doc Miller for my annual physical.

"How'd you get that?" said Doc Miller, probing a small indentation in my skull behind the left temple, hidden under my thick black hair. "Tomahawk?"

He chuckled. I didn't.

"Golf club," I said, trying to keep the resignation out of my voice. "I stepped into somebody's backswing when I was fourteen."

"Ouch," he said.

Doc Miller is a sixtyish man with a rubbery bloodhound face like Walter Matthau's. He put the same questions to me at every annual physical. At first I was annoyed. I was sure he remembered the answers from year to year, but Fred Miller is a decent and caring man and it's not worth carrying a grudge over a tasteless question meant in gentle humor.

"Knife fight?" he asked, finger running gently across a jagged scar on my chest.

"Bamboo tomato stake," I said with a sigh. "It broke when I was shoving it in the ground."

"Ouch. More than one sexual partner?"

"None of your business."

"I'm your doctor, for Chrissake. Not your mother."

"No." The real answer was "Lately, none at all," but I wasn't going to confess that. From time to time I think about answering "Yes," just to hear Doc Miller's celebrated lecture about AIDS, condoms, and needle-sharing. Before he came to Porcupine County Hospital, he ran an inner-city clinic on Chicago's South Side. There was a story in his escape to the north woods, I thought, and someday I'd like to find it out.

"You're a disappointment, Steve," he said with mock lugubriousness, as he does every year. "Otherwise you're in excellent health."

"I've got a question," I said, shrugging into my shirt. The question had been building up inside me for a while, waiting for an opportune moment to be asked, and here was as good a time as any.

"Shoot."

"How can you tell if somebody's got Alzheimer's?"

He looked at me sadly. "Relative?"

"Uh-huh." Despite myself I glanced aside, a sure giveaway that I was dissembling. I kicked myself mentally. Look Doc in the eye!

"We can't tell absolutely for sure until an autopsy, if the family requests it, and if we find amyloid—that's a gummy protein that accumulates in the brains of Alzheimer victims—in two or more brain regions. If the hippocampal and cortical tissue of, say, an eighty-year-old demented patient contains fifteen or more amyloid plaques per square millimeter, it's usually clear evidence of Alzheimer's, as is a hippocampus overrun by plaques."

I got his drift. Doc Miller, I thought, must have lectured in medical school sometime during his long career. "Well, yeah, but—" I said.

"Yes, but what good is a postmortem diagnosis to a patient?" he finished the question. "Still, we can make a pretty good guess while the patient is living."

According to the textbook, said Doc Miller, still sounding like one, the symptoms of Alzheimer's "include losses in four principal abilities: memory, orientation, judgment, and reasoning.

"The failing mind loses the ability to find words and converse, to write a note, to read a book, to identify by touch a leaf or a blade of grass, to recognize orange juice by its taste, or realize that a passing object overhead is an airplane, not a bird. In other words, the patient loses the ability to make connections, and this invites delusions. He might not recognize himself in the mirror. His synapses might make the wrong connections so he thinks he's the devil. But he's not aware of what's happening to him."

"You mean if my Aunt Trudy"—I had plucked the name out of the air—"complains that she's always forgetting things, she doesn't have Alzheimer's?"

"Probably not. It's those who forget things and don't complain who tend to have it."

"How about if Aunt Trudy goes on and on in great detail all the time about the years in which she taught chemistry, yet talks about her dead husband as if he's still alive?"

Dr. Miller glanced up. "You're looking right into the heart of the disease," he said. "In the Alzheimer's literature there's a classic story. There was an eighty-four-year-old woman in a nursing home who had been a concert pianist and a piano teacher all her life. Every afternoon she would sit down at the Baldwin and hammer out show tunes from the forties. Can you imagine what that took? Her brain had to recall millions of rapid, highly nuanced finger movements with exact timing, sequences, pressures. She never missed a note. But she often forgot that she'd played a song and might start it all over again, playing it several times, like an old record with a skip, until somebody tapped her on the shoulder and started her in on a new tune. In other words, Alzheimer's victims usually retain their long-term memory while their short-term memory goes all to hell."

"Ah," I said. Then I had a brilliant idea. "If Aunt Trudy's been a cook all her life, would Alzheimer's make her forget she'd picked up a pot of boiling water to pour into the sink, then carry it into the living room when the phone rang instead of setting it back down on the stove? She spilled the water on the coffee table, ruining the inlaid wood. At least that's what we think happened. She says she doesn't know how the coffee table got soaked."

"Not necessarily," Doc Miller said. "Even with Alzheimer's, a woman who has spent so much of her life in the kitchen isn't likely to lose her long-term memory of the rules of cooking. She'd almost always set the pot back down on the stove before going into the living room."

"But how'd the coffee table get ruined?"

"Who knows?" Doc Miller shrugged. "You can't diagnose Alzheimer's from a single incident. It could've been anything. Maybe a tiny stroke. Maybe she just forgot—that happens, you know. Maybe somebody else ruined that table."

I sighed. "Well, thanks, Doc," I said. "See you next year . . . if I remember."

"You will," he said, raising a skeptical eyebrow over my lame attempt at gallows humor. As I turned to open the door, he looked at me with a grave expression I thought contained suspicion among the sympathy. "I hope everything's okay with your aunt—what was her name again?"

"Trudy," I said, thanking my stars I remembered.

"Trudy."

"Uh-huh," I said, and departed.

18

Ninety-nine percent of the time, Ginny Fitzgerald is a lovely person whose easy agreeableness lifts the spirits of everybody who encounters her. Her honest interest in other people always flatters them. When she speaks to you, you get the distinct impression that at that moment you are the most important person in her life.

But God help you if she finds you ridiculous.

Ginny possesses an extraordinarily disconcerting laugh. It is neither a ladylike titter nor a mannish barroom guffaw, but a rich, double-barreled contralto cataract. It begins with a throaty chortle, dips to the diaphragm where it gathers power and volume, then bursts out of her ample chest in a crescendo that rattles the silverware. She often throws her head back, teeth flashing, tears running down her cheeks. This is a laugh to beat all laughs.

If the occasion warrants, her laugh can be so infectious and irresistible that I have seen perfect strangers rise from their tables, walk over, and inquire timidly, "What's so funny?"

And if the occasion also warrants, her laugh can be so derisive it makes the victim feel smaller than a pebble on a shingle beach. More than once I've seen her knock the emotional props out from under honest, well-meaning, and innocent people this way. It's not deliberate. She just can't see what she's doing.

It took me a while to figure it out, but her booming ridicule is also a means for her to warn people off, to say "Don't mess with me." But I'm getting ahead of that part of the story.

That evening, as I told Ginny at a steak house unsurprisingly named the Sirloin about that day's encounter with the doctor and the earlier morning with the body of Paul Passoja, I had confessed a doubt that slowly had been building.

"Something's not quite right," I said, "but damned if I can put a finger on it. Seems to me Passoja was just too much of a woodsman to have made such a greenhorn mistake as spilling his supper on his tent, even with Alzheimer's. He was still in the early stages of it, anyway, the medical examiner said."

In that equally disconcerting way she has of cutting to the quick, Ginny said, "You mean you think Paul Passoja died as a result of foul play? With a *bear*?"

"Well . . . ," I said, hesitating. There it was finally, out in the open, that ridiculous idea I'd been turning over in my brain ever since the coroner's announcement.

That was all she needed. I sat back glumly as the concert of laughter began and other diners' heads rose in amazement. There was nothing to do except wait until Ginny had died down to a snuffling gasp.

"What are you saying?" she asked, wiping away tears, but speaking softly so the other diners couldn't hear. "Maybe somebody might have a good reason for killing Passoja, but a bear makes the world's worst murder weapon. Sure, maybe if you tie the victim to a tree and throw a gallon of chicken fat on him, then let the bear have his way . . . ?"

Her voice again rose to fill the room. "Oh, Steve!" And she started up again.

Ginny was right, I thought, as I grinned in blushing embarrassment. Everybody knows that bears are too unpredictable.

Just like the present company, I might have added. Suddenly Ginny did that thing with her hair, as if her spectacular outburst had never happened. She may not be a police officer, but as a historian she has a good eye for unexpected possibilities. "But that doesn't mean someone wouldn't have had a grudge against Paul," she said, again in a whisper, leaning toward me.

"What do you mean by that?" I asked. "I knew about his power in this part of the state, but I'm not aware that he had mortal enemies."

"It doesn't take much to piss somebody off in Porcupine County," she said. "Relationships up here go way back, and there aren't many of us. Most of us haven't much money, so all we can hold on to are memories of the way other people have treated us. If somebody does you dirty, you remember it a long, long time. Grudges just fester, like a splinter in your fingernail."

"Well, how would Passoja have angered somebody enough to want him dead? How would one find that out?"

"I don't really know," she said, "but if I were a cop, I'd start with his land deals. Over the years he sold a lot of his family's property, and that was how he touched the lives of many people here."

I had been unable to nail down the means. Maybe a motive would be easier to uncover, if there was one, and it would lead to the weapon— and the killer, if there was one. Without telling my colleagues—their reaction to the worries I had confided to Ginny would have been just as loudly scornful but without her empathy—I set out on an unofficial and unacknowledged investigation into the death of Paul Passoja. As somebody wiser than me once said, "Sometimes you've got to back out of the driveway with your lights off."

Of course I had to do everything discreetly and in between my regular deputy's duties, and the "investigation"—if I can call it that—proceeded agonizingly slowly.

19.

A few days later, on my day off, I visited the Department of Records and Deeds in the courthouse. There I told Laura Stillman, deputy recorder of deeds, that I was interested in buying some land and needed to research the history of several parcels. Cheerfully she led me to racks of ledgers in the records room.

"First you have to look up the parties to the sales in these indexes," she said brightly. I am from a part of the country where civil servants like to be uncivil, doing their best to make patrons feel guilty about taking up their valuable time. Public servants in Porcupine County, however, seem to be so delighted to have good jobs in an impoverished economy that they don't jeopardize their income with crotchety behavior.

Nor was Laura at all surprised that I wanted to go through the records. At any one time there are only three or four lawyers in all of Porcupine County, and they are constantly busy, so careful and thrifty property buyers and sellers often do their own paralegal legwork among the titles and deeds. They copy the pertinent records and take them to the attorneys for their professional once-over and approval, saving both time and fees.

"See, there are two sets of indexes," Laura said. "One lists the names of the grantors first, in alphabetical order, and by chronology. Grantors are the sellers. The other index lists the names of the grantees—the buyers—first. See, each listing contains the page number of a third volume—the deed volume—where copies of the actual deeds are kept."

She pulled down a deed volume and opened it at random. "Right here on each deed is a full description of the property—its dimensions and all that stuff," she said. "All set now? I'll leave you alone with these, and if you need to copy a page, just call me. Each copy is a dollar."

For hours I sat at a long table sifting through dusty old ledgers, looking for transactions between Paul Passoja or the Passoja Land Trust and other parties. I do not have a trained lawyer's eye, but as a cop I have seen enough official records to distinguish unusual things amid the boilerplate, and I know how to read fine print over and over again until I can understand it.

Since the end of the Second World War, Passoja had sold many parcels of land, some of them to locals whose names I immediately recognized. Sheriff Eli Garrow was among them. So were a host of local merchants and bankers and miners, woodsmen and people from Wisconsin, Illinois, and Minnesota, including the late Milton Browne, who had once owned my lakeshore lot.

Out of a sense of proprietorship I carefully examined the Browne deed and the subdeeds attached to it. According to the 1946 deed, Browne's land, three hundred feet of lakeshore frontage, extended only from the beach four hundred feet inland to a point fifty feet from the gravel road that Highway M-64 had been then. Passoja had retained the frontage land along the highway, giving Browne access rights over a dirt track to get to his property.

The frontage clause was clear enough, but it also was buried near the bottom of the description, couched in careful legal language that might have been bafflegab to the layman. In another volume I found a deed dated 1983 in which Passoja had sold the fifty-foot frontage to Browne for far more than the latter had paid for the entire lakeshore property in 1946.

That looked familiar, and I riffled back through the deeds and subdeeds of other lakefront properties Passoja had sold over the years. Sure enough, starting during 1944 and extending well into the 1970s, nearly all these deeds had retained for Passoja a 50- to 100-foot-wide frontage all along the highway. Since then he had sold the frontages to many of the parties to the original deeds.

"There's no mystery about that," Ginny said at her kitchen table that afternoon. "After the Second World War and the founding of the state park a lot of people thought that Upper Peninsula lakeshore property had a lot of commercial potential, especially when M-64 was at last paved in the early 1960s. Many of the families who owned the forest land along the highway worried that it might become an ugly commercial tourist strip. Keeping ownership of that fifty-foot frontage made sure the highway would never become a commercial eyesore."

Lovely as it was, the place never became overrun with tourists, even when summer hikers and campers visited the huge Wolverine Mountain Wilderness State Park, or when skiers and snowmobilers flocked to the park and the remote trails of the national forest next door. The Wolverines are hundreds of miles from the nearest big city, just too far for a weekend jaunt.

"When the years rolled on," Ginny continued, "and everybody realized that tourism would never come to Porcupine County in a big way, those frontages slowly were offered for sale to the other landowners."

"Especially when the frontage owners realized they'd never get rich from selling to commercial developers," I observed cynically. "The prices at which they sold the frontages were hardly token. They were out to get what they could."

Ginny nodded. "They were and are businessmen, after all."

I wondered, I told her, if some of those early buyers may have been unaware that their property lines hadn't extended to the highway. They might just have assumed it, trusting in the fairness of the sellers' lawyers who drew up the land contracts. And since they had easy access between their property and the highway, they may never have suspected a thing for a long time.

And then I remembered something I'd encountered in the courthouse: In the 1960s the Metrovich brothers—the two woodsmen who had found Passoja's body—had bought a lakefront parcel from him. Later that afternoon I stopped at the records and deeds office and had another look. Sure enough, that clause about the highway frontage existed on their deed. And there was no later subdeed giving them possession of the frontage. At the time of his death, Paul Passoja still owned that land.

This, I realized, did not mean the Metroviches had had anything to do with his death, but any homicide investigator will tell you that the first thing in building a list of suspects is to check out the person—or persons—who found the body, as well as those present at the scene, and anyone who might have profited financially from a murder.

I laid them out on the blackboard of my mind.

The first was Marjorie Passoja, who, as far as I knew, inherited everything Paul owned, though the probate attorneys hadn't yet done their stuff. I doubted she was the culprit. She already enjoyed all the things Passoja's money could buy, and nobody had ever whispered a thing about clandestine boy toys. Beautiful as she was, she seemed too shy, too withdrawn, to take up with young hunks, even as a widow. I wouldn't write her off until all the facts were in, but so far I could see no reason to make her a suspect.

Stan Maki? Highly unlikely. He was originally from Wisconsin, had no apparent history with Passoja, and in any event had been playing in an amateur golf tournament at Land o' Lakes for two days before we found Passoja's body. He had taken the third-place trophy. I knew from the chatter at Merle's Café that he had returned to Porcupine City late the night before Passoja's body was found and had had drinks at Hobbs' to show off his prize.

Hank Heikkila? A distinct possibility, but churlishness isn't a crime, and I hadn't seen anything that connected him to Passoja.

Mary Larch? A colleague, an officer of the law. No apparent connection, either.

Garrett Morton? An utter simpleton.

I drummed my fingers. Of the people who had been at Big Trees that morning, the Metroviches seemed the likeliest candidates, for there was a paper connection between them and Paul Passoja. There was a possible motive in those deeds.

20 I had to plan my confrontation with the brothers carefully. This was not yet—if ever it was going to be—an official investigation, and I didn't want to tip either the department or the Metroviches to my suspicions. I respected them too much to risk the genuine friendship we had built over the years. Cops in big cities early on develop a cynical attitude toward the people they supposedly serve and protect, because they usually see only their bad sides. But Porkies like the Metroviches are easy to like and admire.

All their lives the brothers had survived hard times, doing what they had to do in order to put food on the table. They had been born to an old lumbering family that had turned to mining early in the twentieth century when Porcupine County's timber was cut over. In the last two decades of the century the Lone Pine Mine near Silverton had faltered and closed, its copper ore no longer profitable enough to wrest from the earth. Fortunately the paper mill, the county's last remaining industry, found the brothers' multiple skills as woodsmen in the second-growth pulpwood forest valuable enough to add them to the fewer than five hundred workers it employed, most of them part-time.

Frank, the elder by half a dozen years, had raised Bill almost single-handedly after their mother's death from pneumonia, and the younger man as a result was utterly devoted to his brother. Separately, I thought, they might not have been able to remain in such a country of high unemployment, but together they made ends meet.

And in doing so they helped others do the same. Their pickup had a detachable plow that helped them earn a little extra money in classic Upper Peninsula fashion by clearing the snow from people's driveways.

When some of their customers were too broke to pay, the brothers cleared the driveways anyway. And they had been known to drop off a free cord or two of firewood at the houses of old folks who couldn't afford to stay warm in the winter.

Someday the favors were likely to be returned, if only in the form of a cherry pie, a bottle of wine or, more often, a few hours of labor. Once an elderly woman press-ganged her daughters into cleaning the Metroviches' house—a typical bachelor sty—from top to bottom while the brothers were gone for a few days in the woods, and they had returned not only to a sparkling home but also fresh-cut wildflowers on the kitchen table. They were amazed that anybody would go to all that trouble.

But these acts are not simply noble selflessness. People up here try to help others not only out of good-heartedness but also because they can't make it without neighbors to watch over them, too. It's the quid pro quo of survival. Like so many Porkies, the Metroviches may not be rich and sophisticated, but they straightforwardly, even courageously, make the most of what they have—and from some points of view it is a surprising lot.

And that is why I hoped fervently that the brothers weren't the guilty parties. But I am a cop, and I could not look the other way.

Over the next few days I made sure I casually ran into the Metroviches at Merle's or the hardware store and exchanged a few pleasantries. At any time I enjoy talking with them, not least because they speak a soft, almost pure "Yooper"—lots of "dis, dese, dem, dose" and the frequent "eh?" at the end of a declarative sentence that sounds almost Canadian. The genuine accent is slowly disappearing from the Upper Peninsula, thanks to the flattening of regional speech by radio, TV, and the Internet, and most Yooperspeak one hears these days is slathered on like stage Irish by merchants for the benefit of tourists.

Neither brother showed the slightest sign of guilt, and I have long considered them simple and guileless men. I confronted them subtly at breakfast one morning at Merle's in early November, while the proprietor of the same name stood on a stepladder replacing the Halloween decorations with pine boughs, wreaths, and Christmas lights.

"Getting a jump start on the holidays, eh?" I said. This was rare.

Unlike the big cities, where the Christmas commercial push begins not long after Labor Day, Porcupine County still considers Thanksgiving the start of the holiday season.

"Yep," Merle said. "Way the economy's going, I can use all the help I can get."

Shaking my head sympathetically, I slid into a booth behind the Metroviches and turned to face them. "Times are getting tougher, aren't they?" I asked.

"Not so's we've noticed," Frank said for them both. "They're always tough."

"It's been a hard year," I agreed, seguing into reminiscence about that unhappy day at the Big Trees.

"Paul Passoja was quite a fellow, but what kind of a guy was he personally?" I asked casually. "You ever have any dealings with him?"

I gazed out into the street but watched the brothers' reflection in the window for their reactions.

"We bought our property from him away back in 1963," Bill volunteered forthrightly. "Never had any trouble, eh? He treated us like everybody else. We did a lot of hiking in da woods with him, cleared some land for him and even worked on his cribs." Frank nodded in quiet assent. "He paid well, and he'd often shuck his coat and work right along with us, eh?"

Cribs were the low log-and-stone semi-jetties many lakefront landowners had built, or had had built for them, to fight wave-borne erosion of their beaches before the government put a halt to it in the 1970s as environmentally unsound. Milton Browne had himself constructed two cribs on the beach of the property I had bought from his estate, and they still stood after forty years of battering from the waves. They needed repair, however, and the next summer I was going to have to spend part of my vacation sawing logs, hauling rock, and driving spikes. "Yes," I said, "maybe you can give me some advice on *my* cribs. The lake is beating them all to hell."

"No sweat," Frank said amiably. "We'll give you a hand."

I decided to take the plunge. "When you bought your land from Paul in '63," I asked, "I guess he must have kept fifty feet of frontage along the highway, like he did with Milt Browne, who owned my cabin. Did you ever buy that frontage from Paul?"

"No, indeed," said Bill without hesitation. "He offered, but we didn't have the money. He wanted five thousand bucks. It wouldn't have been worth it anyway—it wouldn't have made any difference to us except to tidy things up nice and legal, eh?"

"I've had the idea that a lot of people who bought beach land from Paul didn't know for a long time that they didn't own their land clear up to the edge of the highway," I said neutrally "Was that so with you?"

"It sure was," Frank said without rancor, but his expression betrayed a tinge of irritation over the memory. Nobody likes to be had.

"We learned about it only when the electric company started running a new line of poles along the highway, down the part of the property we thought was ours. They never contacted us, and when we asked about it we learned that it was Passoja's land they were using."

"Didn't that frost your cheeks?" I asked.

"Well, sure, for a while," Bill said. "We did feel kind of cheated. We didn't know how to read a land deed. But lots of others were in the same boat. That was just how Paul Passoja was. He was a smart fellow. He wasn't mean, just a little sneaky, like his daddy before him—now *there* was an operator—and like all those sharp fellas who ran the mills and the mines. And in the long run it made no never mind."

It just did not seem that the Metroviches were lying, although I still felt uneasy. I put them on the back burner of my mind, and for a while my unofficial investigation lost much of its energy.

21 My courtship of Ginny Fitzgerald, however, gathered steam, and in more ways than one. As the nip of oncoming winter chilled the first weekend of November, I found myself at her dinner table again, a cheery blaze crackling in the hearth, the branches of the lovely silver Christmas tree from Jerusalem twinkling in the firelight. Partly because as an assimilated Indian I have no special heritage of my own, the national customs of other people have always attracted me, as if hanging out with them might give me a greater sense of belonging.

So it is with the Finns of Upper Michigan. Even though they have been thoroughly absorbed into American life for many decades—almost all of their old people are at least second-generation Americans—and they have intermarried widely, they have nevertheless hung on to many traditional ways. I'm not talking about folk dances or cooking (although I have grown a soft spot for the sweet holiday bread called *nisu*), but something deeper. I often envy Finns their rootedness, I told Ginny, and I love the gentle satiric humor they are able to poke at their own culture because they feel so comfortable in it.

"You mean like St. Urho?" Ginny said with a twinkle.

"Who's that?" I asked.

"Every March sixteenth," she said, "just before everybody in Chicago turns into an Irishman and drinks green beer on St. Patrick's Day, everybody up here turns into a Finlander and drinks purple schnapps to celebrate St. Urho's Day."

I chuckled.

"And don't forget the Heikki Lunta."

"What's that?"

"It's a snow dance we do, like you Indians with the rain dance."

I looked at her sharply, then relaxed. Casual remarks about my being Indian raised my hackles sometimes. I hated being shoved into pigeonholes where I didn't belong. But Ginny went on unconcernedly, as if she had just stated a harmless commonplace. Indeed she had, I suddenly realized. I look Indian, and there's nothing I can do about that, or anybody else. She just accepted it for what it was.

"The ritual is very specific and demanding," Ginny said in mock seriousness, "but there are minor regional differences. Here in Porcupine County we put on our red long-handled underwear, our swampers and chooks—what you call rubber-bottomed boots and toques—and plunk some polka music on the stereo, good and loud. If we are truly lucky we'll find an accordion player. We'll dance around the yard imploring Heikki Lunta—that's Hank Snow in English, and he's the god of the white stuff—to let 'er rip.

"The performance is best conducted with ample amounts of brandy. Some folks prefer beer, and others feel Mogen David is acceptable. If the dance is done with sincerity and in true faith, Heikki will bless us with a hearty storm. If the dance is halfhearted, though, it invalidates the process, and another performance is required. True fact."

Ginny's expression was so mock solemn and schoolmarmish that I burst out laughing.

"I understand that the famous Finnish sauna is giving way to the California hot tub," I said. "Just last week Tina Hokkanen told me she and her husband had discovered that while they were out of town their high school boy invited the whole senior class to a hot tub party in their basement. They cut class the day afterward and went over to clean up after themselves very carefully, and they would've gotten away with it, Tina said, if she and Toivo hadn't come home the next day to find the house spic-and-span but the dryer running, still full of towels."

Ginny chuckled. "Never let it be said that Finns aren't adaptable. A good soak in a hot tub is great after a long afternoon snowmobiling. And just because some of us have become spa people doesn't mean we aren't hairy-chested Finns. Only our sauna-enhanced blood can handle the water when it's at a full rolling boil."

All the same, she added, saunas still survived all over the Upper

Peninsula. "Younger folks are building electric saunas in their basements now," she said, "but real Finns still do it the old way—with wood fires in little outdoor buildings, log ones preferred. We don't flail each other with birch branches anymore, but the tougher ones among us do run straight from the sauna into the lake."

I shuddered. Lake Superior is cold, even in the summer, although in recent years, as the water level has dropped owing to sparser snowfall and warmer winter temperatures, it can be almost bearable. I've been in a few times in August when the inshore water has warmed to just over seventy degrees.

"How do people sauna in groups?" I asked. "Do you wear bathing suits or do you just go coed naked like California hot tubbers?"

"Finlanders do sauna in the nude," replied Ginny expressionlessly, "but we are very modest people. The sexes take their saunas separately, except for families with very small children. And, of course, married couples and lovers."

I could have sworn she eyed me speculatively.

"Have you ever taken a sauna, Steve?"

"Nope," I said. "Milt Browne didn't build one on his property and nobody's ever asked me."

"Well, now, Steve Martinez, it's time to change that. I'll go start the fire." She pointed out the window at a small, low log structure at the edge of her beach. I'd thought it was a woodshed. Only then did I notice the stovepipe at one end.

"Uh," I said, "I didn't bring a swimsuit."

"Don't need one," Ginny said. "We're adults. We know what boys and girls look like. Besides, you're a sworn officer of the law. I can trust you."

"You're going to sauna, too?"

"Why not?"

"Well . . ."

"Don't tell me you're a prude!"

22 I am not ashamed to admit that the distinct possibility of getting lucky that evening entered my mind. There had been a desultory relationship with a young lawyer after the army, and a one-night stand with an unattached female cop during a law enforcement seminar in Lansing the previous year, but other than that I had led a regrettably celibate life.

There had been opportunities. Middle-aged widows and divorcées who live alone in the countryside sometimes call in handsome younger deputies to obtain services not ordinarily provided on a police department's menu. Unlike one or two of my brother cops, however, I always extricated myself as gently and as firmly as I could from such situations. If it is unseemly for merchants to sleep with their customers, I thought, so it is indiscreet for cops to serve and protect in that particular fashion, especially in a county so sparsely populated that everybody knows everybody else. We might have to arrest a former paramour someday. And, in the worst case, how can you shoot someone you've shared a bed with? I will admit, however, that I often felt tempted—and, boy, at that moment, was I ever.

I resolved not to push matters—Ginny, I thought, was worth whatever patience it took to reach her heart. Nonetheless, when an hour later she beckoned from the low door of the sauna and I trotted over from the house, I was goose-bumpy not only from the evening chill but also anticipation. It had been a *long* time.

Through the door I saw Ginny sitting on a high bench in the cedar-lined cabin, swathed like me in an oversized white terry-cloth robe. "C'mon in!" she said, a cheery smile on her face.

It was, I thought, like stepping into a dry oven, and I gasped as the cedar-scented heat hit me. A large thermometer on the wall proclaimed 110 degrees Fahrenheit.

"Close the door and sit down here," said Ginny, spreading a towel on a low bench, almost painfully hot to the touch. I sat.

"Look outside, through the window," she said.

She climbed back on the high bench. "Okay, you can take off your robe now," she said, "but please keep your eyes out the window."

I obeyed. Then, as I heard her robe slither behind me to the bench, the short hairs on my arms and legs prickled.

But the heat, steadily building up in the room as if it were a wooden pressure vessel, had begun to wilt my impure thoughts. And when Ginny, beautiful naked Ginny unseen behind me, suddenly poured a ladleful of water onto the heated rocks at the side of the room, the sexual tension in the room expired in a flash of steam. It was like being thrown alive into an autoclave. Every sweat gland in my skin suddenly erupted. I began to pant like a beached fish.

"Good, huh?" asked Ginny. "More steam?"

"This takes getting used to," I gasped.

"We'll go easy on you the first time," she chuckled.

Ten minutes passed. I closed my eyes, seeing only red from the window light as the rising steam insinuated its way into my being through every pore I owned. I tried to breathe shallowly in order not to sear my lungs. From time to time Ginny dipped another ladleful of water onto the rocks, further boiling me in my own juices.

I felt agonizingly well-done when Ginny suddenly said, "Time to go! Head for the lake!"

The moon had risen over Lake Superior as I burst out of the sauna in a dead run, robe forgotten on the bench, thundered across the beach and plunged into the water in a shallow racing dive. The lake couldn't have been much colder than about fifty-five degrees—the unseasonably warm fall had kept the water comparatively warm inshore into November—but the effect was like leaping from a deep fryer into a bucket of supercooled ice. Electricity—I can call it only that—rocketed through my body as my pores slammed shut, every one of my nerves protesting the double insult to their harmony.

"WhooooOOOO!" I surfaced with a glorious bellow, triumphant that I had survived. I caught a flash of red hair and naked breast as Ginny herself erupted from the water in the moonlight twenty yards away, her delighted laugh echoing from the woods. I dove in again and sprinted a good seventy-five yards out into the lake, turned, and sprinted back.

I was puffing as I staggered over the rocky inshore out of the water. Again in her robe, Ginny leaned on a crib, gazing away from me to the west down the lake, watching the moon dip behind a bank of clouds. My robe lay on the crib where she had put it, and I donned it, marveling at how so very splendid I felt.

Ginny turned to me. "Now you can introduce yourself as a full-blooded Finlander at the next St. Urho's," she said with a chuckle.

After we dressed—in separate rooms—it felt only natural to say good night. Anything else, I thought, would have ruined a wonderful evening.

At the door Ginny's kiss and embrace were warm, the warmest ever. Her eyes shone as she waved good-bye and I walked out to the Explorer, feeling about as agreeable as I had felt in many, many years.

With flying colors I had passed a test, although exactly what kind I wasn't quite sure.

23 By the time I got home the moon had dipped below the horizon and the stars sparkled in the night sky, diamonds scattered on jeweler's velvet. Up here in the north, away from the lights and pollution of the cities, night is extraordinarily dark and clear, a perfect background for stargazing. I strode down to the water's edge and searched for a constellation I had loved ever since my boyhood.

"The Big Dipper," I could hear my Uncle Fred saying. "The Romans called it Ursa Major, the Great Bear." Fred, who took me under his wing when my adoptive parents died, was an amateur astronomer as well as a salty front-stoop storyteller. One night we peered at the northern sky through his big reflector telescope.

"The Romans had this knockout of a huntress called Callisto," Uncle Fred said. "Jupiter, the boss god, had the hots for her. He took on the shape of Diana, the goddess of hunters, so he could nail Callisto. Afterward she bore him a son called Arcas. But Juno, Jupiter's wife, heard about the rape, got jealous, and turned Callisto into the Great Bear.

"One day Arcas was out hunting, saw the bear and was about to kill it, but Jupiter stopped him and changed him into a bear, too—that's Ursa Minor, the Little Bear, just to the right and below Ursa Major.

"And now the Great Bear and the Little Bear forever rotate around the northern sky without ever setting, just to remind Jupiter of what he'd done."

As I studied the constellation through the telescope, Uncle Fred grasped my shoulder. "There's something even cooler," he said. "American Indians also saw a bear in those stars."

Some tribes told a story about three warriors chasing a huge bear through the forest for many days, many nights, and many narrow escapes. Finally, exhausted, the bear jumped into the sky, but the resolute Indians leaped after it. Now, all year round, the hunters pursue the bear across the northern sky.

What's more, Uncle Fred said, "in the autumn Ursa Major has turned upside down, with the bear flat on its back. That means the Indians have caught it and killed it, and its blood is falling from the sky and coloring the leaves of the trees. In the winter, when they cook the bear, its fat drips and turns the land white. As the moons pass and the sky once more moves towards spring, the bear slowly gets back on its feet and the chase starts all over again."

If two vastly different civilizations could see the same animal in the constellation, I thought decades after my introduction to the magic of the stars, perhaps the Great Bear was a kind of bridge between cultures. Or maybe not. The classical story, full of sex and revenge, clearly reflected an accurate view of human nature. But I liked the Indian tale better, for there was grandeur in its union of the stars with the seasons. And I could relate to the doggedness of those warriors.

I am not ordinarily a spiritual fellow, despite—or maybe because of—my upbringing by Christian missionaries. All the same, as I stood on the shore of Lake Superior staring into the night and recalling Uncle Fred's stories, it seemed as if the eternal Great Bear were beckoning, inviting me into the cosmos, gathering me into the great chain of being where I had so long struggled to find my place.

It suddenly reminded me of a worldlier event—what had happened to Paul Passoja at the claws of a black bear—and that darkened the almost mystical cloud of contentment I had been wrapped in since that sauna with Ginny.

And then, in the cabin, I opened the freezer for a couple of ice cubes. There, in a corner, sat the little Sucrets tin covered with hoarfrost, its gray shard of bacon invisible inside. With a start I thought guiltily, "That's evidence in a murder investigation and I'm concealing it!"

But then common sense won out. There was no murder investigation, just a few loose doubts rattling around in my brain. What really had happened to Paul Passoja, the consummate woodsman? Did a malign disease of old age kill him, or did something else? Why? Who? How? And did anyone care?

I sighed and turned in, sleeping fitfully all night, dreaming of chasing the Great Bear around and around the timeless sky.

24 A week later, before going on duty I played Saturday-morning dodgem with housewives hell-bent on vehicular homicide in the produce aisle at Frank's Supermarket as carols boomed out from speakers scattered around the store. I winced. Every holiday season Frank's elderly manager always turned the music up a couple of notches too high. I suspected that was because he was going deaf. Or maybe the music was making him deaf. I wished I had brought earplugs.

Navigating around a stack of canned cranberries and past a rack of Christmas cards, I nearly cannoned my cart into a tiny, stooped, gray-haired woman squeezing the grapefruit and leaning conspiratorially toward what looked like her twin sister. It was then that I heard the name for the first time.

"It was Karelia," the first woman whispered to the other. "Reino was never the same after." I looked at them blankly as I attempted to squeeze by.

The other noticed my glance and nudged her friend. "Shh!" she whispered sharply.

I chuckled inwardly and sniffed a cantaloupe. Whoever Karelia was, she must have been quite a temptress, I thought, if Reino had never recovered from her. The women still gazed at me guardedly as I turned the corner into the frozen foods section.

25

As I pulled the Explorer into Ginny's driveway just before lunch, a waxed black Lincoln only a year or two old loomed in the parkway next to her muddy Toyota 4-Runner. Michigan plates, I noticed automatically, always the alert and suspicious cop.

A small Detroit Lions sticker sat in a corner of the Lincoln's rear window—a dead giveaway that this was a Lower Michigan car, because the western Upper Peninsula is culturally part of Wisconsin and Minnesota, and people here root for either the Packers or the Vikings. What's more, U.P. vehicles are usually muddy and dusty—keeping a car clean in the north woods is both useless and an extravagance—but the Lincoln's paint was spotless and shiny, except for the bug-spattered hood and windshield, which bore a Grosse Pointe municipal sticker.

An out-of-town car that had come all the way up from Detroit, probably over the Mackinac Bridge, I deduced brilliantly. I should have been a detective.

The front door opened and two men walked out to the Lincoln, where I still stood. Both were middle-aged, balding, and dressed in nearly identical dark suits, expensive by the look of their cut. One of the men was portly and the other wore French cuffs. When you see suits like that in the U.P., somebody is about to be killed, buried, or foreclosed upon. I was prepared to dislike these two men.

"Good morning, deputy," said Portly in a gentle, cultured voice. "I hope nothing's wrong?"

"Nope, this is just a social visit," I said. "Mrs. Fitzgerald home?"

"Yes, she is," said French Cuffs with an amiable grin, like a Lions Club vice president. "The coffee's very good this morning, too."

A slightly awkward moment of silence followed. "Well, we'd best be getting back home," Portly said. "Long drive ahead."

"Nice to make your acquaintance," said French Cuffs.

I nodded and stood aside. The Lincoln drove off slowly, as if in law-abiding acknowledgment of the presence of authority in this part of the world.

Ginny stood in the door, a worried expression on her face and a blue power suit on her frame. It was strictly businesslike, yet smartly cut to accentuate her womanliness. "Donna Karan" came to mind for some odd reason; I am hardly knowledgeable about women's fashion, yet designers' names are part of the worldly flotsam that have stuck in odd corners of my brain. A simple strand of pearls lay on the ruffled blouse that peeked from her jacket. Neutral hose clad her legs—it was the first time I'd ever seen them outside Levi's, and they were shapely—atop alligator-leather pumps. Ferragamos, I thought blindly. Then I noticed the makeup—tastefully understated eye shadow, blush, and lipstick. This astonishingly elegant woman wouldn't look out of place in a corporate boardroom in Manhattan.

"What's wrong?" I said. "Did those men threaten you?"

"No," she said, relaxing only slightly. "Far from it."

"Who are they?"

For a moment she gazed at me speculatively. Then she touched her hair.

"Come in and I'll tell you," she said. "You're going to have to know sometime and I guess it's now."

A shapely seven-foot balsam, not yet trimmed, stood in its stand by the glowing fireplace of her great room, a huge combined kitchen and living room. A splendid aroma of newly cut balsam, burning maple logs, and Colombian coffee enveloped us.

We sat at the kitchen table. French Cuffs was right. The coffee was good.

"Steve," Ginny said, "I know I can trust you never to repeat to anyone what I'm about to tell you."

"Providing it doesn't break a law," I said.

Ginny snorted. "Those men," she said, "are my attorney and the director of my foundation. We meet once or twice a year to sign papers."

"Foundation?" I said dumbly.

"Yes," Ginny said. "I am a wealthy woman. Filthy rich, in fact."

It had been obvious to me that Ginny had some sort of outside income—her home and its furnishings were evidence of that—but I had simply thought her husband had left her reasonably well provided for before his death.

"When John died," Ginny said—it was the first time she had used his name—"he left the whole thing to me. And it was a rather big thing."

He had inherited his father's prosperous electrical parts company and in a few years quadrupled its capital. Upon his death Ginny took over the president's chair, and in a year the company had nearly doubled its income, thanks to John's judicious choice of management, including a whip-smart chief executive officer.

"But I'm a historian," Ginny said, "not a businesswoman. Although the company was thriving, there really was nothing for me to do except chair stockholders' meetings, and I held nearly all the stock. Two years after John died, a bigger company made a very generous merger offer, and I took it with the blessing of his management."

All those millions and nowhere to spend it—and no inclination to, for that matter. Ginny was simply uninterested in money, except for the good things it could do, and with the help of Portly and French Cuffs—who had been her husband's legal and financial advisers—she set up several foundations to distribute her income to worthy causes.

I would have to find out the real names of Portly and French Cuffs someday, I thought—no point in referring to upright, law-abiding citizens as if they were Mafiosi.

"I really wanted to come home and study the history of this place," Ginny said. "And maybe help out a little, where I could, with the foundations."

Within a year her volunteer work at the Historical Society had led to its poorly paid directorship, but no one in Porcupine County—indeed, no one outside the law offices of Portly & French Cuffs and the Internal Revenue Service—knew that she was the head of the foundations that put a new roof on the building, that provided much of the money for the restoration of the 150-year-old lighthouse at the mouth of the harbor, that paid for the new recovery room at the county hospital, that bought new uniforms for the peewee hockey team Mary Larch coached, that put the St. Nicholas Project's Christmas fund drive over the top. "No wonder you're so successful at writing grants," I said with a chuckle. "You fund them yourself."

"Money changes the way people look at you," Ginny said. "I don't want anyone here ever to know that I have it, like Marjorie Passoja. I love this place and I want to be an ordinary part of it. I want to be accepted for who I am, not what life has given me."

"I know," I said. "I do, too."

"You'll never tell?" she said.

"Never," I said. "Not unless you finance a revolution or hire a hit man."

She hugged me across the kitchen table, her eyes moist.

"Thank you, Steve Martinez," she said.

At that moment I loved her mightily and would easily have been swept away, my deputy's duties for the day forgotten, had she just beckoned. But she gazed distractedly out the kitchen window onto the calm and windless lake beyond, watching a fleet of mergansers dive for their breakfasts, popping up hither and yon, a pack of feathered submarines. I had been entrusted and I was not going to jeopardize that trust with a clumsy pass. There would be another moment, I was sure.

I broke the silence. "Speaking of hit men," I said. "In a way I was almost one this morning."

26 As Ginny changed behind her bedroom door, I told her about my odd encounter in the supermarket that morning.

"This Karelia sounds like quite a gal. Who was she?"

Ginny chuckled as she swept back into the living room in her everyday Levi's-and-Woolrich outfit, still in makeup. She was achingly lovely in anything she wore.

"Karelia wasn't a woman," Ginny said, unconsciously switching into historian's lecturing mode. "She was what used to be the eastern region of Finland. But she did cut quite a swath through the Upper Peninsula once."

"Clue me in," I said, consciously switching into detective's listening mode.

Back in the early 1930s, Ginny said, the government of the Karelian Autonomous Soviet Socialist Republic sent agents to upper Michigan, Minnesota, and Canada. They sought to recruit skilled and talented Finnish-American farmers and industrial workers for a better life of opportunity in the worker's paradise of Karelia, a province of largely Finnish-speaking inhabitants that over the centuries had changed hands several times between Finland and Russia. The Karelian commissars, nationalist to the core, thought importing American and Canadian Finns would prevent Moscow from packing the sparsely populated region with ethnic Russians.

"Karelia fever" captured many Upper Peninsula Finns. "We have always been highly political and intensely devoted to our community,"

Ginny said, "and in the old country we had all been Evangelical Lutherans. That was a stern and authoritarian state church, and we all did as it told us to. But over here, as you'd expect, many younger immigrants and second-generation Finnish-Americans had broken away from the old ways. It was the Depression, after all, and many had become radicalized. Some of them were looking for a whole new religion, and Marxism offered a glimpse of heaven."

The traditional churchly Finns, she added, had no illusions about godless communism and railed against the Karelian agents and their "Red dupes." Fistfights broke out at political rallies the recruiters held in halls all over Finnish immigrant territory. Families split, many fathers disowning their radical sons, some of whom had joined the Communist Party, and friendships crumbled as idealistic Finnish-American "pioneers" signed up and departed for Karelia to put their agricultural and industrial skills to work in the brave new world.

Like Americans elsewhere during the Depression, Finns were on the move. Thousands participated in the reverse migration to Karelia, Ginny said, their numbers swelling to more than ten thousand as the Depression deepened.

"Some of them of course were Communists," she said, "but many more were just naïve, terribly poor people seeking a better life. The Upper Peninsula had been hard hit by the Depression, and there was a lot of poverty here."

But when the pioneers arrived, things weren't as they expected. They had to go where the commissars told them to, in jobs that rarely fit their talents. Skilled artisans were put to work digging ditches. They couldn't travel without official permission and were denied access to Western newspapers. The promised land was a prison.

By 1935 Karelia fever had subsided as Stalin decided at last to move more Russians into the region instead of importing capitalism-tainted Finns from North America. The Karelian officials who had dreamed up the reverse-migration scheme were demoted, and when the great Soviet purges began in 1937, they were executed. The Finnish language was banned in Karelia, and when war between Finland and the Soviet Union loomed in 1938, the Soviets clapped into labor camps many of the immigrants from America as potentially disloyal elements. Some died in the camps and others were brutally liquidated. Few survived the Stalinist holocaust to return to freedom in the West.

"That's a horrible story," I said when Ginny finished. "How come I've never heard about it?"

"Simple," she said. "We're ashamed of it. We were suckered. It's a closed subject, even in my own family. A couple of great-uncles took their whole families to Karelia, and only one of them came back—alone. He still lives in a cabin in Baraga County. We never talked about Karelia, partly out of respect for him, because he never brought up the subject—it was just too painful for him. His wife left him, and took the children with her when he couldn't send money back from Karelia. And he lost all his land in America to the banks that grabbed the land for nickels on the dollar at tax auctions. When he came back, the new owner of his home just laughed at him and said he'd made his own bed and had to lie in it. It happened time and again, and many people who haven't shoved the whole Karelian episode under the bed still hold grudges about it."

"Even now?" I asked. "The people who remember Karelia fever have to be in their eighties and nineties."

"Yes, but their children and grandchildren remember, too, because in so many cases they lost their birthrights. There are still people in their sixties and seventies who don't talk to each other even today. Watch them at church and in public places. They may be neighbors, but they don't speak. They don't kill each other in bar shootings anymore, as happened a few times long ago, but they don't speak. It's as if the Hatfields and McCoys decided to hang up their weapons but just can't forget."

"Hmm," I said. Then the obvious conclusion occurred to me. "This could be a motive for murder. In the late thirties Paul Passoja was the right age—in his late teens—and as the son of a big landowner came from the right background."

Ginny looked up. "Still riding that horse, are you, Steve?"

"I'm afraid so," I said with a deep sigh. "It just won't let go."

"Like Karelia," Ginny said.

27 The first time I laid eyes on the Porcupine Township Library I was delighted. I'd never thought such a small town in the middle of nowhere could have such a well-stocked library complete with a couple of Internet computers. As I learned more about Porcupine County, however, I understood.

The county's population, once in the healthy five figures, had dwindled to less than eight thousand—the fewest in the state—as its young people left to find jobs in Milwaukee, Detroit, and Chicago. At the same time, more and more exiles who'd made their pile were returning home to live on their pensions.

And why not? In many ways it was Michigan's prettiest retirement community. Second-growth forest was restoring the countryside to much of its original wilderness. Except for the vast fields of tailings north of Lone Pine Mine, the wounds the copper mines had carved in the woods—now the Ottawa National Forest—had largely been hidden by scrub, brush, and young aspen and birch. The wildlife had roared back to the point where some species, like whitetail deer and black bears, had become nuisances. Timber wolves had returned to the most remote outback more than a century after they had been wiped out. There were even rumors of mountain lions. Most years the stream and lake fishing was as good as the hunting, and so was the snowmobiling and skiing.

Porkies who leave tend to get an education and then good jobs and more than a smattering of culture, and when they come home to retire they want to stay in touch with the outside world. Despite—and maybe because of—their isolation they demand books, magazines, and newspapers. If the library doesn't own a certain book, the state interlibrary loan system will provide it.

Millie Toole, the small, blue-haired dynamo of a librarian, is like so many people in the county a master at writing grants, and while many city libraries languish because their budgets are cut to hold the line on taxes, Millie's collection grows and grows. It's getting so big that she's negotiating for more space in the township building where the library occupies most of the the the ground floor.

As I walked in on my next day off, I spotted the Metrovich brothers sitting in overstuffed chairs across a low table from each other in front of the library's picture window, bedecked with pine boughs, holly, and a mock-Gothic SEASON'S GREETINGS painstakingly lettered in tempera. Their noses were buried in the daily newspapers, Frank's in the *Duluth Mining Gazette* and Bill's in the *Detroit Free Press*. Like most Porkies, the brothers must husband every cent they have, and they often spend their spare moments catching up with the news in the free papers at the library. I shot them a hello, and they waved back. I looked at them closely. Way too laid-back to be killers, I thought.

"Hi, Steve," Millie said from her desk. As a mystery novel addict I'm one of her better customers, but she's jaunty and cheerful to everybody. "What can I get for you today?"

"I'm on a history kick," I said. "I'd like to rummage around in old newspapers from the area. Got any?"

"Yep. The entire archive of the *Porcupine County Tribune*, all the way back to 1890, is on microfilm."

"Could I see the films beginning January 1, 1931?" I asked.

"Sure," she said, and in the shake of a squirrel's tail I was sitting behind a microfilm reader. Millie showed me how to insert a roll of film—I remembered from my college days, but there is always pleasure in watching an expert do things—and adjusted the focus.

"Yell when you need more," she said. I smiled. Millie was not a shusher. Like so many gatekeepers to small-town libraries, she was proud that hers was bright and bustling, not gloomy and hushed.

Rolling through scratched old microfilmed newspapers is a slow job but a fascinating one. It's like peeking into the diary of a departed time. Old stories about people meeting untimely ends always demand full reading. The ads, with their ridiculously low prices—five hundred dollars for a new Chevrolet, eighty-eight cents for a house dress—captivated. The personals, full of pleas for work, implied sad stories, while the "Help Wanted" listings were pitifully meager. As months rolled by, the numbers of official public notices headed NOTICE OF MORTGAGE FORECLOSURE SALE grew in number until in early 1932, the *Tribune* printed almost an entire page of them. Notices of auctions of tax-delinquent lands escalated, too. The Depression had well and truly hooked Porcupine County.

All the while I scanned the stories for the words *Karelia, socialist, emigrate, Finland,* and *workers needed*—as well as the names of anybody I might connect to Paul Passoja. All through 1930 and most of 1931 there was nothing about Karelia, although there were plenty of stories about socialist workers' organizations and Communist hall meetings, most of them slanted in disapproving language.

One was headlined HELP FOR KARELIA SOUGHT. A representative from the Karelian Technical Aid Society in New York was to speak at a workers' hall one weekend in October 1931. There was, said the story—clearly retyped from a press handout—a great need in Soviet Karelia for skilled lumbermen with tools and machines to harvest the vast forests in exchange for badly needed foreign currency. Preference would be given those who spoke Finnish. Those who agreed to go would be assisted in their passage.

I would have expected the *Tribune* to print an occasional story announcing that another party of Finns was heading for the Soviet Union, but it was silent on the matter. Finally, in the issue dated October 24, 1932, I saw this item:

SIX FINNISH PEOPLE
LEAVE FOR RUSSIA

Mr. and Mrs. Simon Talikka, Mr. Arthur Weser and sons Arthur Jr. and Elmer, and Henrikki Heikkila, who have lived at Greenfield for several years, left Thursday for Kontupohja, United Social Soviet Russia.

> A farewell party was given for them at
> the Farmers' Hall at Greenfield Monday
> evening.

That gave me pause, not only because of the creative rendering of the name of the Union of Soviet Socialist Republics, nor the fact that my cabin lies is just a mile west from Greenfield, halfway between Porcupine City and the Wolverines. That name *Heikkila* jumped out at me. The diminutive for the Finnish *Henrikki* is "Heikki," and "Hank" is the English equivalent of *Heikki*. Hank Heikkila had been at Big Trees the morning Paul Passoja was found dead. Could it be?

28

Indeed it was.

"Hank Heikkila?" said Ginny, that gorgeous human card catalog, while we feasted on lake trout at my cabin. "Yes, he's the grandson and namesake of Henrikki, who went to Karelia and disappeared into the Gulag. I'm not certain, but I think you will find that the taxes on Henrikki's farm went delinquent when he stopped sending money back from Karelia—if he ever sent a cent—and that somebody, maybe Einar Passoja, bought it at a tax auction. Quite a few well-connected Porcupine County businessmen turned into tax title sharks in those days."

"What happened to Hank's father?" I asked.

"Urho Heikkila was a teenager when Henrikki left for Karelia," she replied. "Urho was about the same age as Paul. They must have known each other. Urho's family probably went on relief. We do know that Urho joined the army in the Second World War and came back to work in the mines. He died fairly young, not long after his son was born, from alcoholism."

"It's not really relevant," I said, "but what about the grandson's claim that he's also descended from the voyageurs?"

"It's possible," Ginny said. "I think Urho was the one who started the story. It's a historical fact that voyageurs settled in this area and intermarried with Indians—you'll find that some Ojibwa on the reservation near Baraga have French surnames. But a lot of the poorer people in the county like to give themselves a little dignity by dressing up their genealogy and making it more interesting than it really is. Rich people do that, too. We all want to be descended from kings."

29 Sure enough, Ginny was right. The next day it took only an hour at the courthouse to find the records: Henrikki Heikkila's land had been sold at tax auction to none other than Einar Passoja in 1934, barely two years after Henrikki had left for Karelia. In 1940 Einar sold the property for four times the price he had paid.

This time, I thought, I was not going to beat around the bush. Hank Heikkila was so crazy-man-of-the-woods reclusive that he was probably the last person who'd share with his nearest neighbor the details of an encounter with a deputy sheriff. As one of Porcupine County's more notorious bottom feeders, he wouldn't want to call attention to himself in the slightest way.

I knew where Hank's shack was, deep in the tall spruce and balsam second growth in the southern quarter of the county at the end of an old logging trail, but he was not visible when I arrived in my ancient Jeep, trailing a cloud of dust. It was my day off, and I was wearing civilian clothes. This was not an official visit from a sheriff's deputy. Nonetheless, I tucked the .357 into my belt at the small of my back.

Amid a score of traps in various stages of disrepair a dozen fisher pelts hung drying in the sun on a board leaning against the front of the shack. That was grounds for a DNR arrest right there—the season limit for fisher is three per person—but state game violations are not within the purview of a deputy sheriff. I knew, however, that the knowledge might prove an useful lever to get Hank talking, for Molly Schultz, the DNR's Porcupine County conservation officer and Stan Maki's boss, would be highly interested.

The door to the shack was open. I peered inside from the doorway.

Hank's big Springfield rifle rested against a badly cracked pine table piebald with remnants of red and white paint, and the few other sticks of furniture—two rusty gray metal folding chairs and a peeling brown cardboard wardrobe—suggested that no one in this room had ever uttered the word *houseproud*. Animal hair and dried mud lay scattered in the corners, as if chased there by desultory swipes with a broom.

On a nearby bureau missing half its drawers sat a .38 revolver—an old Smith & Wesson Police Special, cylinder open and empty. In Michigan, handguns must be registered, and I doubted that one was, for Hank Heikkila was not the kind to respect the niceties of the law. But I was after something more important than proper paperwork.

I checked the .357 at my back. Though he had never been known to be violent, Hank was the sort of woodsman who could quietly trail someone through the forest for hours, remaining just out of sight and sometimes just a few feet away, like a preternaturally patient Indian waiting for the best spot to attack. Everyone in the county suspected he often did, just to show himself that there was something he could do better than anybody else. It would not have surprised me if from time to time during the stalk he trained the sights of his old Springfield on his unsuspecting quarry, a kind of counting coup over a powerful enemy, perhaps even gently touching the trigger at the moment of greatest glory. If he indeed did that, it was a dangerous game.

"Hank!" I shouted. He had to be close by. He was too smart to go off somewhere for a few days and leave stuff like those pelts and the .38 out in the open.

No answer.

"Hank, where are you?"

No answer.

"You want me to tell Molly about those pelts?"

"Gahhhhhhhh*dammit!*"

Hank stepped out from behind a fat oak, and my nostrils wrinkled as I smelled him. I was yards away, but directly downwind. It had been a while since he had bathed, and he was sweating. I was sure he had followed me as I drove in, cutting on foot through the woods to keep up with the Jeep.

"You're not gonna tell her, are you?"

"That depends," I said. I relaxed. Hank was unarmed, and his hands were out in the open. He knew the fine points of dealing with the cops. He'd been pinched often enough.

"On what?"

"On what you can tell me about Paul Passoja."

"I ain't telling you a fucking thing," he said, defiance smoldering in his reedy voice.

"Those pelts?" He glanced at them guiltily. With his record of poaching convictions, they were good for a few months in the slammer.

"What do you wanna know?"

"How you felt about him."

"He was a shit."

"Why do you say that?"

"You know."

"Know what?"

"What his daddy did to my grandpa. Everybody knows."

"But that was a long time ago."

"Yeah."

"Why are you so pissed off about it?"

"What's it to you?"

"Just curious."

"Like hell."

This conversation was going nowhere. I decided to take a chance.

"Are you happy Paul's dead?"

"Sure. Just like a lot of other people."

"Like who?"

Hank swept his arm around as if to include the whole forest and every living creature in it.

"Did you kill him?"

Hank's eyes smoldered. "A bear did. You know that."

I blinked. Maybe Hank was unaware of the coroner's conclusion.

"Did you help the bear?"

"Oh, sure," Hank said. "I led the bear right up to the tent by the paw and said, 'There he is. Eat.' Who are you kidding?"

I tried another tack. "Why did you hate Paul so when it was his father who took your grandfather's land?"

Hank cracked open the door to his anger. "He never let me forget it. When I was still a kid he would laugh and say, 'Your grandpa was a Red and got what he deserved.'"

That was an unusually long sentence from Hank, I suspect the longest he had uttered in many years.

"And after that?"

"He'd say stuff like 'I was on your grandpa's old farm the other day. Too bad your family couldn't keep hold of it.' He liked to bring it up, to rub it in. He was like that. He liked to be cruel when there was no call for it."

For Hank Heikkila, that was a Johnstown Flood of words. "Sounds like a lot of people might have had it in for Paul Passoja."

"You better believe it."

"Who?"

"I told you."

Hank had purged his tanks and was going to say no more.

"All right," I said. I strode away from the doorway, got into the Jeep and rolled down the window. "Hank!"

"Yeah?"

"We never had this conversation. And I never saw those fisher pelts. Or that .38."

He looked at me, his eyes glowing like coals over the underbrush of his beard. It was just a slight nod, but it was enough.

Hank, I was certain, knew something he wasn't telling. In a place where there are so few people everyone knows everyone else's business, secrets are valuable, for someday they might come in handy—for money or for something else. But what Hank's secret was I had no idea. Nor did I have any idea just then how to go about finding it out. I'd have to file the notion in the cluttered "unsolved cases" drawer of my mind until a better opportunity presented itself—maybe a return visit to his cabin.

My spirits, however, lifted as I drove down the track away from Hank's cabin. Not a hundred yards away a small clearing appeared by the road, and in it was a small bear digging up roots. Quietly I stopped the Jeep to watch. There is something about wildlife of any kind that touches my soul, and these little interludes in the woods often make my day. This one did.

For the little bear was the same one I had seen the afternoon of the day Paul Passoja died, when we tracked down the big one that had given him a heart attack. He looked a little larger than before, but his broad cinnamon face was unmistakable. I wasn't surprised that he was there; the spot where we had killed the rogue bear lay scarcely five miles southwest.

"Hello, buddy," I whispered.

The bear instantly looked up and locked eyes with me. I could have sworn he nodded at me. Some kind of acknowledgment passed between us, but I couldn't for the life of me explain it. All I can say is that it felt almost as if he were saying, "Nice to see you again, friend."

Presently he gave the ground one last swipe of his paw, glanced at me once more, then ambled slowly into the trees and disappeared.

I drove on, smiling.

30

Standing at the kitchen sink, Ginny reached behind her and tucked in the shirttail of her sheer silken blouse with the unconscious candor that comes from living alone, a frankness that outlined her generous breasts against the light from the bright November moon in the kitchen window. The sight brought an involuntary catch to my throat.

I stood up, folded my arms around her, and kissed her graceful neck. She giggled and squirmed against me. I felt my blood rising. It had been soaring all evening and was about to trip the safety valve.

"Bring your toothbrush," she had said that morning.

We had set the Thanksgiving table together and prepared a small turkey, I ministering to the wild rice as best as I could. At the meal we said little, for we were as shy as teenagers preparing to say farewell to their virginity. A delicious tension built slowly but firmly as we savored every bite, every moment, speaking desultorily about nothing at all, looking into each other's eyes and glancing away demurely. By dessert I was as ready as I'd ever be. Ginny's face was flushed, her eyes shining, but she sweetly prolonged the wait, insisting that we wash the dishes.

Then she put her hand in mine. "Come, Steve," she said, gazing into my face with what seemed a mixture of adoration and unabashed lust. We climbed the stairs to her bedroom in the loft overlooking the great room. Her eyes fixed on mine, she drew back the eiderdown comforter covering her huge oaken bed, seemingly four feet off the floor.

"Close your eyes, Steve," she said. I did. Fabric rustled softly.

"Steve."

She stood by the window, its filmy white drapes softly billowing, the reddening autumn light dancing through wind-rustled branches on the joyously ripe body of a woman at the height of her sexuality. I had never seen anything so beautiful, and I gasped.

She smiled. "Come here," she said, and began to undo the buttons on my shirt.

In bed, when I began to draw her close to me, she suddenly stiffened, pushing me away, and burst into tears.

"I can't, Steve," she said. "I can't."

"What . . . ? Why . . . ?" I said, startled.

"Steve, don't! Just hold me, will you?"

In a welter of disappointment, confusion, and frustration I wrapped my arms around her, and after what seemed like hours of silent wakefulness we fell asleep, snuggling like spoons in a drawer.

Some time before three in the morning she stirred and reached for me. This time there was no hesitation, no reluctance, and just as dawn reddened the eastern sky, we slept once more, exhausted.

31

It was after nine when I smelled the wonderful odor of coffee and fresh nisu, the braided Finnish holiday bread made with cardamom. As I stumbled into the kitchen buttoning my jeans, Ginny turned from the stove in her nightgown and embraced me as if she never wanted to let go.

"Sit down, Stephen Two Crow Martinez," she said. "After you eat, I have something to tell you."

She watched every forkful as it went in. Then she did the thing with her hair.

"Ready?"

I nodded.

"It's about last night," she said. "I'm sorry how it began."

"I'm not sorry how it ended," I said.

"You deserve an explanation, though."

"Okay."

"About a year after John died," she said, "I met a man who hurt me very badly."

I placed my hand on hers and waited.

"He was the most incredibly charming man I had ever met, and one of the most fascinating, too. Malcolm was the director of a Baptist refugee agency and told me the most heartrending and hair-raising stories about saving lives in the Gaza Strip and the Balkans. You wouldn't believe the danger he put himself into in places like that.

"The cliché is true—Malcolm swept me off my feet. I'd rather not go into the details, but after a few months we became engaged. He started living with me most of the time, secretly of course because, he said, his church wouldn't have approved. Oh, Steve, I was so bubble-headed, so naïve about it all.

"My best friend, Sheila, who is a lawyer, demanded that she draw up a prenuptial agreement for us. Malcolm was *insulted*. I was, too. 'He's a hero!' I said. 'We don't need one!' But she insisted.

"I was so *stupid*. I didn't notice when Malcolm's lawyer—by now he had hired one—proposed that half of John's company stock go to him in the prenup.

"It was the classic story, Steve. I was a lonely widow and Malcolm paid me the kind of attention no man had ever had, not even John, who was absolutely devoted to me.

"I might have married Malcolm if he hadn't made a stupid mistake. After my accountants delivered my income tax return for my signature, Malcolm so very kindly offered to take it to the post office. Later that day he came back seemingly very upset. He had put down his jacket to play pickup basketball in a park, and it had been stolen. Naturally the tax return was still in it.

"I was unconcerned. Oh, all the accountants had to do was run off another copy on the printer, and I'd sign it. No harm done.

"But a couple of weeks later I went to Malcolm's house on an errand. I needed a pencil to leave him a note, and I opened his desk drawer looking for one. There was my tax return. It had been opened. And there was yellow highlighter across the names of the stocks Malcolm had suggested for his half of the prenup settlement.

"I went to Sheila and told her about what I had found. She didn't say anything. She just handed me a folder. It was from a private investigator she had hired to check on Malcolm. He had not been married just once, as he had told me, but five times. All his wives had been wealthy, and he had taken them for every cent he could. He loved being a hero, but he didn't mind being a son of a bitch, too."

I looked up at Ginny. A single tear coursed down her cheek. I reached up and wiped it away.

"It took me so very long to learn to trust completely again," she said. "Until last night."

I chuckled softly. "And is that the real reason you came back to Porcupine County? You ran away. Just like me."

"Part of it, yes," she said, smiling. "But not all. And *now*, Steve, you know all my secrets."

I wasn't sure about that, but in response I swept her into my arms. She snuggled her head between my neck and my shoulder as I carried her up to the loft. We didn't wake again until almost noon.

32

I had just ticketed the teenage driver of an dilapidated old Chevy that had proved it still could get its speedometer needle to ninety when Mary Larch's voice crackled on the open radio.

"Car twelve-oh to dispatcher," she said. "I'm at Hank Heikkila's cabin. Bring the camera, will you? And send the ambulance, but tell them not to hurry."

By "camera" Mary meant for Joe to send the sheriff's department's evidence kit. By "not to hurry" Mary meant someone was dead. I grimaced. Three weeks before Christmas this wasn't what I wanted to hear on the radio.

"This is Steve," I broke in. "I'm on M-64 near Silverton. Want help?" Like most of the other deputies, I never bother with the protocol of identifying myself by car number. We all recognize each other's voices anyway. Being young and gung-ho, Mary, however, believed in the rules. Gil O'Brien often asked the rest of us why we couldn't follow them.

"Yeah," said Joe. "Mary, Steve's on his way."

Half an hour later I bounced down the logging track and pulled up at Hank's shack. Mary had cordoned off the place with crime-scene tape, although I doubted a rubbernecking crowd would form this deep in the woods.

"Steve," Mary said soberly.

I didn't say anything. Not even "What do we got?"—that hackneyed expression beloved of television detectives. I just raised my eyebrows wordlessly.

"Come look."

I stepped into the shack. On the floor Hank sprawled supine, missing most of his head above the eyebrows. It was spattered low on the wall behind him, a stew of blood, brain matter, and bone shards still dripping slowly to the floor. His Springfield rested on his stomach, muzzle pointing toward his mouth. Powder burns blackened his lips. He was fully dressed except for bare feet.

"Whatever happened to holly and mistletoe?" I asked nobody in particular. "Just what we wanted to see at this time of year."

A sheriff's deputy is bound to encounter violent death from time to time, especially on the highway. A car wreck does terrible things to the human body. Cops develop a protective emotional carapace against such sights.

But suicide has always been hard for me to keep at arm's length, because my first thought is to wonder what inner demons could have driven a fellow human being to such a despairing act, to wall himself off with such finality from society. Donne was right: "Ask not for whom the bell tolls; it tolls for thee."

Mary evidently heard the tolling, too. She looked drawn and white. I suspected that she had lost her lunch while I was on the way. I doubted that she had ever seen a gunshot death, though she had encountered plenty of traffic victims.

"Looks like he put the barrel in his mouth and used a toe to press the trigger," Mary said, as if I needed to be told the obvious. She was not brazen about it, but she sometimes subtly treated her brother deputies as if we were not as quick off the mark as she was. It didn't matter. Smart young people tend to be smart-ass, too. I used to be that way myself. We grow out of it.

"Find anything else?" I asked.

"This note," Mary said, pointing to a table. "I haven't touched it."

"That's good, Mary," I said.

She bristled slightly.

"I'm not being sarcastic," I said. "You'd be surprised at how many country cops would disturb a possible homicide scene without realizing it. We just don't get that much experience."

I looked at the note, faceup on the table. It contained three words in crude block printing: **LIFE IS SHIT.**

Next to it was a half empty fifth of Jim Beam, the cap beside the bottle.

In the wilderness, suicide is not uncommon. Up here many people use alcohol to pacify the resentments of poverty, loneliness, and hard winters. Booze easily triggers depression, and every year two or three people in Porcupine County decide they've had enough. Mix despondency with a few drinks, and a quick bullet sounds good. It happens in the cities, too. And Hank already had been halfway there. Some people might say he had heard voices from the beyond, beckoning him to join them. Others might declare he only had needed his medication adjusted. In either case I would have been sorry.

"Anything else?"

"No."

New seeds of doubt sprouted in my mind. Where was that .38 I'd seen a few days earlier? Why hadn't Hank used it instead of that clumsy Springfield? True, a .38 slug is much lighter than that of a big .45–70, but in the fashion Hank had apparently chosen for his exit, it would have been just as effective—and a lot easier.

The revolver was nowhere to be found among Hank's mess, and I did not mention it to Mary. I had filed no report of my unofficial and unauthorized visit to Hank's shack, and I was not about to tell my superiors about my equally unofficial and unauthorized quasi-investigation—if you could call it that—of a case that had been closed.

But someone, I was certain, had taken that Smith & Wesson, and I was equally sure that its disappearance had something to do with what Hank Heikkila had not wanted to tell me. I prowled around outside. The fisher pelts I'd seen were gone, and so were all of Hank's traps. Perhaps he'd sold the pelts and left the traps in the woods, but a few traps always sit in pieces around a trapper's shack, awaiting repair. "No traps," I told Mary. "That's odd."

She caught on quickly. "Possible robbery-homicide. That's enough to call the blues, isn't it?"

Rural sheriff's departments don't have the resources for any but the most elementary criminal investigations. The state troopers do have the goods, and when we know we're out of our depth we call them in. Often they take over a case entirely, usually with the swift agreement of the sheriff. One fewer headache for him.

I radioed Joe, who spoke to Gil, who authorized him to call the Michigan State Police post at Wakefield, fifty miles southwest of Porcupine City. The thirteen-trooper post there includes an evidence-gathering team of uniformed technicians all too happy to drop their daily routine of traffic stops on U.S. 2 and fight crime instead.

Soon two troopers arrived, siren blaring and blue lights flashing. The drive up from Wakefield had taken them just forty minutes. They'd kept the pyrotechnics on even while bouncing down the narrow logging track in the middle of nowhere. At least the siren drowned out the sound of their big highway cruiser's undercarriage thumping on the ridges of the deep ruts. State cops like to make an entrance. Deputy sheriffs would, too, if they knew how.

I told them what I thought. They shrugged.

"Anything could have happened to those traps," said one after carefully examining the scene. "Trappers trap, after all. They're probably out on the line. Look, here's a bit of cash in a drawer. The place doesn't look as if it's been tossed.

"Looks like suicide," said the other trooper. "Open . . ."

"And shut," said the first.

"No shit?" I said. Though I knew their real names, I privately called them Monoghan and Monroe, the dirty-mouthed wiseguy detectives who always are first at the opening murder scene of a cop novel by Ed McBain, whose books I had devoured in high school.

I kept the skepticism out of my voice. We have to get along with these folks, who, like state cops everywhere, tend to look upon country deputies as a bunch of dim bulb clodhoppers who can't write a legible traffic ticket. Sometimes, though, even their smart evidence guys—and these two, for all their airiness, were really quite competent—quickly reach a conclusion and then find the facts to back it up, missing a detail that might cast a little doubt. They're only human.

And they didn't know about that .38.

"Mary," I said.

"Steve?"

"What brought you out here in the first place? This isn't part of your regular patrol run."

She shook her head. "I got bored and decided to extend it a little. Besides, any reason to go into the woods."

She loved them as much as I did.

"Makes sense."

I nodded, then climbed into the Explorer and keyed the mike. "Joe?" I said. "Steve. Returning to patrol now."

"Ten-five," Joe said.

"Ten-*five?*"

"I get tired of saying 'Ten-four' all the time," he replied.

Despite my mood I laughed. Joe *never* says "Ten-four."

But I felt glum again as I drove back down the track. I hadn't said a word to my superiors about that bacon shard in the freezer, I hadn't said a word about my suspicions about the death of Paul Passoja, and I hadn't said a word about my earlier visit to Hank or that old .38 on his table. This was not acceptable behavior for a sworn police officer, and I knew I was digging an awfully deep hole for myself if ever the department found out.

33

"Anything could have happened to that .38 in the three days since I saw Hank," I told Ginny at her kitchen table that evening. She had confided her secrets in me, and now I was returning the compliment—which, when you think about it, is more of an intimacy than the sharing of a bed. "Maybe he sold the gun. Or lost it in the woods somewhere. Or maybe somebody came along and saw it and stole it. Maybe it *was* suicide. Damn, I wish I'd had the presence of mind to write down its serial number. Maybe it *was* suicide."

Ginny folded her arms and gazed out the kitchen window. "But you don't think so," she said.

"No."

"Why?"

"I don't know. Intuition, I guess. Cops sometimes get hunches for no good reason at all. When they pan out, we're geniuses. When they don't, we're dummies."

"And you men make fun of women's intuition!" Her smile, however, was sympathetic. "Now what are you going to do?"

"Maybe I've been making a mistake trying to find an obvious motive for killing Paul Passoja," I said. "Maybe I'm barking up the wrong tree. Maybe I should be looking at the means instead."

"The bear?" Ginny sounded doubtful. "How? Tracing a bear isn't like tracing the ownership of a gun. People don't register bears. They belong to the woods."

I nodded. The carcass of the bear that killed Paul Passoja—or, rather, frightened him to death—had long been buried beneath tons of garbage in a landfill. The rangers had been unable to discover where the bear had come from. Wisconsin wasn't missing one. Neither was Minnesota. The university biology departments had drawn a blank, too. It looked as if the bear had never been counted and tagged, although it had once worn a radio collar. That was odd—researchers who collar bears almost always tag them on one or both ears for easy identification.

It looked as if all leads to this murder weapon, if it indeed was that, had simply vanished as effectively as if it had been tossed off a ship crossing the deepest trench in the Pacific.

"Maybe not *the* bear," I said, "but *a* bear."

"Hmm?" Ginny said.

"If I can prove that *a* bear can be induced to kill somebody, maybe that will lead somewhere."

"And how do you propose to do that?"

"I've got an idea."

34 The next morning I pulled up before a red-brick university building in Marquette and looked up Dr. William Ursuline on the register. I had called ahead to his secretary, asking for an appointment, and at the elected hour his office door swept open.

I must have gaped. Before me stood the most bearlike man I had ever encountered. He was not tall, perhaps five-seven, but thick, muscular, broad-shouldered and, except for his pink pate, astonishingly *hairy*. Curls of dark fur peeked above his collar and around his cuffs, and a magnificent full black beard adorned his strong chin.

"Ursuline," I thought. That must come from *ursa*, the Latin for "bear."

The human bear smiled and held out a paw. "Bill Ursuline," he said with twinkling good humor. "It's not true what you're thinking."

Was I that obvious? I blushed.

"People may grow to resemble their dogs," he said, "but biologists don't necessarily look like the animals they study. Jane Goodall hardly looks like a chimp, does she?"

Dr. Ursuline, however, resembled his lissome and celebrated fellow field biologist in at least one way: for years he had studied his subjects intimately, living with them and becoming an accepted part of their world. He spent weeks and even months in the woods following the animals, chronicling their every waking movement and publishing his findings regularly after he got home and washed away the smell of bear.

At first people thought he was crazy, but as the fame of the "Bear Man" spread far and wide, he soon became acknowledged as the leading scholar in his field. Huge universities proffered lucrative professorial chairs, but he refused them—he wanted to stay close to his bears in case he took the yen to spend a weekend with one. Next to Dr. Ursuline, a state bear wrangler like Stan Maki was a kindergartner.

"Well, Deputy Martinez, what can I do for you?" he said.

I started in surprise. I had not identified myself as a law enforcement officer when leaving the message on Dr. Ursuline's answering machine asking for an appointment. All I said was that I was a concerned citizen with a bit of information the biologist might be interested in.

Dr. Ursuline smiled shrewdly. "You don't think I'd check up on strangers who want to come see me?" he said with a chuckle. "All it took was a call to the Porcupine County sheriff's department. A fellow named Joe Koski assured me you weren't a lunatic or a Jehovah's Witness."

It stood to reason that before heading into the wilderness, the biologist would make sure law enforcement all over Upper Michigan knew what an apparent wild man in the woods was up to, and would know whom to talk to in every cop shop.

But I was unhappy that Joe knew I'd contacted a bear expert in Marquette. Maybe I could minimize the damage.

"Well, yes, I guess so," I said. "But I'd really rather you didn't talk about my coming, if you don't mind."

"You're investigating a crime?" Dr. Ursuline said forthrightly.

"Not exactly," I said. "Not officially, anyway. Just tidying up some loose ends." That was perfectly true.

He leaned back in his chair and studied me frankly. "This has to do with Paul Passoja, doesn't it?"

"How the hell did you know?" must have been written all over my face.

"Elementary, my dear Martinez," said Dr. Ursuline with a laugh, not waiting for me to respond. "What would a cop want to see a bear man about, except something having to do with an unfortunate event, such as the demise of a very important Upper Michigan personage?"

I shook my head. "That case has been closed," I said truthfully.

"As for the case I'm unofficially working on," I added, lying only by omission, "I'm sorry, but for legal reasons I cannot share the details with you. I know you probably will wonder why, but I can only ask you questions—I cannot answer any of yours. If ever there comes a time when I can talk about this with you, I will. That's a promise.

"And I am going to ask for full confidentiality about our meeting. I hope very much you won't even tell other people that we met."

Dr. Ursuline didn't hesitate for a moment, but looked me straight in the eye. "Yes, of course," he declared. "It won't leave this office. You have my word."

I sighed in relief.

"Now," he said briskly, "how *can* I help you?"

"What I came here to find out is whether a bear could be trained secretly to attack a human being, and if so, what it would take to make sure it would really do the job."

Dr. Ursuline's eyes widened. He shook his head slowly, but leaned back in his chair, lost in thought.

"They're too unpredictable, aren't they?" I asked after a moment.

"Not necessarily," he said. "There are a lot of myths about bears. For instance, there's never been a documented instance of a mother black bear defending her cubs by attacking a human being.

"Unpredictability is largely a myth, too. Bears are creatures of habit, just as we are. And like us they're individuals. Every bear lives by a set of habits that are both similar to but also appreciably different from those of any other bear. If you know a bear well, you can generally predict what it will do at any old time. It's the bear you don't know that's unpredictable."

I waited. "Bears are easily conditioned," Dr. Ursuline said. "It doesn't take much to turn one into a garbage bear—just two or three encounters with food waste will do. They're pretty smart about that. They're smart enough to understand that where humans are, there will be easy food. And you know that if humans get between them and their lunch, that's when they can turn dangerous.

"If a bear wants food and you won't hand it over, it's likely to forget its natural fear of humans and go for you in anger. It wouldn't be hard to figure out how to piss off a bear. Stake one to a tree, or hold it in a cage, and starve it for a bit while dangling wonderfully smelly food just out of reach. Now where could this be done? Let's say a remote place deep in the forest where nobody goes except once in a long while.

Perhaps a week, perhaps two weeks, and you'd have a large and ugly killing machine that needs only to be baited."

"Could you be absolutely sure a particular bear would kill in a given situation?" I asked.

"Could you be absolutely sure a particular *human* would kill in a given situation?" he replied, quickly adding. "I'm sorry, I'm not supposed to be asking the questions."

I laughed. "I can answer that one. No, of course not. But given certain facts, the odds would be in favor of that happening. You just need the right opportunity."

"There you go," said Dr. Ursuline. "Same with bears."

I stood up. "That's all for now," I said. "Thanks. You've been very helpful."

"If it's possible," said the bear man, "I'd like very much someday to know exactly how."

"I promise," I said, and took my leave.

On the drive back to Porcupine City I felt as if I had achieved a major step forward in the case. Maybe I didn't yet have motive, but I very likely had nailed down the means. With a little help, a bear could make an excellent murder weapon—one, if things went as expected, that could disappear into the woods under its own power, as this one had—almost.

Yes, Paul Passoja had been killed by a heart attack, but if the hand of a human being had been behind the bear assault that ended in his demise, I had a good case for homicide—maybe even murder one.

I just wished Joe Koski, Porcupine County's biggest gossip, didn't know I'd gone to Marquette.

35 Swish-*clunk*. Swish-*clunk*. Swish-*clunk*. Though my breath hung visibly on the cold air, I had fallen into a soothing, sweat-oiled rhythm at the chopping block in my backyard, the broadax rising and falling in graceful arcs upon maple bitts, splitting them into manageable chunks for the cast-iron wood stove with which I heated my cabin. The hickory handle felt hard and dry inside my tingling hands. It was a chore I looked forward to every day.

Half an hour a morning at the woodpile provides me with enough fuel for the long cold season, October through April, and the exercise keeps my wrists, arms, and shoulders supple, limber, and fit while relaxing the tensions of life. Chopping wood salves the body and calms the mind.

Like most Upper Peninsulans who live along Lake Superior, I keep a small propane tank and furnace in reserve for the times when I can't be in residence, but a pile of wood the size of a couple of Buicks—mostly maple and oak that has escaped the pulp logger's chainsaw—is the most economical way, as well as the healthiest, to stay warm in the winter.

The shore of Lake Superior in winter is as windswept and desolate as any Arctic coast, but in the warmth of summer and fall it teems with wildlife—bear, deer, otter, fishers, bald eagles, Canada geese, canvasbacks, mallards, mergansers, and loons.

And garrulous little chickadees. Constantly they talk to one another, *"chick . . . chick . . . chick a dee, dee,"* over and over, keeping in touch with one another, a close-knit community brimful with belongings. *"Chick a dee, dee, dee,"* I called, immediately answered by a *"dee?"* in the big maple above me.

You could carry on entire conversations with these birds, and I often did, to Ginny's considerable amusement. But she understood my feelings: in our "chats" these little birds gathered me into their fellowship of the woods, as they must have some long-ago ancestor of mine. At times like these I felt almost as if I had come home.

I was not surprised to hear the sudden rising beat of large wings, gathering power as they drew closer. I looked up just as a loose formation of a dozen Canada geese flashed past just offshore, scarcely a foot off the water, honking frantically as they bore in like feathered torpedo bombers for my closest neighbor's crib three hundred yards east on the beach. Following close aboard were scores—no, *hundreds*—of honkers. The sky darkened as they swooped by and splashed down into a bobbing flotilla around the crib. In an ordinary year they would have been long gone to southern climes for the winter, but the extraordinarily warm autumn—and the lack of violent storms that signaled the time to depart—had delayed their migration.

I looked at my watch and smiled. Four-thirty, feeding time. You could set your clock by Sheila Carnahan; a wide-bodied widow who, every day at that hour, spring through autumn, waddles out from her house with twenty pounds of cracked corn and spreads it along the shore. The geese wade through the shallows and up the sand as if it were Omaha Beach, honking and hissing, bobbing and nodding like humans at a dinner party. As the geese pecked for their dinner, frantic gulls dove and darted in to contest possession. The noise was deafening.

These days naturalists advise us not to feed wild birds or animals, for that, they say, upsets the normal routines of nature. That makes sense, but Sheila is all by herself a normal routine of nature, and I can't see that her indulgence of geese affects their lives, except perhaps to make them a little cushier while they hang around.

I returned to my task. Swish-*clunk*. Swish-*clunk*. Swish-*craaack!*

A maple limb twelve feet away at the level of my head exploded in splinters, followed an instant later by the heavy report of a powerful rifle. I dove into an untidy heap behind the woodpile toward the lake, rolling in the sand, my elbow bouncing off a boulder as I reached for a revolver that wasn't there but in its holster on the kitchen table. That damned sidearm! Never there when I needed it! For several seconds I lay still, nuzzling a man-sized pine log, sand gritting my teeth, pain shooting up from my abused elbow. No sound except the sigh of the breeze and the echo of honks from down the beach.

"Who's there?" I called at last, raising my head cautiously above the woodpile.

No answer.

"Show yourself!"

No answer.

I took a deep breath and gathered my wits. Judging from the brief but definite interval between the smashing of the branch and the sound and location of the shot, the shooter must have been three or four hundred yards away through heavy scrub—hardly a distance at which a man deliberately tries to kill another, not unless he's using artillery. Most likely it was just a random shot from an overeager hunter keeping his eye sharp at target practice. But bear season had ended a month ago, firearms deer season the week before—except for antique muzzle-loaders, and that shot hadn't come with the heavy whump of a black-powder weapon. This wasn't a time to hear the crack of modern big-bore rifles. Somebody was getting careless.

I stood up, rubbing my sore elbow, and strode back to the cabin, counting the charges I'd file against the trigger-happy idiot if I ever caught him.

36 In the early afternoon, as I drove to the sheriff's office, that familiar feeling of uneasiness wrapped itself around my entrails. And it settled in to stay as Joe Koski gave me the big hello through the lumpily decorated little Douglas fir that obscured the top of the dispatcher's desk.

"Steve!" he boomed cheerily, all heads in the squadroom rising as one. "What are you doing, getting ready for next year's bear season? Did the Bear Man tell you the best places to find 'em?"

Joe's jocularity told me he didn't suspect the real reason for my visit to Dr. Ursuline, but now I was sure everybody and his grandmother in Porcupine County knew about it. I kept my voice light as I responded, "I'm thinking about changing jobs and learning how to live with bears. It might pay better than this one."

Everyone laughed and returned to work. Porcupine County deputies hardly drew excessive salaries and they were often the subject of bitter humor. I hoped the joke had deflected their curiosity.

The phone rang, and Joe answered it. His expression turned somber. "Steve," he said, "that call from was from Union Bay campground. An eighteen-foot outboard boat that was launched from the ramp there hasn't been heard from since last night. Four people aboard. Time to hit the air. I'll have Mary cover your patrol area."

I nodded. From time to time, even on a perfectly pleasant day like this one, Lake Superior can change its mood almost without warning. Small boats launched from the public ramp near the campground at the Wolverine Wilderness Park sometimes get into trouble with high waves or stiff winds, and the warm autumn meant more campers had extended the fishing season long past a sensible time.

The nearest Coast Guard helicopter station is at Traverse City in lower Michigan, two hundred thirty miles to the southeast. It takes the Guard's Dolphin helicopters almost two hours to make the flight to Porcupine City, so when somebody gets in trouble off Porcupine County, the sheriff's department usually is the first called to mount an air search. Small planes flown by Civil Air Patrol volunteers from nearby airports also help, as does the Gogebic County sheriff's department just west of Porcupine County.

At the airport I rolled the Cessna out of its hangar, quickly did the preflight chores, and ten minutes later rose from the runway, heading for the lake. Since small boats often are driven onshore by bad weather—and the waves the previous night had pounded the beach from the north—I decided to start the search along the lakeshore. Maybe the boat had gone aground somewhere along the thirty miles of park shoreline, uninhabited except for summer and fall hikers who used a couple of rustic cabins near the beach.

Banking west two hundred feet out from the shore, I held the Cessna's altitude at three hundred feet above the waves and carefully watched the sand and tree line for signs of life. All I saw for nine miles was the occasional agate hunter out on the stony beach, then civilization disappeared as the Union Bay campground passed beneath my left wing. Mile after mile passed, the only visible living creature an occasional deer that spooked and dashed into the tree line as the roaring aluminum eagle swooped close overhead.

After crossing the mouth of the Presque Isle River, the westernmost boundary of the park and my jurisdiction, I keyed the radio on the departmental frequency. "Porcupine Sheriff six-eight-six-Papa-Quebec from Presque Isle," I said, giving the airplane's registration number, 686PQ. "No joy on the shoreline. Starting grid search of the lake now." In the air I followed radio etiquette. The Feds demanded it.

"Charlie-Alpha-Papa-seven-five-niner-Sierra-Echo from Ironwood to Porcupine sheriff's aircraft," my receiver crackled in response. It was a Civil Air Patrol volunteer. "Copy. No joy either west of Presque Isle."

Climbing to two thousand feet, I began a steady sweep farther out from the shoreline, extending the pattern half a mile with every reciprocal change in course. The waves grew choppier and choppier the farther out I flew. Two miles, then three, then four. At six miles from shore, almost directly north of Union Bay, I spotted the overturned white hull of the boat, bobbing wildly in the surf. First I marked the location on my handheld global positioning satellite receiver, a little electronic instrument that reads signals from man-made birds orbiting in space and locates my exact spot on earth with an accuracy of three feet. Then I wrote down the coordinates and called them in to the sheriff's department and Coast Guard helicopter, still a hundred miles to the southeast.

Dipping down to a scant hundred feet above the waves, I circled repeatedly, looking for survivors. I could see none. No one who had gone into the fifty-degree water the previous day was likely to have lived more than a few hours before dying of hypothermia—unless they'd had the sense to dress in waterproof thermal "dry suits," which few sport boaters owned. It was going to be a search for bodies now, and that was a job for the Dolphin from Traverse City as well as the Coast Guard cutter from Houghton fifty miles to the east and the smaller sport boats from the Guard auxiliary in Porcupine City.

When it arrived—it was still a good half-hour away—the Dolphin would use the overturned boat as a reference point for its search, flying two ever-increasing circles in a bow-tie shape, using the boat as the "knot." The boats would sail a course much as I had flown, running parallel to the shore for five miles, then turning ninety degrees out from shore half a mile and sailing the reciprocal course until reaching a point five miles offshore. They'd repeat the pattern farther down the shore until they either encountered survivors, bodies, or nightfall. Once darkness came they'd almost certainly give up all hope, trusting to currents and waves to wash the bodies onto the beach within days or weeks.

Sadly I banked the 172 away from the boat, my job done, heading for base. I did not fly southeast straight to Porcupine County Airport, but directly south toward the shore of Union Bay, where I'd turn east toward my destination. Flying over open water in a single-engine airplane makes me nervous, as it does most sensible pilots—we often hear imaginary misses and catches from the engine—and I will go miles out of my way to get "feet dry" as soon as possible.

Before turning toward the airport, I decided on a low flyby over the Lone Pine Mine tailings fields, a desolate moonscape of sterile, rocky leftovers from processed copper ore, a wasteland speckled with ponds of poisoned water three miles wide by five miles long left by nearly a century of mining and smelting. Until very recently, astronauts could have used the tailings to train for landings on inhospitable planets. Now environmental laws had frog-marched the mine company into seeding the area with fast-growing ground cover from the air, hoping to heal decades of industrial rapine. That would, I thought, take many generations.

For years, however, the fertile forest floor had slowly crept over the outer edges of the tailings, and that, the sheriff thought, might be a likely place for criminal entrepreneurs to grow small crops of marijuana. I throttled back to seventy knots and dropped to three hundred feet above the tailings, gazing into the narrow verge of dry brush and brown grass between the tree line and the moonscape.

Almost immediately I saw a large dun patch, maybe a hundred feet by seventy-five feet, standing out from the evergreens around it. Even this late in the year, enough leaves remained to reveal regular borders, almost squared off. Crapped-out sheriff's aircraft don't boast night-vision devices and high-tech thermal-imaging gadgets that allow DEA and state police aircraft, usually helicopters, to spot the heat emitted by pot farming, from indoor grow lamps to moving bodies and disturbed earth, from thousands of feet in the dead of night—but at low altitudes in daylight in any season the old Mark One Eyeball still has its uses.

In summer and early fall the color of marijuana is unique, an almost iridescent green with such a bold hint of blue that novice spotters sometimes confuse it with blue spruce, among which it is often grown to camouflage it from the air. From low altitude pot—which can be anywhere from a couple of inches high to eighteen feet tall, with three-inch trunks—looks spiky, like a prehistoric shrub. Growers plant it just about everywhere, from cornfields and swamps to backyards and gardens. Often perps who think they're being clever will scatter clumps around the inside rows of a huge cornfield, trusting the tall stalks to hide the pot from prying eyes at the verges of the field. From the air, however, the bushes stand out like zits on a teenage beauty.

Porcupine County is too far north, its growing season too short and its soil too clayey, for commercial corn farming. If a warm summer is forecast, however, dairymen and gardeners sometimes will plant corn on the southern sides of tree-lined roadways, protected from north winds, mostly for cattle silage and a little for sweet eating, and once in a while pot entrepreneurs will try to hide their handiwork among the rows. In Porcupine County we airborne pot-spotters more commonly find our quarry in small clearings and along forest edges, usually close to natural water sources like ponds, streams, or swamps. Water buckets, plastic fencing, trails, and vehicle tracks are also clues.

I circled over the patch, snapping photographs with the old Minolta and two hundred millimeter lens that was part of the plane's law enforcement tool kit. Maybe it was nothing, just an illusion, but the dried-up patch ought to be investigated, and despite the lateness of the season and my antipathy for drug laws I decided to report what I'd seen; a few of us might have to follow up the next day on the ground just to see if any clues remained. I marked the position on the GPS.

Thunk! Something—a small bird?—struck the right wing. I leveled the Cessna and eyeballed everything I could see. The instruments reported nothing out of the ordinary and the controls behaved as they should. All the same, I decided to break off the search and return to base immediately to check out things. I hoped the leading edge of the wing hadn't taken on a big dent; that might require a trip to the mechanic at Land o' Lakes some forty miles south for expensive aluminum reskinning. The plane had suffered bird strikes several times; such are the perils of low-level searches over wilderness.

After taxiing up to the hangar and swinging around the tail, I stepped down from the plane, walked around to the right wing, and immediately saw the two holes. One—30 caliber, by the look of it—punctured the underside of the leading edge not much more than a foot inboard of the wingtip, and the second had butterflied out through the aluminum skin on top. Fortunately, the bullet had struck no ribs or spar, and a simple riveted patch would make the fix. A few inches of duct tape could serve as a temporary repair.

I picked up the mike to radio the department and call out the troops for an armed search of the woods near the tailings for the shooter, who likely was the cultivator of the pot crop—if that is what it was. Second thoughts, however, won out.

This was the second time that day I had been shot at. Fool me once, shame on you; fool me twice, shame on me. Thanks to Joe Koski, that one-man loudspeaker system, the whole town—including whoever set up Paul Passoja—by now knew I had an unusual interest in bears.

But was that someone really trying to kill me, or just send me a message? If the shooter who blasted the maple branch while I was chopping wood was the same person who holed my wing, he didn't seem to be trying very hard. Furthermore, there are much better ways to ambush somebody. It would have been child's play for a halfway decent marksman with a scoped rifle to pick me off from the brush on the short walk from my cabin to the Jeep in the driveway, or to put a bullet into the slow-flying Cessna's fuselage right under the pilot's seat.

How serious a target was I, really? Did the other guy know I was on to him, or was he just trying to draw me out, toying with me until something cracked?

I sighed. Going to the undersheriff meant I would also have to report my suspicions about a closed case without a shred of solid evidence. That wasn't likely to result in anything but derisive laughter in front of everybody else and a full-bore drill-sergeant chewing out behind closed doors, maybe even suspension without pay. Things may be different on TV cop shows, but law enforcement brass does not like lone-wolf officers, regarding them as loose cannons on their tight ships. A cop's first duty if he wants to keep his job is to keep his superiors informed.

Sure, reporting the bullet strike on the airplane would bring everybody out to hunt the shooter by the tailings, but he likely would have disappeared. If he had anything to do with Paul Passoja's death, a raid would just cause him to go to ground for a good long time.

And there was no point in giving that good-hearted blabbermouth, Joe Koski, something else to gossip about.

I was going to have to do this alone.

37

But I did not feel lonely. Not with Ginny Fitzgerald by my side: my sounding board, my sidekick, my Sancho Panza, my love. For a long time now we had been an Item for the town gossips from Joe Koski on down, and now everybody thought of us as a couple, even though we did not yet live together. "Bring that fine young deputy of yours with you," people automatically would say while inviting Ginny to dinner.

Before then, few of them would have thought of inviting me alone, sometimes because I was the law, sometimes because I was not a white man, and sometimes because I tended, consciously and unconsciously, to keep people at arm's-length.

Increasingly I realized that the protective standoffishness in which I had wrapped myself for years did me more harm than good. As a biological Indian and a cultural white I often felt part of two worlds, but not completely at home in either. When I was exceptionally far gone in self-pity—thankfully a rare event—I thought of myself as a restless misfit endlessly sailing the oceans looking for a safe harbor.

Sometimes I failed to recognize an offer of friendship, thinking instead that it was a patronizing gesture toward my Indian-ness, or maybe a calculated act of manipulation because I was a police officer. Sometimes I could be my own worst enemy.

In some things, I was beginning to see, Ginny was very much like me. And we were both slow learners.

At her invitation I had moved in my toothbrush, but that was it. Sometimes I'd spend the night, especially if I was off-duty the next day; sometimes she'd spend the night. Every day I saw her at least once, if only fleetingly, and we had dinner together several times a week. Our relationship settled into a comfortable routine, ripening slowly, neither of us making demands on the other.

In different ways we both had been hurt by circumstance—I by being wrested from my biological heritage and she by loss and betrayal—and, mutually, silently, we had agreed to heal slowly so that our cures would be complete. We had all the time in the world.

38 On the tenth day of December I stopped at Merle's for breakfast. Even before the sun came up holiday lights twinkled in the storefronts all up and down Main Street, MERRY CHRISTMAS and HAPPY HOLIDAYS blazing from shopwindows. Inside Merle's the faces, however, looked as dark as the predawn chill outside. "Who died?" I asked as I sat down at the counter next to Joe Koski.

"Maybe all of Porcupine County," Joe said gloomily. "We've just been watching the Weather Channel, and the forecasters predicted no precipitation for the next three weeks. You know what that means."

"Ouch," I said. The Upper Peninsula of Michigan—indeed, the entire northern reaches of the Western Hemisphere—had been experiencing its third consecutive unseasonably warm autumn. We hadn't seen even the usual three-day October blow out of the northwest off Lake Superior, a vicious forty-knot wind that slams shutters like pistol shots and chases the last summer people south. In the papers Alaskans had complained that the permafrost that served as their basement was melting, their roads rolling and cracking in mush underneath, and engineers worried that the oil pipeline south from Prudhoe Bay would crack and spill black stuff all over the landscape. For the southern shore of Lake Superior, the warming trend meant no snow, except for a light dusting, might fall until after the New Year.

I had no idea whether the culprit was global warming thanks to greenhouse gases or just one of nature's mood swings, but whatever it was, the consequences could be disastrous to Porcupine County's economy. Last year the first heavy snow didn't fall until December 28, meaning the ski slopes at the state park and the snowmobile trails didn't have enough pack until it was too late to attract the Christmas and New Year's skiers and snowmobilers from Chicago and Minneapolis. Several restaurants and motels, dependent on the holiday trade to stay alive, went under. A second consecutive snow drought could mean curtains for the county as a viable economy. "Porcupine County needs white stuff to make green stuff," people often said.

I shook my head feelingly. I am not a fan of snowmobiles, even though I own one just to be able to get into the woods over unplowed tracks when going by cross-country skis just takes too long. Snowmobiles are noisy, smelly beasts, and they often awaken me on Sunday mornings when stoked-up snowmobilers roar past my cabin at blinding speeds along the frozen berms beyond the beach. Snowmobiles and booze seem to go together like fish and water, and every winter I have to clean up after messy accidents. In Porcupine County at least three or four snowmobile fatalities occur every winter—usually involving a drunk zooming off-trail into a barbed-wire fence or to the bottom of a lake whose ice is too thin to support the weight of a speeding machine. When I carry on about snowmobiles, however, it is always when I am alone with Ginny, who has the insouciance to remind hypocritical old me that I like to drive annoyingly noisy, smelly beasts, too—those with wings and a propeller.

But I'd never knock snowmobiles in public. Porcupine County's merchants depend on the money visiting snowmobilers spend, and many volunteers belonging to the Wolverines Snowmobile Club devote hours to grooming snowmobile trails leased from local landowners.

"There's something else, though," said Joe. "Yesterday Gail Sheehan came up with the idea of having a Christmas parade, with floats and fireworks and everything, on the twenty-third." Gail was the operator of the local day-care center and a civic-minded lady.

The café's patrons visibly brightened at Joe's words.

"It's a great idea," said Merle, smiling maybe for the first time in weeks.

It was. I could see that getting people together for a public celebration of the birth of Christ, or the winter solstice, or just generally the holidays, depending on one's religious belief, was a way of drawing wagons into a circle against adversity. Even if the first big snow was too late, a Fourth of July–style festival might help folks' resolve to tough it out—and possibly could bring in visitors from outside the county, visitors who might spend a little money.

"What are the rules?" I asked.

"There's only one rule," Joe said. "Only one Santa for the entire parade, and he's to ride on the fire engine. No use confusing the kiddies, Gail said."

"Makes sense."

I paid for the eggs and toast and left, the gloom in Merle's having lifted at the prospect of a parade.

39 "Be careful, Steve," Ginny muttered sleepily as I slipped from her bed well before dawn the next morning. I didn't have the luxury of time. I had to nail the killer of Paul Passoja before he nailed me.

And so, at cold daybreak on my next day off, two days after the Cessna took the bullet, I jounced in my Jeep southward up a rocky track through the forest leading to the western edge of the mine tailings. When I was still half a mile away, I pulled off into the brush, backed the Jeep out of sight, and concealed the tire tracks with evergreen boughs and twigs. I would hoof it the rest of the way.

Around my neck dangled the Minolta and telephoto, which looked like a standard woods photographer's equipage. If I should encounter anyone—unlikely at this hour and in this place—I was merely indulging in my notorious new hobby of bear-watching, and had they seen any that hadn't yet gone to ground, hibernating for the winter? My .357 nestled behind quick-release Velcro tabs in a fanny pack, ready for action. To blend in with the brush as well as protect myself against the thirty-degree chill I wore a camouflaged canvas hunter's jacket over a warm down inner coat and a similarly colored Elmer Fudd hat with earflaps—a typical nature shutterbug's outfit.

For half an hour I threaded my way through the trees, avoiding footpaths, treading softly on the balls of my feet, not the heels, silent as an . . . an . . . an *Indian*, grinning to myself at the irony. The dead brown grass was so dry that my boots kicked up dust as I moved diagonally through the tree line. Even this late in the year a careless spark could start a wildfire.

I tiptoed past a large field of stumps arranged in neat rows, fat ones and thin ones, like a company of soldiers lined up according to size. It was a freshly harvested Christmas tree plantation, one of scores in Porcupine County, and though its produce had long been wrapped in netting and trucked south to Milwaukee and Chicago, the sharp sweet smell of pine tar still hung in the air.

Presently, through the edge of the forest the desolate, bare tailings loomed high above me, green-stained copper-bearing rocks mixed with crystalline slag from the old smelter. I pulled out the GPS and took my bearings. The suspicious patch I had spotted two days before still stood three-quarters of a mile away.

I had full confidence in the device, although they'd led us deputies on some merry chases. A few years before, when handheld hikers' GPS receivers first came on the market, a local merchant became the first Porky to buy one. He was an unpopular man who frequently abused his wife. She often called us in mid-beating, but never would press charges.

Shortly after the merchant boasted about it to everybody one day in Merle's Café, he disappeared into the mountains. When he didn't come home by the next morning, his wife called the sheriff, and we had to mount a six-hour search-and-rescue operation before we found him deep in the hinterlands, thoroughly lost.

Worse, the following weekend, having declared that he *really* had learned to use the GPS, he vanished into the woods again. And again we had to tramp around for hours to find his sorry ass. "I'll never know why Sylvia ever bothered to call him in missing," Koski said afterward. "I'd just have let the bears eat the idiot."

Thanks to my aviation experience with the GPS, I wasn't likely to get lost in the woods. Carefully staying out of sight within the tree line, I trudged slowly southward, picking my way over log falls and boulders and skirting thick copses, until the GPS had led me almost to the spot I had marked in the air. It was a wide low expanse of dry, spiky brush eight feet high, harvested many weeks ago. Peering carefully in all directions, I bent down, plucked a withered brown leaf from the ground, crumbled it between thumb and forefinger, and sniffed. *Cannabis sativa*, sure enough, and probably of high quality as well. After bagging several leaves for evidence, I turned back to the woods, glad to get out of sight again.

Instead of retracing my route along the edge of the forest, I plunged directly east, hoping to find evidence of cultivation—tools, irrigation pipes, empty fertilizer bags. I saw none, but a hundred yards away through the brush, half a mile east of the tailings, the outlines of a rough cabin and outbuildings took shape. I saw wood smoke curling from a chimney at the same time I smelled it. Someone was around.

Drawing upon all the woods lore I had learned in the army and from the *Boy Scout Handbook*, I tiptoed toward the cabin, hiding behind spruces and pines, breathing shallowly, making not a sound, waiting after each step to see if I had been discovered. My .357 hung heavy in its fanny pack. I briefly considered drawing it, but decided that I did not yet have sufficient evidence of wrongdoing.

Then I saw him as he emerged from the cabin. It was Garrett Morton, the hulking and not overbright summer ranger who had arrived at Big Trees with Stan Maki the morning Paul Passoja had been found dead. This was a surprise. What was Garrett doing here in the backwoods of the Upper Peninsula in early December instead of playing forward for Kalamazoo College's basketball team? I had not seen him since he and Stan had captured that bear at the Cackle Shack, and assumed he'd gone back to school.

I stayed hidden, mulling over this new discovery. Garrett wore jeans and a bright blue down parka, was unarmed, carried only a heavy rucksack, and did not seem a present threat to my safety or anyone else's. Quickly I decided not to make myself known. Other than the presence of the cabin half a mile east of the tailings, there was nothing to connect Garrett to the marijuana patch or to the shot fired at my airplane. Better be sure before moving in on him.

By himself Garrett didn't behave like an overeager puppy, but he still stumbled about like a clumsy suburban kid who didn't quite fit into the woods. He shouldered aside saplings and shuffled noisily through fallen leaves and twigs as he strode to a low outbuilding. He wrenched open a ramshackle door, its hinges creaking in protest, and in a moment drove out in an ancient, rusty yellow Scout, its loose tailpipe rattling as it bounced onto the track and then northward toward M-64, three miles away. I waited, still as a Sioux scouting an enemy, until I could no longer hear the rattle.

Before I could move toward the cabin, a lone doe nearby snorted, causing me nearly to jump out of my skin. When deer think there's something they should be seeing, they often blow, or snort, to see if they can't startle it into moving. They always nailed me.

I had no warrant to search the place and doubted if I could get one, even if I was on an official investigation. I was tempted to go ahead on my unofficial own, but didn't want to taint a possible legal case. I could, however, look as much as I wanted so long as I didn't touch any doors or enter any buildings. I peered in a window past a rough burlap curtain.

A table, chairs, bed, cabinets no doubt holding canned and dried food, and water jugs—the typical layout of a hunting cabin, which this one obviously was. Clothes lay draped over the folding metal screen standing to the left of the fireplace, where smoke rose still. Not very smart—an ember could pop into the room and start a blaze. This was not a seasoned woodsman who lived here, or even a tenderfoot with half a brain. Nor was this anybody who planned to celebrate Christmas here—there wasn't a wreath or ornament of any kind.

Eureka! In a corner lay two large bags of fertilizer with a roll of flexible PVC irrigation pipe. There was the link to the marijuana patch.

Double eureka! In another corner was propped a well-worn bolt-action Winchester Model 70 with a powerful scope. I would have bet everything in my wallet that the rifle was a .30-'06 and the same weapon that not only scared the daylights out of me while I was chopping wood but also ventilated the right wing of my Cessna.

I had my man, I was certain. But I couldn't go blundering in just yet. I needed more evidence—evidence I could use in court—and a solid motive as well.

Still, I now had the advantage: I knew exactly who my quarry was.

Wishing mightily that I could break into and search the outbuildings, I started back through the forest, paralleling the track to the highway but remaining well clear of it, out of sight and out of earshot.

Within an hour I reached my concealed Jeep and was on my way back to civilization, smiling to myself for having stolen through the woods unseen and unheard until I had encountered my prey and, in a modest sort of way, counted coup. Crazy Horse would have been proud.

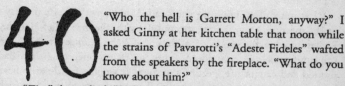

40 "Who the hell is Garrett Morton, anyway?" I asked Ginny at her kitchen table that noon while the strains of Pavarotti's "Adeste Fideles" wafted from the speakers by the fireplace. "What do you know about him?"

"Zip," she replied. "He's not from around here, after all. Where did you say he played basketball?"

"Kalamazoo, I was told when I met him at Big Trees," I said.

"I've got a friend in the Kalamazoo Historical Society," she said. "Let me give her a call and see what she can turn up in the local papers."

I blinked. "I've got an acquaintance down there, too," I said. "Cop who went through the state training program at the same time I did. I'll drop a dime on him. May I use your phone?" I didn't want to make the call from the department where I might be overheard.

Just ten minutes passed before Sergeant Ted Conover of the Kalamazoo Police returned my call. "Steve," he said, "been a while. What can I do for you?"

I took a deep breath and decided to trust Ted. "I'm involved in a very unofficial homicide investigation," I said, "and I'd appreciate it if you kept this under the rug."

"Sure," Ted replied. "Who do you like for the deed?"

"Nobody just yet—I'm still sifting a list of possible suspects. One of them is a young man from Kalamazoo College named Garrett Morton. Basketball player."

"Know him sure enough," Ted said. "Big palooka, quite a forward on the freshman team last year, the varsity's best hope this year. Let me punch him up on the computer."

In a moment Ted was back. "No real record," he said. "I busted him once last year, for possession of small amounts of pot at a wild frat party with a bunch of others. His rich and connected daddy, who's a big auto company executive, got the case dismissed.

"Before then he got into a bar fight and laid out a couple of kids pretty good, but they wouldn't press charges. I think Daddy bought 'em off, too. But he doesn't sound like a hardened felon to me, just a kid too big and strong for his own good and not too bright besides. That's all I got for you."

I thanked Ted, hung up and headed into town to start the day's work, meeting Mary Larch to consult with the fire chief, Dudley Richardson, on the origin of a blaze at Gitche Gumee Tractors and Implements on the east side of town. A transformer in a shed had shorted and caught fire, gutting the shop. It wouldn't ordinarily have been considered suspicious, but Jack Pillanpaa, the proprietor, was such an incorrigible, much-disliked jerk that arson had to be ruled out.

I'd had a run-in with Jack when I was a young deputy and stopped by to rent a chainsaw. He refused, saying he didn't have any available—though half-a-dozen well-used McCullochs sat on his counter—and I chalked that up to anti-Indian prejudice.

Dudley sounded disappointed when he told me the fire had been started by ancient and frayed electrical wiring. "Ought to have been fixed years ago, but Jack is such a cheap bastard he wouldn't have spent the ten bucks for new wire."

Mary laughed. "He wouldn't have spent *five* bucks," she said. "I can't stand him. He screws people every way he can, including himself. Oh, I could tell you about the run-ins I've had with him."

Joe Koski, who had stopped by on his way to work, cut in. "You're telling me," he said. "Years ago he wouldn't sell me a new carb for my lawn tractor because I didn't buy the tractor from him."

People, I suddenly realized, are often the way they are because of what they are, not because of who *you* are. In fact, an unpleasant encounter with Jack Pillanpaa was a kind of initiation into Porcupine County society. This place, like everywhere else, was bound to have its share of disagreeable human beings. Nothing to do with me.

Mary broke my reverie. "You okay, Steve?" she said, eyeing me closely.

"Oh, yes, thanks."

"You seemed far away."

"I get that way sometimes. Don't you?"

"Nothing's happened?"

"Not a thing."

"Okay." She didn't sound as if she believed it. "Take care."

She climbed into her cruiser and drove away.

At the end of the shift I decided to bask in the presence of an extremely agreeable personage, the exact opposite of Jack Pillanpaa. I stopped in at the Historical Society, and spotted Ginny sitting in her office at the back of the cavernous room, packed floor to ceiling with displays of artifacts in glass cases. A life-sized diorama of a Finnish Christmas of 1900 occupied one corner, a bewigged mannequin in lumberjack dress handing a gift to a small child in front of a potbellied woodstove. The gift-shop counters groaned under their burden of holiday sweetmeats, some of them Finnish, some of them Croatian, some of them Cornish.

Ginny waved as she saw me, pulled me into her office and closed the door.

"I have something good for you, Steve," she breathed sexily as she melted her body against mine and planted a thorough and lingering kiss on my lips.

"Not here!" I protested when we came up for breath. "There are people out there!"

"I didn't mean *that*," she said, giggling, doing the thing with her hair, "although you could be a little more adventurous, you big stick-in-the-mud. Sit down."

I sat, puffing slightly.

"I got through to my friend in Kalamazoo, and she came up with some interesting stuff about Garrett Morton. There were a couple of columns in the newspaper there about why he hadn't returned this fall to play basketball. He was that big a star on the freshman team. It was a huge disappointment to the whole college that he didn't return.

"One of the stories said that his grade-point average his freshman year was so low he might not be eligible for sports that season, not without a lot of remedial courses. He could have taken them and played, but he chose not to return—the columnist speculated that like so many student athletes he just wasn't college material, even for a basketball factory like Michigan, let alone a small school like Kalamazoo.

"The second column—are you ready for this, Steve?—reported that Morton had told a friend he wasn't coming back because he'd found a girl in Upper Michigan. It offered no further details."

I rubbed my jaw thoughtfully. "Who the hell could that be?" I said. "Up here everybody knows everybody else and who's doing what with whom. But I haven't heard a thing about Garrett Morton and any locals. Have you? And what possible reason could he have for wishing Paul Passoja dead?"

Ginny shook her head. "I think when you find out who the girl is, Steve, you'll have the solution to that mystery right in your lap."

She's beautiful, smart, and encyclopedic, my Ginny. And, let me add, remarkably prescient.

"What do you plan to do now, Steve?" Ginny asked with concern.

"Nothing much," I said, "Just a little breaking and entering."

41

I was going to have to swallow my legal pride and break into Garrett Morton's cabin if I was to get to the bottom of this business, but any information I gathered illegally could never be used in a court of law. All the same, I figured, blindly poking a stick into a hornet's nest seems reasonable when you are the target of a man who may or may not have homicide on his mind, and maybe an unlawful act or two would shake out enough independent evidence to convict. I didn't have much choice.

And so shortly after dawn on my next day off, I took the long way around the tailings, driving west to nearly the entrance to Wolverine Park and then south to the old mining town of Lone Pine. There I entered the mine property, waving to the lone watchman at the gate who was unsurprised that a deputy might have business there. County officials come and go all the time. I took a rough track eastward past the southern edge of the tailings and into the forest, where I parked the Jeep in the bushes again. This time I would approach Garrett's cabin from the south just in case he had the presence of mind to watch the road from the north.

On the fourth day of December no snow had fallen. Even so I could see no trail through the thick second-growth forest, clotted with dry thimbleberry bushes and grasping brush, even with my Indian's eyes, so I used white man's medicine—the handheld GPS—to find my way. For three miles and two hours I trudged due north, walking slowly not only to make as little noise as possible but also to keep my footing on the rough, stumpy ground. These were the low hills leading into the Wolverines, full of bare escarpments that bore visible traces of the copper that had attracted men by the thousands during the nineteenth century.

The going was slow, often almost straight up and down and sometimes through muskeg swamp, and as the bright sun rose into a cloudless sky I was thankful for the crisp, chilly air. Hiking in this place during the height of summer, as I sometimes have to in order to fulfill my professional duties, can be an exercise in navigating the seventh circle of hell, fighting off swarms of blackflies—tiny winged demons brandishing fiery pitchforks.

So intent was I on walking an accurate track that I tended to keep my head down, eyes on the GPS, that from time to time I collided with a tree or stumbled over a stump, swearing softly. I was looking down when I heard the low whimper through the brush to my right. I looked up and immediately spotted the rusty steel cage ten yards away, half hidden by tall grass. Inside it was a brown furry shape. Stepping over, I saw that it was a small bear, and then it looked up. It was my little acquaintance, the one with the cinnamon face.

"Hello, friend," I said. It was odd, I thought, to see a bear up and awake that late in the fall. Nearly all Upper Peninsula bears turn in for the winter by the end of November. But the unusually warm autumn had delayed hibernation for many.

In response the little bear gave a soft rolling growl and examined me quizzically, seemingly unperturbed at either my presence or its entrapment in the cage, about eight feet wide by ten feet long. A bag of dog chow and a nearly full tub of water sat in a corner by a large, straw-lined rustic cedar doghouse, the kind lumberyards up here sell ready-built to summer people for their Labs and golden retrievers. The bear was being carefully cared for, that much I was sure about—the doghouse doubtless was intended as an artificial den for the winter's hibernation—but I doubted that whoever had captured and caged the bear had complied with the necessary legal paperwork.

The little bear's calm was unsettling. No wild animal I had encountered showed such apparent trust in human beings. By rights it should have been pacing nervously, snarling, trying to reach me through the steel mesh, protesting against its imprisonment.

The brush suddenly rustled behind me and I caught a whiff of a heavy rank odor. I whirled, and my bowels melted when in the next instant I saw a massive dark shape through the dry saplings, stamping and whoofing angrily, getting ready to charge. It was a full-grown black bear, and it was furious.

As I reached around for my .357, fumbling with the Velcro tabs, the bear crashed forward, bellowing and slavering, yellow teeth bared to bite into my neck. Involuntarily I shut my eyes and scrabbled at the fanny pack, hoping to get the Magnum out and bring it around in the second before the animal struck.

Twaaaaaaaannnngggg! Scarcely six feet away the bear suddenly lifted and crashed into the ground, rolling, scrambling to regain its feet, knifelike claws tossing up clods of dirt. It charged again, and the heavy chain that bound it to a tree twenty feet away once more brought it up short. Like a dog fastened to an outdoor stake, the bear stood on its hind legs scything its forepaws, still trying to get at me, flashing a crescent-shaped splash of white fur on its broad black chest.

Were it not for the chain, I realized, the bear could have slashed me to bits before I wrapped my finger around the trigger of the .357, and even so powerful a handgun slug might not have worked. The bear was a tall and mature specimen, skinnier than it should have been for the hibernating season but still weighing about 250 pounds. Only a well-placed shot through the mouth to the brain might have stopped it. And at the best of times I am only an average marksman.

On hands and knees, my heart thumping, I scratched my way well clear of the bear, now sitting on the ground, its huffing subsiding only slightly. It sat right in the middle of the path I had trod through the tall dry grass. The little bear's whimper had drawn me outside the range of the chain. Suddenly I realized that I owed my life to that animal.

It did not take the acumen of a Dr. Bill Ursuline to figure out that someone had chained the large bear to the tree for a purpose—no doubt to turn it into a lean, mean killing machine.

Squatting in the brush, I considered the situation. The bear's charge had made a lot of noise, and anyone within half a mile would have heard the ruckus. I withdrew behind a tree and waited silent and still, counting off thirty minutes on my watch. No one came.

Carefully I stood up and sidled around the tree to which the bear was chained, keeping well out of harm's way even though the animal, seemingly having lost interest in me, was now snoozing in a patch of sun.

It didn't take long to find the Tupperware container that had held the bacon grease, and it didn't take much longer to find drying grease splattered on saplings in a wide circle just a couple of feet outside the bear's reach. The frantic animal had trampled the grass into an almost perfect circle trying to get to the saplings.

It had not been completely starved. Not far from the Tupperware lay a rancid sheet of butcher paper still sodden with the juices of raw meat, probably hamburger, judging from the shreds that stuck to it. Whoever was tuning up the bear knew just how far he could go and how much food he needed to keep it going. And when a few yards away I found the sharpened, spearlike eight-foot sticks, tufts of fur sticking to their tips, I realized that the bear had been physically tormented as well, no doubt to keep it furious and focused on human beings.

How long the bear had been made to suffer I didn't know, but I guessed at least a couple of months, judging from the deep grooves rubbed in the stout maple to which the bear's chain was padlocked. There was no doghouse or lean-to for a winter den. Somebody had plans for this bear and they didn't include hibernation.

Twaaaaaanggggggg! The bear had awakened and lunged at me through the grass again, and even though I was a good ten feet out of its reach I still leaped clumsily into a low berry patch, barking my shin on something hard and metallic.

Groaning softly, I rubbed my shin, drew aside the curtain of brush and saw an ancient bear transporter, decades old by the look of it. Careful not to disturb the brush or the ground, I examined the long cylinder. Orange rust crept over its faded green paint and dried leaves filled both ends, the heavy mesh doors lying open. Its tires were nearly bald. But the wheel bearings had been recently greased and the door hinges oiled.

I looked upslope through the trees and in the brown sedge grass saw the double tracks the transporter and whatever vehicle pulled it had made. Following the tread marks a few yards, I saw that they emerged onto a rough, stony road that would have tested even my tough little Jeep. The road pointed toward Garrett's cabin just under a mile northward through the forest.

I am not a gambling man, but I would have happily laid ten to one that the transporter had spent some time recently up near Big Trees. That the bear was the one Stan Maki and Garrett Morton had tranquil-ized and hauled away from the Cackle Shack a month before. That it was being starved and harassed to anger it into an assault on someone, that someone quite possibly—make that probably—being me. And that the person who was doing the deed was none else but Garrett Morton.

I felt certain that Morton planned to load the bear into the trans-porter and in the dead of night release it at a spot very close to my cabin. Did he really aim for the bear to kill me? I still doubted it—I could think of at least a dozen smarter ways to dispatch, or perhaps just divert, a nuisance cop who was coming uncomfortably close to the truth. Maybe Garrett was playing some kind of weird game toying with his quarry.

But he didn't seem bright enough for that—he was, so far as I could see, a dim sort of fellow who charged ahead blindly without regard for nuance or consequence. And, maybe, I suddenly realized, he was also the kind of fellow who was happiest doing what he was told. Maybe by whatever girl he had taken up with.

Suddenly the notion of breaking into his cabin didn't seem like such a good idea, at least not just yet. That could wait, now that I had some idea of Garrett's plans. I was now certain that he was the shooter who had put a bullet into my airplane and another into a tree limb while I was chopping wood, and I was also now certain that he wasn't trying to dispatch me by gunfire.

Instead of going to him, I thought, the best thing to do was let him come to me—and to be ready. For a moment I considered freeing the little bear from its cage, but that would have revealed my presence. Any-way, he had enough chow and water for several days, and Garrett likely would keep him fed and watered.

"I'll be back," I whispered to the little bear. He gazed at me with unearthly calm.

Slowly and quietly I withdrew, backtracking along my original route, taking pains to steer clear of the large bear and carefully rear-ranging the disturbed brush behind me to conceal my presence.

Back home that evening I went to the gun cabinet and withdrew my prize Browning 12-gauge over-and-under shotgun, a heirloom bequeathed me by Uncle Fred and with which I occasionally hunt pheasant and grouse. I oiled its action, loaded both barrels with deer-slug shells, switched on the safety and propped it by the door. At close range and put into the proper place, those slugs could stop anything, two-footed or four-footed.

42

As I shaved the next morning, the phone rang. "Steve?" It was Joe Koski. "Eli wants you to come into the shop as soon as possible."

"The sheriff wants to talk to *me*?" I replied. That was rare. Usually Garrow dealt with deputies through the undersheriff. Laid-back as he was in personal and political habits, he believed in the chain of command.

"Yes," Joe said, "and he doesn't look happy."

Had the sheriff somehow put together what I was up to?

On the drive into town I turned over a number of scenarios in my mind, and the curtain in each fell with me handing in my star and sidearm and stalking in disgrace out the door, my career in law enforcement forever stained.

But when I walked into the squadroom the deputies waved casual hellos from their desk, and Undersheriff O'Brien barely looked up from his. "Hiya, Steve," said Joe from behind the holiday tree at his counter, his tone unconcerned. "Sheriff's in his office."

I knocked.

"Come in," Eli boomed.

I barely suppressed a sharp intake of breath as I saw Garner Armstrong sitting next to the sheriff's desk with a sour expression. The county prosecutor is a good one and an upright man, although highly ambitious—it's clear to everyone that he looks forward to a long and fruitful career in Congress.

"We've got a problem, Steve," Eli said. I steeled myself.

"It's my aunt," Garner said. "Cordelia."

I looked up in surprise. "What's happened now?"

Cordelia Armstrong, sister to Garner's uncle, Congressman Armstrong, was another singular Porcupine County eccentric, a Vassar-educated former New York bank officer who'd had a nervous breakdown after hitting the glass ceiling, come home to recuperate, and never left. Now aging and almost toothless, Cord lived alone amid rusting automobiles, broken farm machinery, and assorted trash on the old family farm on clear-cut land deep in the southern part of the county.

Rumor had it that when her cow barn burned down during the coldest weeks of winter she had sheltered the beasts inside her rotting old farmhouse, and when the manure rose too high, moved into a single-wide trailer she'd found in an auto graveyard. According to the story, she vehemently denied that she had a soft heart for animals. Those cows, she said, represented money in the bank.

Few people visited Cord, an exceptionally cantankerous sort who often threatened to shoot any passerby who trespassed upon her property, often brandishing a rifle to make her point. She loudly included state police, sheriff's deputies, and, indeed, any government official among her potential targets, and none of us looked forward to what seemed an inevitable confrontation with this crazy old lady.

She was not a recluse, but she drank so much you could have garnished martinis with her eyeballs. She had been bounced from every bar in town, except Hobbs'. Ted Lindsay refused to overserve her, which was why she didn't go in there much, except to start a binge. When she did that, Ted always made sure that when she left she was not armed. He had yet to find a weapon on her, but there was always a first time.

Cord was most notorious for her long-running feud with Ettie Lahti, her neighbor, whose house lies just a couple of hundred feet from Cord's. The war had started years before when a few dozen of the hundreds of rabbits Ettie raises and sells for meat escaped from their pen, squirted through the wire fence separating the two farms, and went to work on Cord's lettuce. Instead of complaining to Ettie and asking restitution, Cord took out her shotgun and blasted the rabbits—and what remained of her lettuce crop—to kingdom come. Ettie took offense and threatened to sue, and that was the beginning of the county's most notorious border dispute.

Garner had paid Ettie for the loss of her rabbits out of his own pocket, although she didn't have much of a legal case against Cord. All the same, little by little Cord had escalated the hostilities, once knocking down Ettie's mailbox with her tractor and scattering its contents over the windy meadow. Now, every time Ettie drove by on her way to town, Cordelia would burst out of her house, fling a loud hail of four-letter words in her rival's direction, and give her the finger.

What's more, Cord had screwed a phony security camera to a fence post, pointing it directly at Ettie's house a hundred feet away. First Ettie had bought thick new shades and drapes for the windows in the side of the house facing Cord's, then had an eight-foot-high, sixty-foot-long cedar board fence erected along the property line. Two days after the fence went up, the word **ASSHOLE** appeared on Ettie's side of the fence in three-foot-high barn-red letters.

What could we deputies do? "It coulda been anybody," Cord said defiantly, and she was right. Everybody in the country has a can of barn red paint in the garage.

Ettie had complained often and bitterly to the sheriff, but, mindful of the miscreant's relationship with the prosecutor and the congressman, Eli did nothing. Garner, to his credit, often tried to defuse the situation. But neither sweet reason nor outright threat moved Cordelia, who never missed an opportunity to berate Ettie whenever and wherever they met, in town as well as the woods and fields.

"Now it's gone too far," Garner said. "The other day Ettie and Cord ran into each other at the checkout line in Straki's Grocery and in front of God and everybody and a lot of small children, Cordelia called her a cunt."

"It gets worse," Eli said. "Ettie has lawyered up with a downstate attorney and he's threatening to expose us for nonfeasance if we don't do something. You remember that case a couple years ago in Standish when a young fellow was convicted of public obscenity? You know, the one who said 'fuck' in front of a bunch of kindergartners and their teacher watching from a bridge when his canoe flipped over? The lawyer says he's gonna cite Garner and me for not upholding the law."

That case had made the papers nationwide. The young canoeist had been convicted under an obscure 1897 law that prohibited cursing in front of women and children. The judge declared the "women" part of the statute unconstitutional, but upheld the "children." The canoeist protested that the river was freezing and anyway he had cussed only a couple of times, but the jury believed the witnesses, who said he had spread the F-word hither and yon at the top of his lungs at least ninety times by their count. That water must have been *cold*.

He could have been sentenced to ninety days in the pokey and a hundred-dollar fine, but the judge, mindful that the American Civil Liberties Union would appeal in the name of free speech, slapped his hand with four days of community service and a seventy-five-dollar fine. The ACLU was right. On appeal the law was declared unconstitutional and the conviction thrown out. Garner and Eli well knew that the most Cordelia could be hit with were charges of personal harassment and disorderly conduct, a catch-all that almost never went to trial. But those were legitimate beefs Ettie's lawyer could claim the Armstrongs had failed to follow through on.

"Worst of all," Garner cut in, "that lawyer's threatening to tip the Detroit papers to the story. And the election is next year."

It didn't take a brilliant scholar of journalism to behold the comic possibilities in the great back-fence feud of a couple of rubes, one of them politically connected, in a far north wilderness county. And Geoffrey and Garner Armstrong, for all their virtues, have no sense of humor about political matters.

"So you want me to bring her in?" I said.

"Yup," said Eli, Garner, and Gil simultaneously. The undersheriff had wandered into the boss's office in the meantime.

"Why me?"

"She's said she respects you," Garner said. "She told me she'd seen you toss a bunch of drunken bikers out of Hobbs' without drawing your weapon, using just words."

Now I remembered. Cordelia was the old woman who had flashed me the thumbs-up as I left Hobbs'. She *did* favor digital communication, I thought, concealing a smile.

"She likes that kind of thing," Garner said, "and you know she never says anything good about anybody. I think she'll come with you without any trouble. If anybody else goes out to arrest her, she'll just barricade herself in her trailer with those guns and who knows how many boxes of ammunition."

He handed me the warrant.

"Okay," I said. "I'm on my way. Anything else?"

"Take Larch for backup," O'Brien said as I departed the sheriff's office. I hoped the sheriff, undersheriff, and prosecutor could not see the expression of relief on my face.

43

Mary slipped into the right seat of the Explorer. "I hope this isn't going to be fun," she said, pulling a face as we pulled out of the lot. "I don't love it when people point guns at each other."

I chuckled.

We drove silently for a while, enjoying the crisp and sunny morning. Feeling amiable, partly because the prosecutor had paid me a compliment, partly because the sheriff had not confronted me with my unofficial investigation, and partly because a pretty colleague I liked rode in my presence, I opened up a bit.

"How much longer do you have to go to get your sheepskin?" I asked Mary, forgetting that she didn't like personal questions.

"Just a year," she replied, gazing out the window at the passing forest. I realized what I had said, and looked over at her. Her expression—almost always grave, alert, and professional—softened, and her eyes sparkled.

"And after that?"

"Oh, I don't know. But since you asked"—she turned and looked at me directly—"I'll tell you the possibilities."

In a couple of years, she said, she might apply for a job in a small city, like Muskegon or Grand Rapids, and work her way up, maybe eventually going to Lansing or Detroit. But lately she was thinking about trying for a scholarship to law school, having done well in academics as a part-time undergraduate.

"After that, who knows, maybe the FBI?" she said. My already warm opinion of her ratcheted up a notch. I approve of dreams.

"What about marriage and a family?" I asked, swiftly wishing I hadn't.

Surprisingly, she laughed. "I could ask you the same question. We're all wondering about you and Ginny."

I glanced out the driver's window, trying to hide the blush, and was almost glad to see the carcass of the deer in the middle of the road ahead.

I stopped the Explorer and Mary and I got out. The deer, a mature doe, was dead, but the blood around it was not fully dried. It had probably been struck not an hour before. I wondered if the driver had called in the accident. Many of them don't bother, especially those who don't carry collision insurance on their old trucks and automobiles. It's mostly those with newer cars and full insurance who report deer strikes in order to collect on their policies.

It didn't annoy me that the driver hadn't attempted to move the deer off the road, as most will. Probably it was a senior citizen without the strength to drag a 120-pound animal across the pavement. I sighed. Dead deer on the road are a problem in the Upper Peninsula, not only because there are so many of them but also because nobody wants the responsibility for hauling them away.

The county road crews say that belongs to the DNR, for it is notorious for telling people that the deer belong to the state and that you have to pay the state for them. But the DNR doesn't have enough rangers to do the cleanup job. At one time the sheriff's department decided to take on the job itself, because deer carcasses on the road are a safety hazard. We deputies were ordered to stop and pick them up, toss them in the trunk and haul them away to the dump.

That policy was short-lived. There's nothing like a rotting carcass and a deputy with a dry-clean-only uniform staring at it in disgust. Then, too, the smell of decomposing meat as the temperature climbs and the sun bakes the trunk can be too much to take.

In the summer, local residents will do the job themselves, dragging the corpses into the woods away from their property.

Mary and I had no choice. We each donned latex crime-scene gloves and in each hand grasped a leg, hauling the creature to the side of the road.

"Let's get it to the tree line," I said. "That'll protect the eagles."

Bald eagles, those symbols of tribes and nations, may be glorious to behold on the wing, but on the ground their feeding habits are less than pleasant. They're opportunistic scavengers some ornithologists think are more closely related to vultures than hawks. They will eat carrion, especially in the winter when the rivers and much of the lakeshore are frozen, and they often feast on roadkill.

Eagles need about twenty feet of "runway" to take off and climb above the danger zone of an oncoming car, and sometimes they get hit. Sometimes they gorge so much that they can't get into the air at all, and have to walk around on their talons for hours until they've worked off enough ballast to get airborne.

A partridge inside the tree line loudly drummed its wings, annoyed at our intrusion, startling us.

"Don't you just love the sights and sounds of nature?" I said. Mary and I grinned at each other. Then she gave me an odd glance, as if she were sizing me up. For a moment I wondered if I had made a breakthrough—if she was on the verge of allowing me into a deeper friendship, the kind in which the parties share things they don't tell other people. Then Mary looked away, and the moment disappeared.

The job done, we drove off, and within half an hour pulled up by Cordelia Armstrong's junkyard of a homestead.

"Maybe you'd better stay in the Explorer until we know what she's going to do," I said. "But be ready to back me up if I need it."

"Gotcha," Mary said, unclipping the strap on her holster.

I walked the few yards to Cord's door and knocked.

"Yeah?" came an irritated voice from inside.

"Steve Martinez here," I said. "Sheriff's department business."

"Okay, just a minute," Cord said almost meekly. "Be right with you."

In such a situation, some cops would draw their sidearms. Sensing that Cord would cooperate, I didn't. The sight of a .357 in my hand, I figured, might trigger an alarm in her disturbed mind.

The door opened and Cordelia stood in it, her hands empty.

"What can I do for you?"

"I think you know why we're here, Cord."

She looked past me, saw Mary, and nodded.

"Ettie's stirring up trouble again, eh?"

"I'm afraid so," I said. "She's filed a complaint of harassment and disorderly conduct, and I've got a warrant. I'll have to take you in and book you, but Garner will make bail right away. Somebody will drive you home. It'll take only a couple of hours."

"All right," Cord said. "But one thing."

"Yes?"

"Do you have to handcuff me?"

"It's the regulation," I said. "But I won't put them on till we get to the department."

She thought a moment. "Fair enough," she said. "Let me get my teeth."

She got her purse as well, climbed into the back of the Explorer, and we were off.

For much of the way we drove in silence.

"Is that your camera on the dash?" Cordelia suddenly said.

"Yup." I had taken to carrying the Minolta, its long telephoto attached, everywhere on duty and off, just in case someone asked about my interest in bears. And Cord naturally had heard the gossip.

"For bears?"

"Yup."

"See many?" Mary interjected.

I glanced at her. "They're never around when you're looking for them. Mostly just the ones at the Cackle Shack." That was perfectly truthful.

She chuckled.

"Why are you so interested in them?" she said.

I had prepared a little speech just in case. "They're fascinating animals," I said. "Do you know that they have individual personalities? Some of them are laid-back, some of them are timid, some of them are vicious, some of them are just cranky . . ."

"Like me," said Cord in a rare flash of humor. Sometimes she could be almost rational.

"Have you ever had any personal experiences with bears?" Mary cut in, her expression intent.

Before I could go on, we arrived at the sheriff's department. I was almost sorry; my little speech was quite truthful. I had grown interested in bears for their own sake, not just because of the jam I was in, and I could have gone on for a while.

We got out of the Explorer, Cordelia meekly presented her wrists for the cuffs, and Mary and I escorted her to the women's lockup. Within an hour the judge met with Cord and her court-appointed lawyer for the arraignment, after which Garner paid the hundred-dollar bail. At her court date next month, everyone agreed, she'd plead guilty to disorderly conduct and pay a fifty-dollar fine, and, everyone hoped, that would end the matter.

I had my doubts. Cord Armstrong wasn't the kind of person who'd easily let go of a satisfying mad. She ate, slept, and breathed anger at the world.

Another deputy drove Cordelia home, and that was my day. I felt it had been a productive one, full of good police work. The safety of the public had been upheld and the wheels of justice had been set in motion without anyone getting hurt or having to raise their voices. I'd even done a little bonding with a colleague. I'd almost, but not quite, forgotten my predicament.

44

Shortly after midnight two days later I was returning in my Jeep from a holiday poker evening with colleagues in the Gogebic County department at Watersmeet, an hour south of Porcupine City, when my high beams glinted off a vehicle hidden in the brush around a curve of U.S. 45. Probably nothing, I thought, an old junker abandoned off the highway, but habit called—on duty or not, cops just have to check out unusual sights. I slowed the Jeep, then returned to the spot where I'd seen the vehicle. I alighted, a big four-cell Mag-Lite in hand, and panned it across the dry brush by the side of the road. In a moment the beam skipped across yellow metal screened by a thick grove of bare aspen shoots.

I stepped off the road, grumbling softly as my spit-shined, tooled Western boots—one of my few sartorial extravagances—sank into unfrozen muck. I'd missed the nearby track, rough but high and dry, leading off the highway and into the aspen grove. Not fifty yards inside it sat a rusty yellow Scout. I felt its hood. Still warm; it had been parked within the hour. Only one person in all of Porcupine County drove a yellow Scout, so far as I knew, and that was Garrett Morton. But he was nowhere to be seen. What could he be doing this late at night and why was his Scout parked like that?

Emerging from the grove, I took my bearings. The moon had risen, softly illuminating the landscape. The aspen rose hard by a creek that led across a meadow to an abandoned farmhouse and tumbledown barn I knew well, having rousted partying teenagers there more than once. That reminded me with a start that one of my fellow deputies lived not two hundred yards away on the other side of the grove. Mary Larch.

Just a year before she had leased a bit of land, parked a used double-wide house trailer on it, and had a well dug.

Was Garrett Morton stalking her?

Swiftly I returned to my Jeep and fished the Magnum from the glove compartment. I returned to the grove, .357 in one hand and a smaller, pocket-sized pilot's Mag-Lite with a red lens in the other, and found the track through the dead grass Garrett had trampled. It led toward Mary's trailer. Carefully shielding the Mag-Lite to conceal my presence—its red beam did not harm night vision—I slowly followed the path across the meadow to Mary's double-wide, soundless as a Shawnee, stopping at every tiny scrabble of pebble and rustle of twig to make sure I had not been seen or heard.

A dim light burned from within the double-wide. I squatted in the shadows a few yards away and listened. Bing Crosby was singing "White Christmas" on a tape deck somewhere in the trailer, and a soft murmur—Mary's voice—wafted intermittently through the window. She did not sound troubled. But then I heard another low voice, harsher, more masculine. Garrett? I couldn't tell. But then there was a soft gasp, followed by a sharper one, then a moan. Was she being attacked?

I crept forward to the trailer. A curtain in the rear, I saw, had not been completely closed. I stood up, holding the .357 before me, and peered into the window.

The room was dark, but inside it the light from the new December moon outlined a Scotch pine festooned with tinsel and stockings hanging from an impromptu mantel nailed to the flimsy interior wall. Three large boxes trimmed in Christmas wrap sat before the tree. But the inhabitants of the double-wide weren't snug in their kerchiefs dreaming of sugarplums.

Through the open door on the far side I could see Mary.

Her back was to me. She was nude, straddling a supine and equally naked man whose face I could not see, on her double bed. Her pelvis rose and ground in abandon, her back arching as her gasps softly increased in volume and frequency.

Inwardly I blushed. I am not a prude, but neither am I a voyeur, and I hate to intrude on other people's intimate moments. I had started to draw back from the window when the man's head rose into my view.

It was Garrett.

"What the—?" I muttered to myself as I squatted back out of sight. Mary Larch and *Garrett Morton*? Mary Larch and *anybody*?

Unbelievingly I stood up again to make sure I had seen what I thought I had seen. What I then saw shocked me to the core.

A naked blond woman, shapely breasts swinging, walked into view. A concupiscent leer wreathed her face as she sat on the edge of the bed and kissed Mary with an open mouth. It was Marjorie Passoja.

"My God," I thought.

Swiftly I considered what I had seen. A ménage à trois is none of my business, either personal or professional. But Mary and Garrett, Mary and Marjorie? My mind raced, my thoughts tripping over one another.

Both women are fully a decade older than he, and a lot smarter and more ambitious besides. Maybe I was wrong that Mary was repressed and asexual. Maybe she was merely a single woman in her full ripeness using a brainless young stud for pleasure. That must be it. But Marjorie? Yes. She and Mary were lesbian lovers. It fit. Their connection was a battered women's shelter. They had been friends, then had become more than friends. Maybe Marjorie had introduced Mary to the joys of bisexuality and had suggested they find a suitable boy toy to share.

Then it hit me. If those two women were involved amorously with Garrett, they could be—no, make that probably, even very likely— involved in other things with him. Such as conspiring to thwart and maybe hurt, even bump off, a curious deputy sheriff who wouldn't let go of the Paul Passoja case.

Mary? I couldn't believe it—didn't want to believe it. But there it was.

Quietly, crouching low in the grass and stopping frequently to make sure I had not been made, I retraced my steps to the aspen grove, then the highway where I had parked the Jeep. Keeping the lights off for half a mile and driving slowly so that my brake lights wouldn't flash and reveal my presence, I returned to Porcupine City, stewing all the way.

45 "What can you tell me about Mary Larch?" I demanded the next morning as Ginny came down for breakfast. I'd waited hungrily for her, for the previous evening she'd made prune-filled Finnish Christmas tarts, one of my favorites, and the scent of fresh butter pastry still filled the air.

"Aren't you going to kiss me good morning first?" she said. I hung my head in mock guilt and chuckled. Even bundled in green quilted robe and matching flip-flops, red hair askew and eyes heavy-lidded with sleep—or maybe because of it—Ginny looked extraordinarily desirable.

"Sorry," I said, and complied thoroughly with her request. So thoroughly that when she came up for air, Ginny said through her gasps, "Mmm. Let's go back upstairs." So thoroughly that I forgot all about Mary Larch and Marjorie Passoja and Garrett Morton.

An hour later Ginny awakened, poked me, and said, "Now what about Mary?"

I told her what I had seen the previous night.

At first Ginny started to snuffle with suppressed mirth, the rolling teakettle building up pressure for one of her patented spells of hilarity. I steeled myself.

"Mary Larch?" she said. "Mary Larch and *Marjorie Passoja?* Mary Larch and *Garrett Morton?"*

But almost instantly Ginny's bubbling subsided. Her eyes widened and her grin faded. "A three-way?" she said. "Maybe it's not so surprising about Marjorie. She does come from that anything-goes Southern California background. Three-ways wouldn't have been uncommon among bored young people in Beverly Hills and Brentwood. And when you're widowed and lonely you grasp at straws. You do dumb things just to connect with others.

"But Mary? Not only doesn't she seem the type, Garrett doesn't seem her type either," she said. "Or Marjorie's, for that matter. I have to agree with you about that."

"So it's just sex, you think?" I replied.

"No. Think about it," Ginny said. "Would a female sworn officer of the law, an intelligent and promising one like Mary, take up with a much younger and not very bright lout, let alone a lesbian relationship with a woman as prominent as Marjorie? This is a big county with a small population, and that kind of hanky-panky is bound to be discovered sooner or later. Not that there's anything hugely wrong with it— none of the principals is married—but it's exactly the kind of thing people like to gossip about."

"So there's got to be more to it?"

"There must."

"But what?"

Ginny lay back on the pillow thoughtfully. "I don't know," she said. "Let's put Marjorie aside for the moment and consider Mary. She was born and grew up here, like her parents. Her mother was from a Finnish family, her father an English one. He was a storekeeper in town, one who like so many of them up here just made ends meet. After he retired they sold their house in town and lived in an old farmhouse on cutover land out near Ewen. They died about a dozen years ago."

"You think Mary's father abused her?"

"We never heard anything like that," Ginny said. "I think that would have gotten around."

"And they had no link to Paul Passoja?"

"I'm sure they knew Passoja and his family, as everyone else did, but I don't know of any harder connection."

"I don't, either," I said. "I can't remember seeing the name Larch in any of the Passoja land records I turned up last month."

Ginny lay silent for a moment. "Maybe there never was a land sale," she said. "Maybe they rented their house from Passoja. Maybe something went on there."

I nodded. "It'll be easy to find out who owns that land, and who owned it before."

Without a word we lay together for a minute. Then the comforter rustled downily.

"You're such a wanton," I said.

"Aren't I?" she said.

Joyously we wasted—if you want to call it wasted—the rest of that Sunday morning.

46

Ten minutes at the courthouse and I had my answer: Paul Passoja had owned the land Rudy and Tillie Larch rented and still lived on at the time of their deaths a little more than a decade ago, she first and he a few weeks later. But what was the connection between Passoja and Mary Larch—if there was one beyond her parents?

That was what I had to find out now. But how? I couldn't go brace Mary and demand to know, nor could I throw Garrett up against a wall. The scant evidence I had was purely circumstantial, much too weak to overcome the trouble I was bound to get into if the sheriff's department learned about my rogue investigation.

For the next couple of days I either ran into Mary at the department or waved to her as she passed by in her cruiser. She waved back pleasantly with an unconcerned expression. Either she did not know I knew—or did, and didn't care.

Late the evening of the second day I stayed at the office after everyone except the night dispatcher had gone home, on the pretext of having to catch up with my paperwork. When the dispatcher left to make his rounds of the cells, I quickly fished Paul Passoja's file out of the drawer containing closed cases. Except for the stuff having to do with his death, there was nothing in the file except a single sheet reporting that at age twenty-two he had pleaded no contest to a disorderly conduct charge as a result of a drunken brawl in a town bar. That told me nothing. Half the men in Porcupine City must have at one time or another in their lives thrown a sodden punch at the wrong guy.

But the coroner's report contained Passoja's address in La Jolla as well as Porcupine City. That gave me an idea. I'd call the police in La

Jolla. If Passoja had spent winters in California for many decades, maybe he had a record there.

Clearing off my desk, I bade the dispatcher a good evening and went home to make the call, because I'd be hard-pressed to explain a long-distance item on the sheriff's dime to Gil O'Brien, who kept a suspicious eye on the phone logs in case a deputy tried to hang a personal call on the county. A sheriff's department in a poor rural county has a very, very tight budget, and every pencil, pen, and Post-It must be accounted for, let alone every gallon of aviation gasoline.

"Deputy Steve Martinez, sheriff's department, Porcupine County, Michigan," I told La Jolla's chief of detectives, giving him my star number. "I'm calling in connection with a homicide investigation here. Can you tell me if you have a sheet on a fellow called Paul Passoja, P-A-S-S-O-J-A, address 1382 Camino Real del Norte, La Jolla?"

A few minutes later the chief returned to the phone, having checked out both the files and my bona fides. "Yup," he said. "There's one. I'll fax it to your department."

"I'm going to ask a favor, Chief," I said. "I'm calling from home, and time's a-wasting. Can you just read me the highlights?"

"Sure. There isn't much, just one arrest and charge of statutory rape fifteen years ago. It was pleaded down to misdemeanor disorderly conduct in exchange for psychiatric counseling and a five-hundred-dollar fine. That's all."

"How old was the girl?"

"Fourteen. Guy said she looked eighteen. They all say that."

"Thanks."

I put down the phone and sat in a puddle of sudden understanding. Paul Passoja had been the fellow who assaulted Mary Larch when she was a girl.

I hopped into the Jeep and rolled down to Ginny's. She was still awake, having a cup of tea in the kitchen. I told her what I'd discovered.

Her eyebrows rose. "Mary was a Girl Scout at the time Passoja started taking them on overnight hikes," she said. "Five gets you ten she went on one of them."

"Do you think he might have done something?"

"If what you said happened in La Jolla is true, it's not just possi-ble—it's almost certain."

"Ever hear of him doing anything like that here?"

"Nope. If he had been caught, we'd all know about it. This is a small town. But La Jolla's a pretty good-sized place, full of rich people with both the knowledge and the money to keep things quiet."

I drummed my fingers on Ginny's kitchen table.

"And Marjorie?" I said.

We spoke at the same time. "The Andie Davis battered women's home!"

"That has to be it," I said. "Paul abused Marjorie in some way. Maybe not physically. Maybe she found out about his habits and he threatened her. Maybe he didn't beat her but abused her emotionally. It's logical that she would find something more in a women's shelter than just a place to donate her money. She'd find someone to tell her story to. And that probably was Mary. And having exchanged secrets about Paul Passoja, they'd work up enough anger to seek revenge."

Ginny nodded silently.

"Now what?" I said.

"Now what, indeed?" she said.

I looked at her. "I've got means, and now I've got motive. But I still haven't got a stick of evidence except some very circumstantial stuff."

She nodded again. Clearly she found the scenario hard to believe, but there it was right in front of her.

"Looks like I'll have to take a stick to that hornet's nest again at Garrett's cabin. Maybe this'll be third time lucky."

But I wasn't in a rush. I could wait for him—and Mary, if indeed she was connected—to deal the next hand. If there was anything I had inherited from the genes of my Indian ancestors, it was patience.

47 In the middle of that week Garrett finally rewarded my forbearance. Ginny had come over to my cabin to spend the night, parking her Toyota next to my Jeep and the department's Explorer in the driveway, so that I could roast a leg of lamb on the grill for us. I was still in bed the next morning when I heard her gasp and shout from outside, then the back door slam, followed by a thump that shook the cabin.

"Steve!" Ginny called from downstairs. "We've got a bear on the deck! And it's a big one!"

I scrambled into my jeans and thundered down the stairs barefooted. "Where?"

Another huge thump against the back door.

I pulled back the curtain. The bear, foam on its lips, scrabbled and slashed the screen door, ripping the metal screening to shreds. It already had made short work of the grill on which I had cooked the lamb. I doubted that it could get past the sturdy maple inner door, though it could easily burst through the glass windows if it had enough intelligence to figure them out.

Ginny squatted well out of sight, breathing fast but not panicky. "This one's a rogue, Steve," she said. "I was out in the backyard gathering boughs and cones for the kitchen table when it charged me. I made it into the cabin just in time. It's not going to go off into the woods after a while."

With a splintering sound the bear tore the screen door from its hinges.

I nodded. "I'll call Stan."

Maki answered on the first ring. "Mean bear in my backyard," I said. "It's got us trapped. Can you bring the bear kit?"

Within fifteen minutes Stan, who lives just five miles west at Silverton, arrived in his pickup, transporter jouncing behind, and parked it behind our vehicles. Almost immediately the bear turned from destroying the deck and charged the pickup, covering the twenty yards before Stan could get out of the vehicle. With a mighty crash it collided with the driver's door, denting the metal and starring the glass.

By then I was out on the deck, shotgun cocked, trying to avoid stepping in my bare feet on the sharp metal shards from the back door screening and the wicked splinters from the door frame. Behind the bear scrabbling to get into the pickup Stan, trapped in the driver's seat, saw me. He nodded, raised his hand, cocked his thumb and pulled an imaginary trigger.

I whistled.

In one swift motion the bear whirled, saw me, and leaped. I fell to one knee and aimed carefully at the crescent-shaped white patch on the charging animal's chest. The shotgun boomed and the bear stopped. Another shot and it dropped. Quickly I broke open the Browning and reloaded. But the bear lay motionless in a furry brown heap.

"Put another in its head," Stan said anyway. Unable to wrest open the sprung driver's door, he had emerged from the passenger door, rifle in hand.

I administered the coup de grâce and stood back, panting, as Ginny walked up behind me, my .357 in her hand. "We won't need that," I said. She nodded and removed her finger from the trigger. Gently I took the revolver from her.

Stan squatted by the carcass. "I've seen this bear before," he said. "It's a big one, but it ought to be a lot heavier for this time of year. It's past the normal denning time, you know."

Ginny cut in. "I'd wondered about that, but the warm season has delayed things, hasn't it?"

"Yeah," Stan said. "See this mark?" he added, pointing to a faint ring in the fur circling the bear's neck. "Radio collar."

I knew what that mark really meant and where that bear had been and who had put it in my backyard, but it wasn't yet time to let Stan in on the truth.

"Maybe it's a roadside zoo bear," I said. "Owners closed up the place, brought it up here and dumped it in the forest?" That was a possibility. Northern Wisconsin is full of highway tourist traps of that kind.

"Yeah," Stan said. "But I think that bear's been starved."

Then it dawned on him. "Hey, that's the bear Garrett and I took down at the Cackle Shack when you were there. See the blaze on its chest?"

"Yep," I said.

"Not surprised it came back from where I had Garrett drop it. Twenty miles isn't much for an adult bear to cover once it's made up its mind."

"You didn't go with Garrett to let it loose?"

"Naw, it doesn't usually take two of us to release a bear, or even many brains. He dropped me off at my house on the way."

We contemplated the carcass in silence.

"Better get it out of here," Stan said. "I'll take it to the DNR station. We'll have the vet look at it."

I helped Stan winch the carcass onto the bed of his pickup and waved as he drove off.

Once he was out of sight, I said to Ginny, "I bet I know where Morton set that bear loose."

We strode west across the backyard and a hundred yards into the woods to a small lakeside clearing on the next property. A sandy road led from the clearing to M-64 another hundred yards away. The damp sand revealed two sets of fresh tire tracks, one pair clearly made by a heavy vehicle, the other obviously made by a lighter one with nearly bald tires. Three large imprints of bear paws in the sand, pointed toward my cabin, clinched it.

"Time to pay an official visit to Mr. Garrett Morton," I told Ginny.

At the cabin I dressed in my deputy's uniform, strapped on the Magnum and reloaded the Browning with buckshot, stuffing extra shells into my shirt pocket. I'd left the riot gun at the sheriff's department so a gunsmith could install a new firing pin, for the old one had bent during the last monthly target practice. The two-shot Browning and the .357 would have to do.

This time, I had probable cause: the presumption that Morton had assaulted Ginny with a bear. I wouldn't need a warrant to get into his cabin legally, although I still would have plenty of explaining to do: how I had first seen that bear with the white crescent on its chest chained in the woods and why I had not reported it to the DNR, let alone the department.

Most of all, I would have to justify not calling in for backup. No intelligent cop goes after an armed felon without at least one fellow officer riding shotgun, preferably the entire department. But the only other deputy on duty at that hour of the day was Mary Larch.

And Garrett Morton was the most dangerous kind of bad guy: a stupid one who'd act—no, react—without considering the consequences.

I sighed. No more scouting, no more parleying. It was time to put aside patience and ride against the enemy.

"Be careful, Steve," Ginny called as I strode out to the Explorer in full deputy's uniform. This was going to be official.

"*You* be careful," I retorted.

"I will, Steve," she said, adding almost under her breath, "but I've got your back."

I was too preoccupied to ask what she meant.

48

This time I drove all the way up the track to Morton's cabin, parking the Explorer directly behind his Scout and trapping it against the tumbledown outbuilding. He might break out on foot, but he wasn't going to escape on wheels.

No one was in sight. I alighted, shotgun in hand, the Explorer's broad bulk screening me from the cabin thirty or so yards away. "Garrett!" I shouted, taking care to keep the Explorer between me and his front door. "Sheriff's department!"

No answer.

"Garrett! Where are you?"

The curtains in a front window twitched as a sash shot up. A rifle muzzle emerged, and I ducked below the Explorer's hood, behind the heavy engine. Not a lot of armor, but it would have to do.

"Show yourself, Garrett!"

The rifle answered with a heavy bark and the police radio antenna atop the Explorer sailed into the woods end over end.

A .30-'06 for sure. Now calling for backup, whether it was Mary or not, was utterly out of the question. It was going to be *mano a mano*, Morton against me, alone in the woods until one of us either was hit or ran out of ammunition—or both.

I held my fire. No point in wasting the few rounds of buckshot I had, and a .357 with a four-inch barrel wasn't accurate beyond fifteen yards or so. I had to get closer, where the Magnum slug and Double-O could do their best work.

I peeked around the front of the Explorer, spotted the glint of the heavy scope under the sash and quickly ducked back as the rifle coughed again, the bullet splintering the plastic bumper cover.

"That's damage of public property!" I shouted. "You're just adding on to the charges against you, Garrett!"

"Yeah?" he answered from the window. "What are they?"

It's a small psychological breakthrough when the subject shows a little curiosity. Maybe I could work on that a little, perhaps weaken his resolve, at least distract him some.

"Cultivating marijuana!" I said. "Resisting arrest! Assault! And, most of all, murder!"

Morton wasn't a bad shot, and at any good distance that scope would help. But up close it would make the rifle clumsy to swing and hard to sight.

An ancient oak with a six-foot-thick trunk stood to the right of the Explorer, six or eight yards closer to the cabin. I safetied the shotgun, cradled it loosely, and erupted into a crouching sprint around the rear bumper. Within an instant I hit the ground by the tree and rolled up against the trunk, flicking off the safety, the shotgun ready for action. At least half a second too late Morton's rifle barked, the bullet kicking up a clod of dirt a good six feet behind me. A big Winchester with a powerful scope was no close-quarters weapon.

Morton had fired three times. A Winchester Model 70 chambered for the .30-'06 cartridge carries four loads in its magazine and one in the chamber. Two left, unless he had reloaded, and I doubted that he had either time or presence of mind. It was a good moment for me to deliberately draw fire.

I unsheathed the Magnum and checked its load. Taking a deep breath, I quickly dodged into view around the right side of the tree, keeping my body behind the trunk, and hastily squeezed off a bullet that shattered the window two feet above the rifle muzzle I aimed for. As I ducked back the muzzle swung and coughed, Morton's bullet splintering the bark a good eighteen inches above where my head had been.

One left.

Morton's small woodpile, scarcely three feet high and six feet across, lay five yards closer to the cabin, just to the left on a line from my oak to his front door. It would partly screen me from his view if I took the chance and ran for it. I did, and Morton's last bullet—if indeed it was that—thunked into the soft ground in front of the woodpile a nanosecond after I fetched up against it with a heavy thump. At almost the same instant I shrieked in mock pain, and let a long moan trail off.

This time I lay motionless, shotgun at the ready, .357 in its holster with the strap undone. Though the window was out of sight I could see a sliver of the front door through the haphazardly piled logs. Five minutes passed.

And another five.

Morton lost patience. "Martinez!" he yelled.

I did not answer.

"Martinez!"

I lay silent. Then the door swung slowly open. Two more minutes passed before Morton's head and shoulders sidled into view a good six feet behind the door. I waited. He waited. Then he emerged into full view, rifle at his shoulder, its muzzle pointed toward the woodpile, his eyes scanning the forest behind me.

I stood up suddenly, Browning at my shoulder. Just before I loosed both barrels, one after the other, I heard his Winchester's firing pin click on an empty chamber.

The first charge of Double-O missed, splintering the door frame, but the second caught him in the left leg, spinning him out of sight inside the cabin and sending the Winchester skittering across the floor.

Quickly I dropped the empty shotgun and hurdled the woodpile, .357 at the ready, and burst through the door.

49 Morton lay slumped against the wall in a heap, tears streaming down his face.

"You've killed me!" he sobbed as he cradled his bloody thigh.

With a double-handed grip I kept the .357 trained on him.

"I'm gonna die!" he whimpered.

Nineteen-year-old infant or not, he had to be searched. Swiftly slapping his hands away from his leg, I said, "Garrett, put your hands on top of your head."

Still crying, he did so. Within seconds I'd rolled him over and tossed his clothes. Nothing except a penknife that I slipped into my hip pocket.

"Get me the ambulance!" he shrieked.

"It'll take a while for that," I said. "You shot off my antenna, remember? And there's no phone here."

Morton keened and rocked like an old woman at a Greek funeral, grasping his thigh above the wound.

"Shut up and let me take a look," I said.

I ripped open his trousers and examined his leg. Flesh lay exposed and torn and blood oozed copiously, but the heavy buckshot had not hit an important sinew or artery. The wound looked a lot worse than it really was. He'd recover, though he'd limp for a good while.

I didn't tell him that.

I tore apart a bedsheet and bound the wound. The bleeding had dwindled to an ooze. Often people in pain and shock will spill the beans easily, and I decided to work on Morton while I could, before he regathered whatever wits he had.

"Before I get the ambulance," I said, "let's have a little talk, Garrett."

"I'm dying! There isn't time!"

"I'll get you to the hospital faster if you tell me a few things first."

"You greaser shit!"

I might have been a shit, but that "greaser" offended me—all racial and ethnic slurs do. I am a minority, after all, even if I'm also a honky by adoption. I decided to be even more of a shit.

"Greaser, Garrett?" I said in my best bad-cop voice. "I'm an Indian, not a Mexican. That's much worse for you. Do you know what we used to do to captives? We liked to stake them out on the ground naked in the hot sun and let the fire ants eat their privates. Then we'd take their scalps. Slowly."

He shrieked.

"Oh, Jesus," I said. "You baby!"

I sighed, holstered the Magnum, settled into a rocking chair, then drew the little laminated Miranda card from my shirt pocket.

"You are under arrest, Garrett Morton. You have the right . . . ," I ..ted.

"Do you understand?" I finished.

"Yeah, yeah, hurry up, damn it!" he whined.

"Why did you kill him?"

Morton panted as sweat coursed down his face.

"He found the bear," he said. "He came in here and said he knew what Mary and I had done."

"Who?"

"Hank."

"Hank Heikkila?" I said, surprised. It was Paul Passoja I had had in mind.

"Yeah. He said he was going to find you and tell you."

"Mmm."

I settled deeper into the chair. That must have been the secret Hank had nursed. He must have encountered the bear with the blaze on its chest some time before our conversation at his shack, afterward putting two and two together and figuring that Morton had planted the first bear near Big Trees. But would Hank, who has absolutely no respect for authority, have come to me with that information?

Maybe. Hank, for all the torment in his mind, was an intelligent fellow. He probably figured that telling me what he'd found would buy him some much-needed goodwill. It's too bad, I thought, that he hadn't reached that conclusion during my visit to his cabin. If he had, he might still be alive.

"For God's sake, let's go!" Morton whimpered.

"You put that Springfield into Hank's mouth and pulled the trigger, didn't you? And then you arranged the body to make it look like suicide?"

"Uh . . . Mary told me to."

A lock clicked into place in my brain.

"Was she there at Hank's?"

"No."

"Where was she?"

"I don't know. Out somewhere at work, I guess."

"What did you do with his .38?"

The tears stopped briefly and he looked directly at me. "You know about that?"

I nodded.

"It's in the bottom drawer there. Hurry up, for God's sake."

I strode over to a cracked old bureau, pulled open the drawer and fished out the revolver, careful to thread a pencil through the trigger guard to protect the prints. If Morton's prints were mixed on top of Hank's, that was pretty good evidence. And so were the fisher pelts crammed underneath. The forensics guys could easily tie those to Hank. Then there was all the pot-growing paraphernalia in the corners—as well as the game traps. I had Garrett Morton nailed six ways from Sunday. Sure, I'd still be in deep shit for my lone-wolf investigation, but I had the goods, and that was what counted.

"Now, Garrett," I said, as if talking to a child would keep him acting like one, "it's almost time to go. But first you tell me about Paul Passoja."

"We weren't planning to kill him," Morton said, "just—"

"*Shut up!*" a female voice barked from the doorway.

I turned and gazed right into the wicked little muzzle of a nine-millimeter Beretta. Directly behind it stood Mary Larch, trimly pretty in her deputy's uniform, with a fierce expression on her face. I had seen it only once before, the day we picked up the child molester, and I was very sorry that it was aimed at me along with the pistol.

50

"Take your piece out of the holster with your fingertips and slide it to me," Mary ordered. I did so as gingerly as I could. Quickly she thrust the Beretta into her belt and trained my .357 on me, then strode over to Morton, still whimpering on the floor. "You'll live, blabbermouth," she said with icy contempt.

She turned to me. "I'm sorry, Steve," she said.

Regret tinged the steel in her expression.

"Just doing my job," I said, trying to keep my tone reasonable.

"I know."

"What are you going to do now, Mary?"

She didn't answer immediately but gazed at Morton thoughtfully.

"I don't know just yet," she said, "but I'll think of something. You stay right there and don't move."

Doubt. When subjects show doubt, work on it, keep them talking—maybe they'll talk themselves into surrendering. That's what we were taught in the hostage situations class at cop school. Of course, now I was the hostage. But still . . .

"Mary, can I ask you something?" I spoke in a friendly voice, trying to make her think I was on her side.

"What?"

"How did you know I'd come out here this morning?"

"Heard Stan on the CB talking about the bear in your backyard."

I decided on a frontal assault. "What did Passoja do to you?"

She looked at me in surprise.

"How did you know he did anything to me?"

"Just police work, Mary. Why don't you tell me?"

Her face clouded, that twisted expression of hatred returning to mar her pretty features. "The son of a bitch."

"Yes," I said. "It must have been awful."

"I was thirteen," she said, her emotional dam bursting in slow motion, like a levee giving way to floodwaters. Maybe she was planning to kill me, but I am sure she wanted me to understand why she had done what she did, as if my knowing the truth would somehow ease and even justify my death. Or maybe she was getting ready to do something else. I'm no psychologist.

"He'd taken five of us Girl Scouts camping in the woods for two days. On the morning of the second day he asked me to go to a spring with him a mile away to fill the canteens, and when we got there he told me I was very pretty and that he wanted me to do something special for him."

Her jaw trembled. It was hard for her to revisit the memory.

"He made me take my jeans down, and he touched me. Then he opened his pants, and—"

Involuntarily I reached a hand to her. For a moment she turned toward it, then away.

"It was awful. I can still remember the taste."

She shut her eyes tightly, then opened them quickly, keeping the Magnum trained on my chest. They were dry. Whatever grief she had shed for her innocence had been shed long ago.

"I am so very sorry, Mary," I said, honestly meaning it. For the briefest instant I *was* on her side, no longer the cop, feeling deep down that Paul Passoja had gotten what he deserved.

"Then he said if I ever told, he'd throw my family off his land. He said he knew we had no money and had nowhere to go."

She was telling the truth.

"The bastard," I said with feeling. "Where in the woods did this happen?"

"Big Trees."

My eyes widened.

"Later on, when I was old enough," Mary continued, "I found four other women he did the same thing to when they were girls. I tried to

talk them into bringing charges, but they were too scared of him's
power. He could have destroyed them if he wanted.

"And it was only my word against his. Who would have believed me?"

I nodded. "You were in a terrible jam, Mary," I said. Agree with her.
Build up the mitigating factors. Build up hope that she might escape the
worst consequences for her acts. It was an old trick, and I doubted it
would work with a cop as smart as she, but there was nothing else to do.

"From time to time, even after I became a cop, I'd run into him,
and once when we were alone I told him I would get him some day. He
laughed and said, 'You just try.'

"From then on, every time he saw me he would chuckle and shake
his head. That man was not just evil, he was contemptible."

Just as Hank Heikkila had said. Men rape to achieve power over
their victims, and strengthen their hold by tormenting the victims afterward. What Passoja had done to Hank was also a kind of rape, a rape of
the soul.

"What about Marjorie?" I asked.

Her jaw dropped. "How did you know about that, too?"

I told her. She had the grace to blush.

"Last year," she said, "Marj and I got to talking, and she told me
that she'd discovered Paul in their bedroom in La Jolla, having sex with
an underage girl. He threatened to kill her if she ever told, but he
couldn't leave it at that. He kept telling her that she was too old, she
wasn't as good in bed as the young stuff and that she loved his money
too much to leave him. He broke her spirit."

Mary told Marjorie about her youthful experience with Passoja,
and the shared shame drew them closer together. They fell in love.

"It was Marjorie's idea to use Garrett, but together we figured out a
plan."

Calmly Mary told the story. Early in the summer she had met Garrett Morton on one of his bear-catching jobs with Stan Maki. With a
young jock's blind cockiness he had come on to the pretty deputy, and
in the beginning Mary swiftly discouraged the much younger man. She
told Marjorie how Garrett had hit on her, and Marjorie suggested that
Morton, for all his denseness, had had enough intelligence to absorb a

bit of knowledge from Stan. The women began to hatch a plan. They'd entice him the best way Marjorie knew how and use him to do the dirty work.

It was not hard to figure out why Mary had rowed back across that river of pain—sex—that Passoja had thrown her into at such an early age. Rape is about control, and its victims sometimes try to retake control of their lives in the same way they were victimized. The same thing went for Marjorie, but in a different way. That desire for control also explained why the women would try to get back at Passoja in the woods, on his own territory.

"Passoja boasted so much about camping without a gun and knowing what to do with bears. But we didn't really expect the bear to kill him. We thought he'd just be chewed up a little and the whole thing would embarrass the hell out of him."

Whatever their intent, a human death had resulted, and the charge—if I could get Mary to surrender—still would be murder. Maybe in the second degree, but still murder. Maybe a good attorney could plead it down to aggravated manslaughter, but there was the matter of that second bear, the one Garrett had sent after me.

"Think of it, Steve," she said, almost enthusiastically. "A bear as a weapon? So unlikely! Who would ever think somebody would use it for that? And how could it possibly be traced?"

"But aren't bears unpredictable?" I said. "What made you think you could train one well enough to go after somebody?"

She smiled ironically. "Same way you figured that out, Steve," she said. "You went to see Professor Ursuline. In the library at Houghton, between cop classes, I read one of his monographs on the behavior of bears and the regularity of their habits."

I realized I could have done the same thing and avoided a lot of publicity. I kicked myself mentally.

"Keep your hands in your lap, Steve," Mary said. "I'm telling you this because I think you have a right to know, before . . ."

She let the sentence trail off, doubt in her eyes. She was thinking, I was certain, that she would have to kill me, but was not sure if she really wanted to.

"Yes, Mary," I said. Keep her talking. "Go on. What happened then?"

After she and Marjorie had finally hooked up with Morton, Mary continued, they had persuaded him with little difficulty to buy an old bear transporter at a junkyard in Wisconsin and drive it at night to the empty hunting camp where we now sat, hiding it in the copse where I had found it. The bear they planted on Passoja was a woods itinerant Morton had baited and shot with a tranquilizer gun borrowed surreptitiously from the DNR and returned before anyone missed it. He had done the same thing with it that he did with the bear that had surprised me near his cabin, chaining it to a tree with a heavy leather collar.

"It took just two weeks to starve it, teasing it with bacon grease, until it was ready. When I heard Passoja tell the Metroviches at Merle's that he was going into Big Trees, I had Garrett take the bear into the woods that day and let it loose as close as possible. That turned out to be only about a mile, right at Mills Creek."

I looked at Morton, staring sulkily at Mary but saying nothing.

"What did you do then, Garrett?" I said.

He had emerged from shock and slowly picked up on her unspoken thought that I was being honorably informed before the disposal.

"Sneaked up on him while he was cooking and baited the tent with grease. Then I left and went home. Nothing more to do."

I nodded. "Pretty easy to figure out what happened then."

Then I remembered Heikkila.

"What about Hank?" I asked. "We were talking about him a while ago."

"Mary told me to kill him."

"I did no such thing, you idiot!" Mary said. "I told you we'd take care of him later."

She turned to me. "He hears what he wants to hear."

"But I thought . . . ," Morton protested. Now he turned to me.

"It was an accident," he said. "We wrestled with the rifle and it went off. I didn't know what to do and tried to make it look like suicide."

Morton was changing his story, trying to make things look better for himself, even though Mary had the drop on me and presumably was going to kill me before long. That meant doubt had fogged whatever remained of his resolve, or maybe it was just loss of blood.

"You said Hank found the bear," I said. "Which one was that? The one you planted on Paul or the one you planted on me?"

"On you," Morton said.

"Why me?"

"You were too close," Mary said. "We had to do something. And if a bear worked once, it might work again. We were hoping it would hurt you badly enough so you would have to quit and go somewhere else."

"You didn't want it to kill me?"

"Not really."

I wanted to believe that. Maybe it was true. "I don't know whether to be disappointed or pleased."

"You're a nice guy, Steve. You're just in over your head."

The room fell silent. There seemed to be nothing more to say.

A pickup door slammed loudly outside.

Mary turned to the door, the muzzle of the .357 in her hand following her eyes. That was a mistake.

51 I leaped, aiming my head at her lower right rib cage as I reached for the Magnum with my left hand. Whether by design or by blind luck, my aim—and my timing—was perfect. The collision scattered furniture in a clatter across the room. The wind whooshed out of Mary as I tore the revolver from her hand just as she bounced against the wall and collapsed, struggling for air. Before she hit the floor I had wrested the Beretta from her belt.

I am not that fast. I will always believe that something good, something honorable, rose from her heart and told her to slow down, to allow me the advantage, to end it.

"Steve! Are you all right?"

Bright sunlight diffused Ginny's trim form in the doorway, but there was no mistaking the sharp outline of the saddle carbine at her shoulder, eye steady on the sights and the muzzle locked on Mary. Behind her loomed Stan Maki, his big-bore rifle on Morton.

"What did you hear?" I said, puffing, still winded from my exertions.

"Plenty," said Stan.

"How long were you out there?"

"No more than five minutes," Ginny said, "but enough to know what happened at Big Trees last month and twenty years ago."

"Smart move, slamming that door."

"Stan's idea," Ginny said.

I shot her a "what the hell do you think you're doing?" look.

She smiled back sweetly.

Mary's breathing had returned to regularity, but she was sobbing. I helped her, tears streaming down her face, into a chair.

"There's a hard way, and there's an easy way, Mary. You're a cop. You know that." I kept my tone as gentle and sympathetic as I could. "Despite what you've done, there was a reason, and I think that reason may help you. If you cooperate, I'll do my best with the prosecutor."

"My life is over anyway," she said.

"Maybe not," I said.

"Okay." She nodded.

Stan harrumphed.

"What got into you, Garrett?" he said disgustedly. "I trusted you."

Morton gazed dumbly at his boss from the floor. His bleeding had long stopped and so had his whimpering, replaced by an expression of confused incredulity. He didn't answer.

"It's time to go in and get that leg taken care of," I said. "Ginny, would you call the department on the CB and get the ambulance and some backup out here? Oh, never mind. I'll do it."

I reached Koski. "This is Steve," I said. "Put Gil on."

The undersheriff's voice crackled over the radio. "What's going on?"

I took a deep breath and told O'Brien where I was. "There's been a firefight and a shooting, and it also involves two murders."

"Of whom?"

"Paul Passoja and Hank Heikkila."

"Who're the killers?"

"Garrett Morton. And Marjorie Passoja. And"—I hesitated for a moment—"Deputy Larch."

"Holy shit!"

There was a moment of shocked silence, then Gil said, "I'm going to take a chance and believe you, Steve."

"Thanks," I replied. "I'll explain the whole thing when I get back. Now send somebody out to bring in Marjorie Passoja, will you?"

"I'll go myself."

The radio clicked off. I hoped Gil would reach Marjorie before the whole eavesdropping county showed up to watch the arrest.

Thirty minutes after I made the call, two squad cars carrying the department's three remaining deputies—swiftly called in from their off-duty pursuits—and the Porcupine County ambulance arrived.

Quickly I filled in the deputies, and they gently but firmly placed

Mary, docile and handcuffed, into the backseat of a squad for the trip to town.

"I'm really very sorry, Mary," I said before the door closed on her. "Up to this you were a good cop." She nodded stonily.

"How did you find out, Steve?" she said.

"It was that piece of bacon I found by the tent," I said. "I didn't think Passoja was so far gone in Alzheimer's that he'd forget old habits that easily."

"Bacon?" Morton cut in from the stretcher as the paramedics carried him by. "I dripped a few spots of grease on the tent, but there weren't no pieces of bacon in it." He was too dense to understand he was digging his hole even deeper.

Ginny and I stared at each other. Paul Passoja *had* helped do himself in. Fogged by dementia, he had spilled his supper on his tent. Life is full of little ironies.

52 As usual, Eli Garrow cheerfully tried to take as much credit as he could. Honeyed "we," "my deputy," and "my department" dripped from his lips as he held forth to the press from all over Michigan, Minnesota, and Wisconsin, crowded into the sheriff's tiny squadroom. He had dressed the place for the occasion. A fat little spruce, ten times the size of the one on Joe Koski's desk, squatted in the corner and a huge cardboard cutout MERRY CHRISTMAS had magically appeared on a wall. Eli the old pol was at work, and the reporters looked about and jotted in their notebooks what they saw.

At "we dug out the cancer in our midst" I tuned him out. Sooner or later the reporters would work it out for themselves.

Gil O'Brien wasn't fooled. After I had handed in my report, Mary had signed her confession and both Marjorie and Morton had lawyered up, the former with a nationally famous criminal defender and the latter with a high-powered Detroit attorney—thanks to the fast footwork of his well-connected father—the undersheriff shot me an "I'll deal with you later" look.

But both he and I knew I wasn't in for more than a pro forma tongue-lashing in his office. Nothing neutralizes the consequences for what we might call "procedural irregularities" like solid results.

And the outcome was not in doubt. Shortly after the news broke, spreading like a shockwave across Porcupine City thanks to the CB conversation I had had with Gil, one of Mary's sister Girl Scouts came forward, saying she'd testify that she'd been molested by Passoja, too, now that death had muffled his power to hurt anyone. Garner Armstrong, visibly moved by her story and those of Mary and Marjorie, hinted broadly that he'd plea-bargain the charges against the women, maybe to aggravated manslaughter, especially if they cooperated in the case against Morton. The women would have to do time, but with good behavior they'd be paroled in a few years. There would be no further career in law enforcement for Mary, but I thought that with her drive and intelligence she'd succeed somewhere. I hoped Marjorie and her lawyer would see the light and take a plea, too.

Morton, however, was lucky that Michigan did not have the death penalty. He was looking at life without parole for murder one for the Heikkila killing as well as long sentences for murder two in the Passoja death and attempted murder on the deck of my cabin. Almost as an afterthought there was that marijuana patch. He didn't have a prayer.

As for Ginny, in midafternoon she and I drove out of Porcupine City, the first few miles in silence. Then I couldn't stand it anymore.

"Whatever possessed you to come out to Morton's cabin?" I demanded. "You're not a trained cop! You could've been killed!"

"Is that a thank-you?" Ginny replied. "If so, you're welcome."

"I'm sorry," I said. "I just can't stand the idea of you getting hurt."

"Oh, Steve," she said, as if I were a small boy. "I shot my first deer when I was fourteen. Dressed it, too. I've seen blood, and I've spilled it."

Ginny placed her hand on mine. "I'm not stupid, though. When I saw Mary driving hell-for-leather west on M-64 this morning, I guessed where she was heading, and I figured you needed the cavalry. I called Stan and filled him in on the way. He never doubted me, not for a moment."

At that I had to chuckle. "Cavalry. The cavalry rescuing the Sioux."

"You'd have been up that famous creek without a paddle, just like Custer at the Little Bighorn."

I sighed and inclined my head toward her. "Yes. Thank you."

"You're welcome again."

My mind drifted to the twenty-fifth of June in the year 1876, and to Crazy Horse, Sitting Bull, Two Moon, and Gall, the Lakota allies who had waited patiently for the Seventh U.S. Cavalry to blunder into the trap they had laid.

"My people called it the Battle of the Greasy Grass."

Ginny glanced at me. "Your people?"

"Yes. At the moment I'm feeling like a victorious warrior. But ask me again tomorrow."

Then I started. "Hey! We're forgetting something!"

"What?"

I told her about the little bear in the cage out at Morton's cabin. I'd forgotten all about it during the excitement of the morning. "We've got to go out and let it loose."

"Yep."

53

"It's so darling," Ginny said as we contemplated the little bear. It sat in a corner of the cage, seemingly contemplating us in the same way.

"Stand aside and I'll open the door," I said.

Then I had second thoughts. "This bear has been around people a lot," I said. "What do you think will happen to it?"

"A hunter will kill it next season, probably. Or, if it's lucky, it'll become a garbage bear and get killed the year after that."

"I don't want that to happen."

"Why?"

"I owe it my life."

"You do?"

I explained. "We could relocate it."

"Where?" she said dubiously. "There isn't really anyplace in Upper Michigan where hunters don't go."

"How about the Boundary Waters Wilderness?" That's the back country of northeastern Minnesota, just around the western corner of Lake Superior.

"Hunter's paradise."

"Hmm."

"Steve, I've got an idea. Ever hear of the Red Lake Reservation?"

"That's in northern Minnesota, isn't it?"

"Yes. The Ojibwa who own it don't hunt bear there, I know that for sure. It's a big place, more than eight hundred thousand acres of woods and swamp. This little guy would have a better-than-even chance of growing up to be a big bear there."

"We'd never get the permits." We'd need one from the State of Michigan to remove the bear, one from Wisconsin to transport it across the state, one from Minnesota to accept it, as well as veterinary documents and God knows what else.

"Somehow, Steve, I don't think that'll stop you." She was right. I wasn't a stickler for proper procedure. I'd gotten away with it once and I'd get away with it again, or so I hoped.

"Or you."

"I'm in," she said, and hugged me. "Now I've got to make a call. I've got a friend on the reservation."

Luckily Morton's camp stood on a rise high enough to be within cell phone range. The connection was weak, but good enough.

Ginny turned off the phone. "She knows exactly where to let the bear go."

"She?"

"Old college friend."

"Is there anybody you don't know?"

"Probably not."

"How long does it take to get there?"

"It's three hundred fifty miles. About eight hours."

"But how are we going to smuggle the bear all that distance cross-country? My Jeep isn't big enough."

"We'll use my van," she said. "I've got a traveling cage big enough for two or three dogs. The bear will fit into it with room to spare."

"Hope we don't get caught." I said. I didn't relish the thought of tangling with Gil O'Brien, let alone the natural resources departments of three states.

"You leave that to me."

Within an hour I'd dropped off the Jeep at my cabin, called Joe Koski to tell him I'd be out of touch for a while, and returned with Ginny in the Historical Society's van. We'd removed the two rear seats from it to fit in the rusting dog cage, one of the society's enormous pile of useless gifts donated by people who thought they had value just because they were old.

"You don't think the society will mind?" I asked. "Isn't it supposed to be in the Christmas parade tomorrow?"

"It won't know a thing," Ginny replied. "With luck we'll be back in time. Besides, I gave it the van."

"Do you have a dog tranquilizer in that mighty kit bag of yours?" I asked. "How are we going to get him into the cage without getting an arm or two ripped off?"

Out of a paper bag Ginny pulled a bottle of Dramamine and a baggie of raw hamburger. "My dad used this to sedate his Labs for long car trips," she said. "Puts them right to sleep for a few hours. We'll give it a fifty milligram pill, the same standard human adult dose Dad used on his dogs."

I was dubious, but she was right. Within fifteen minutes after we dosed him, we'd coaxed the woozy little bear from its enclosure into the smaller cage and lifted it with two mighty grunts into the rear of the van. Small as the animal was, it was round and fully packed, ready for hibernation, and had to weigh at least 150 pounds. Fortunately it was cooperative, moving when we wanted it to, and once the cage was man-handled into the van it settled down and fell soundly asleep.

"That bear really is trusting," Ginny said.

"Yeah. See what I mean?"

"One more thing," Ginny said, disappearing behind a tree. I went back to the enclosure, scooped up a bucket of dog chow and a bucket of water, and placed them inside the cage, covering it with a ratty old army blanket. The little bear didn't stir.

Ginny returned and we gingerly shut the van's rear doors, careful not to wake up our cargo.

"Let's go," she said, glancing at her watch. "It's four o'clock. If we don't stop except for gas, we should be there by midnight."

54

For the first four hours we made good time on U.S. 2, the northernmost national highway. I carefully stayed at or slightly below the speed limit, hoping not to provoke police curiosity. Underneath the army blanket the bear slept quietly, now and then stirring and huffing gently, like a teakettle on low heat. It sounded to me as if he was just trying to be companionable.

Early into the trip a rank smell wafted up from the rear of the van, and I turned up the fan and cracked the driver's window to the cold air outside.

"That little bear speaks softly and carries a big stink, doesn't he?" I observed.

Ginny chuckled throatily. I didn't envy her the job of cleaning up the van once we had returned. We'd spread a plastic tarp over the floor of the van and shoveled in sawdust from my woodpile, but that smell was the kind that penetrates and hangs around for weeks.

Night had just fallen as we were rolling out of Duluth at eight o'clock, the town's Christmas lights fading in the distance, when a siren screamed and blue beams flashed in the rearview mirrors. I checked the speedometer. Forty-eight miles per hour, and we were in a fifty-mile-per-hour zone.

"Shit," I said. "Driving While Indian." Many cops in states with large reservations profile Indian drivers, especially after dark, partly because of widespread alcoholism and drunken driving and partly because they don't like Indians in general. Several times since my boyhood I'd been stopped just because a cop took exception to my looks.

I pulled over and the Minnesota trooper nosed his cruiser behind the van.

"License and registration, please." He was polite enough.

I handed them over and showed my star.

"On the job, deputy?"

"Not really."

He chuckled, but it was a friendly sound. "Bit out of your jurisdiction, eh?"

I relaxed. I wasn't going to be asked to step out of the van and walk a straight line.

"I was wondering what a commercial van with Michigan plates was doing in Minnesota, that's all," the trooper said.

Sure.

"What's in there, anyway?" Brother officer or not, he was still doing his job.

Damn.

"A bear," Ginny piped up. "We're transporting a young bear to Redby."

I shot her an "I hope you know what you're doing" glance.

"No kidding?" The trooper peered into the back. "Can I have a look?"

Legally we weren't obligated to open the van, but if we refused, the trooper would interpret that as a suspicious act and keep us there until another brought a warrant.

I got out, opened the rear doors, and pulled aside the army blanket. The bear, having been awakened by the small commotion, stuck a wet nose through the bars and wiggled it quizzically.

"Cute little guy, even if he kinda smells," said the trooper. "I suppose you got papers."

Busted! I thought.

"Right." said Ginny. "You want to see 'em?"

I tried not to gape at her.

"Why not?" the trooper said.

"Just a sec." She rummaged in the back of the van and returned with a large plastic Ziploc bag containing a thick, brown-spattered manila envelope. She opened the bag. The odor that had followed us all across Michigan and Wisconsin suddenly billowed into an unbearably intense cloud. My eyes watered. The trooper took a step backward as if stunned.

"What the hell is that?"

"I'm sorry," Ginny said. "I accidentally dropped the papers into poop when we were putting him into the van. They're pretty gross, aren't they?" She opened the flap of the envelope.

"Never mind, never mind," said the trooper, hand to his mouth. He took several steps to the side of the road and breathed deeply. "I don't know what that bear's been eating, but he's not fit for polite company."

"I'm sorry," Ginny said again, a winsome expression on her face.

"Have a good trip," said the trooper suddenly, spinning on his heel and returning to his cruiser with as much dignity as he could muster. Then he laughed.

"I hope you make it before that stink kills you."

"So do I," I said. I wasn't sure we would get there. My knees had grown weak.

The cruiser's blue lights snapped off and the trooper wheeled around in a U-turn, unnecessarily tossing gravel, heading back to Duluth.

Ginny tossed the noisome mess back into the plastic bag and zipped it shut.

"Get rid of that," I suggested.

"No. We might need it again," she said.

"That's not bear crap, is it?"

"No. It's liquid hog manure. There was a jar of it at Garrett's place. He'd been using it to fertilize the marijuana."

"You're brilliant."

"Aren't I?" she said. "Now move over. I'll drive the rest of the way."

55

Just before midnight we arrived in Redby, the largest village in the reservation belonging to the Red Lake Band of the Ojibwa Nation. I'd returned to the wheel an hour before when Ginny began to nod.

"Pull up at that filling station," she said. "We're being met there."

A strikingly good-looking, brown-skinned woman in denims, long dark hair pulled into Indian braids, stood in the light of the doorway. NOEL winked in neon above it. "Ginny?" she called.

"Sheila!" The two women embraced, laughing. "It's been years!"

"This is Steve Martinez," Ginny said. "Sheila Prudhomme. My college roommate."

Sheila extended a graceful hand. "I've heard a lot about you," she said. "You're Stevie Two Crow. My Ojibwa name is Standing Deer, but they call me Runs With Scissors."

Ginny laughed. "Sheila's a kindergarten teacher in the reservation schools. It was a joke but it just stuck."

"Let's have a look at the bear," Sheila said.

I opened the rear doors and pulled back the blanket. Sheila bent close and whispered something in Ojibwa. The bear chuckled happily and stood up. I quailed as she extended her fingers through the steel mesh and wiggled them. That's a good way to lose a pinky. Bears, after all, are wild animals. But he just licked Sheila's fingers.

She saw my concerned glance. "I wouldn't do this with just any bear," she said. "But it's okay with this one. My people and I have a special relationship with bears."

She didn't explain, but shined a penlight into the bear's eyes and examined them intently.

"That's a cute face," she said. "He looks healthy. Tell me about him."

I did, keeping the story as brief as I could.

Sheila nodded slowly. "A very good reason to let him go free here. It's important to us."

"Why?"

"I'll explain on the way."

We climbed into the front seat of the van, Ginny in the middle and Sheila on the right. Immediately Sheila pulled a U.S. Geodetic Survey topographic map from her jacket and switched on the dome light.

"See, this dirt road goes to the northwestern corner of the reservation. That's where we take problem bears when they get too close to people. It's far enough away so that they don't often return. We'll let him go there." She pointed at a spot near a small lake.

I nosed the van onto the gravel track.

"Now, Steve," Sheila said as the van nosed through the night, brilliant light from its headlamps boring under the canopy of leafless branches over the road, "there are seven clans in the Red Lake Band, each named for an animal indigenous to the reservation. My family is a member of the Bear Clan. It is against our belief for any member of the Bear Clan to hunt, kill, or eat bear. We save them whenever we can. That, according to our tradition, is a holy deed. They trust us, and we trust them. Most of the time, anyway. There are exceptions sometimes."

For an instant I heard an echo from Professor Bill Ursuline's office.

"What about the other clans?" I asked. "Are they bound not to hunt bears?"

"No," Sheila said. "But in practice we all respect each other's clan animals. It's part of how we get along. This is a very poor reservation, and we need to keep our ties with each other to survive. Yes, there are casinos, but we're a long way from the interstate highways, so they don't produce a lot of money."

I was silent for a while, absorbing the information. Then I nudged Ginny. "No wonder you suggested this place."

It was two in the morning when we arrived at the spot on the map.

Swiftly the three of us pulled the cage from the van and set it on the ground by the side of the track. We looked at each other and nodded.

"Let me," Sheila said. She opened the cage door. Calmly the little bear emerged, walking unhurriedly to the tree line. The Dramamine had worn off hours before. It stopped and peered around.

Softly Sheila began chanting in Ojibwa. The bear watched her intently, and when she was finished it glanced at Ginny, then me, and swiftly disappeared into the brush.

"It's way past time for him to den," Sheila said. "Not far from here there's a ridge with a lot of downed pines. He'll find a warm spot to hibernate in one of the deep root holes."

I looked up at the sky. The new December moon shone brilliantly and the stars twinkled. In the north I found Ursa Major and watched as the dark veil of an oncoming front from the northwest that extended from horizon to horizon slowly extinguished its starlight.

"A snowstorm's on the way," Sheila said, shivering.

"I hope so," Ginny said.

56 Within an hour we had returned to Redby. "Come on in," Sheila said as we arrived at the filling station, "and have some coffee before hitting the road."

We entered and Sheila opened a door to a back room. Inside, under a grimy wall festooned with greasy gas station girlie calendars, sat four Ojibwa, three men of middle age and one an ancient, playing penny-ante poker around a cracked oaken table so decrepit that it looked as if it must have arrived on the reservation with fur traders two centuries before. Perry Como was singing a Christmas medley from a boom box atop a stack of old tires.

"My brother Jack," she said, introducing the biggest. "He owns this place." Jack stood politely. Like me, he was tall for an Indian, with yard-wide shoulders, and he wore his hair like his sister, in braids.

"Mike and George and Grandfather," Sheila added. "Meet Steve Two Crow. He's Lakota."

Mike and George nodded gravely, but Grandfather stood, muttered something sternly in Ojibwa, gestured at the roof, and stalked out of the room.

"What did he say?" I asked.

"He said, 'Don't let the Lakota leave this room alive,' " Jack said, his expression stony.

"Jack!" Sheila punched her brother in the shoulder. "Stop that!"

Jack threw back his head and laughed gleefully. "He actually said, 'I'm going to bed. Don't wake me before noon.' " The big Ojibwa extended his hand. "We're honored to have you. Have a cuppa."

Mike and George made room, shoving aside stacks of bald tires, and we all sat. Sheila told the others what we had been doing that night.

"Well," Jack said, "that bear sounds like a peace offering."

I looked at him quizzically.

"Did you know, Steve, that in the year 1765 just a few miles from here at the mouth of the Sandy River, the Ojibwa and the Sioux fought their last battle, and you guys left these parts for the Dakotas and became horse Indians?"

"I admit I wondered how you'd feel about a Lakota coming onto the Rez."

"Oh, all that happened a long time ago," said Jack. "Now we Indians have to stick together against the whites." He winked at Ginny. "Present company excepted, naturally."

"It's after three," Ginny said presently. "Time to go. If we keep driving, we'll make the Christmas parade."

We all stood. Jack laid an enormous hand on my shoulder.

"Stevie Two Crow, on behalf of the Red Lake Band of the Ojibwa Nation, I appoint you a honorary member of the Bear Clan." There was no levity in his voice, only gravity.

"Hear, hear," said Mike and George, thumping the table. Sheila clapped.

"I mean it," Jack said. "*Mii-gwech*. That's Ojibwa for 'Thank you.' "

Sheila hugged Ginny and me warmly, as if she had known us all her life, and we set off into the night.

57

A blinding light, then a clearing in the forest. In it a gigantic bear, a good thirty feet tall, sat on its haunches.

"Stevie Two Crow," it said benevolently.

I gaped. The bear spoke in a rolling, sonorous voice that sounded as if it had come out of Harlem by way of an Italian opera. I could think of nothing but De Lawd in *The Green Pastures*, Marc Connelly's once beloved but now hopelessly dated Negro spiritual play from the 1930s.

"Thank you, bro, for bringing Little Bear back to us."

"You're welcome."

"That was a very Indian thing to do, you know," the bear said.

"But I'm not really that much of an Indian."

"Oh, you are, more than you know."

"How?"

"It's hard to explain. Indian-ness is a state of mind more than it is a state of being, if you get my drift."

"I'm confused. People think I'm Indian but I was brought up white. I think white, even when I want to be an Indian."

"*You're* confused? I'm a bear but I think like a human. Talk about fish out of water, excuse the metaphor."

"What am I supposed to do?"

The bear shrugged. "Who knows? You'll find a way. Maybe you've found it and don't know it yet."

"You're not sure?"

"I'm only a bear. I'm not God, or even a shrink."

"I thought maybe you were one of those."

"See? We're never what others expect us to be."

"Yeah, but . . ."

"Look. You just solved a mystery and brought three criminals to justice. Doesn't that count for something? Makes you a pretty good deputy sheriff, in my opinion."

"Thank you. But that's only part of me."

"Feeling fragmented, are we?"

"Yes. I'd like to be more of a Lakota than I am."

"Then you'll have to consult a Lakota spiritual advisor. I'm not licensed in that department. I'm only a paramedic, so to speak."

"Why did you call me into your presence, then?"

"Who says I did?" said the bear. "It's *your* dream. You conjured me, not the other way around."

He was right.

"What am I doing here, anyway?" I asked plaintively.

"Finding your way, of course. It's a process, not a phenomenon."

"You do sound like a shrink."

"Now, now. Just think of me as a guide."

"What's your advice? If you have any."

"Just this: You're doing fine. Go home and carry on. And cherish that Ginny. She's a keeper."

"That she is, that's for sure."

The bear elaborately consulted a pocket watch with a face the size of a kitchen clock.

"I've got a dinner date," the bear said, "with three of your kind. I never look forward to it, but tomorrow is always another day. Ta-ta."

Just before the bright light again flooded my eyes, the bear said: "*Mii-gwech*, Stevie Two Crow."

58

"Did you know that you talk in your sleep?" said Ginny from behind the wheel as I came awake. Day had broken and the van's headlights punched weakly through heavy, driving snow. A good six inches had fallen, and more was on the way. Through the thick white veil I could make out a line of taillights, some of them on snowmobile trailers and some of them on SUVs bearing skis on their roofs.

"Where are we? What time is it? What did I say?"

"We've just entered Michigan, and it's almost noon," Ginny said. "You've been sleeping for six hours, and you didn't make much sense."

"I just had the weirdest dream," I said. "I was talking to an enormous bear that sounded like James Earl Jones."

"What happened?"

"I don't know exactly," I said, "but it wasn't a nightmare at all. In fact, I feel pretty good."

"I know. You were grinning in your sleep."

"Somebody's been doing the Heikki Lunta," I said with a chuckle. "The gods have been listening. Looks like this is going to be a big snow."

With a start I realized that from a certain point of view, what I had been doing the last twelve hours was itself a kind of propitiation, unconscious as it may have been. I kicked myself mentally. What a preposterous notion. But then it started to grow on me. Who can explain spirituality, anyway?

"Hey, slow down!" The snow tumbled down so thickly we could see barely fifty yards ahead. Ginny braked gently, keeping the van in its lane.

"We'll just make the parade," she said.

We didn't stop at our respective cabins, but kept on into Porcupine City, where at the river bridge late in the afternoon the first marchers and floats of the Christmas parade were about to step off for the quarter-mile-long trek down Main Street. Right in front of our van Santa sat atop the cab of the town's big yellow pumper, PORCUPINE COUNTY VOLUNTEER FIRE DEPARTMENT emblazoned on its doors. Through the fake beard I saw the cherubic cheeks of Dudley Richardson, the fire chief. He waved cheerily at us.

"'Bout time you showed up!" said Joe Koski, resplendent in dress uniform, clipboard, and pencil. "We thought you'd run off for the weekend after all that excitement yesterday."

"Something like that," I said.

"Just a sec," said Joe. With duct tape he affixed large cardboard signs to the van's front doors.

"What do they say?"

"Get out and take a look."

HONORARY PARADE MARSHALS, said the sign. MERRY CHRISTMAS FROM STEVE AND GINNY, PORCUPINE COUNTY'S WORLD-FAMOUS DETECTIVES.

"Aww," I said. Ginny's eyes glistened.

"I really shouldn't tell you," said Joe, who never in his life had failed to tell anyone anything they shouldn't have been told, "but guess who were going to be the honorary marshals up to yesterday morning?" The Porcupine County parade tradition was for committees to make such announcements on the day of the celebrations.

"No!" said Ginny, "You're putting us on!" She is a lot quicker on the uptake than I am.

"Yep. Larch and Passoja."

My jaw dropped, then closed in a broad grin. That did make sense. The two women had done the county a great good in their work with the Andie Davis Home. And some might say they had done the county an even greater good by relieving it of Paul Passoja, but I was not about to debate, even with myself, such moral relativities. I was enjoying Joe's unexpected irony too much.

"Go say hello to your fans," Joe said, wrinkling his nose as he took in a sudden whiff of pig poop. "*Where* have you b—"

Ginny drove on before he could finish the question.

As the snow diminished into a few huge flakes parachuting slowly through the air, we drove down Main Street at a stately pace, waving to the crowds under the Christmas lights. The stores stood open, their windows packed with holiday decorations, some of them seasonal and some of them religious. Crowds lined the curbs. I'd never seen so many people at a Porcupine County Fourth of July parade, and this is highly patriotic country.

Christmas hymns filled the downtown air from the chimes in the steeple of the First Methodist Church on the east side of town. Old holiday standards boomed from the exterior speakers on Ulla's Antiques in midtown. Inside the North Woods Bank next door glittered a huge Christmas tree, a six-foot-high pile of gift-wrapped packages before it. I smiled. The St. Nicholas Project was at work. Run by civic-minded folks with assorted affiliations, it placed trees inside the banks of the town. To the trees the St. Nicks affixed paper mittens, each containing the sex and age of a needy child and a suggested gift—and there were hundreds of them—to be plucked by bank patrons and replaced with presents.

In front of the bank a uniformed Salvation Army officer imported from Houghton swung a handbell, smiling and nodding as passersby filled his kettle. Men and women on motorcycles zoomed past, bearing stuffed animals for the Marine Corps toy drive.

A small crèche filled the front window of the village hall as it had every Christmas for more than a hundred years. The sight always brought a grin to my face. During the last few years the Wise Men had smiled down on Baby Jesus from under a Star of David, and a menorah, its electric candles alight, stood prominently in one corner of the window. A crescent hung unobtrusively in the other. There wasn't a Jew or a Muslim in town, but the city fathers knew how to appease the American Civil Liberties Union as well as the Lord. No busybody from the big city could possibly complain. Garner Armstrong, who knew his constitutional law, had seen to it.

Seemingly all of Porcupine County had showed up, and much of Gogebic and Iron Counties as well. They were there to cheer on the snow, they were there to cheer on the holiday season, and they, i seemed, were also there to cheer us on because the Passoja case had put the county on everybody's map.

"Steve! Ginny!" the crowd called delightedly as the van passed. I couldn't speak for her, but an odd feeling suddenly crowded my heart. Was I coming home at last?

Not really, I realized suddenly. The sentiment of the moment simply had overtaken me. Tomorrow I'd be the same confused fellow—50 percent white, 50 percent Indian, 100 percent dissatisfied.

"Things could be worse," I heard the Great Bear growling from somewhere deep in my head. "Enjoy the moment, numskull. It's a gift. You want it tinsel-wrapped? Take it or leave it."

I took it, and waved to the crowd. A man in clerical collar, scarlet vest, and tartan slacks waved back. He was Father Ted McGillicuddy, rector of St. Matthew's Episcopal Church, Scotland's most prominent contribution to Porcupine County.

"Hey, Steve!" he called. "We haven't had so much fun since the moose got loose on Main Street!"

With that, a salute of Roman candles shot into the sky from the piers on the nearby Porcupine River, followed by bright, sky-filling starbursts. The crowd cheered. Fireworks for Christmas! Only in the Upper Peninsula . . .

Later, when we pulled into the driveway of my cabin, the front had passed south, opening the skies, and a vermilion scrim wreathed the setting sun. Red squirrels chattered and scolded as they chased one another through the trees, and a woodpecker jackhammered a snag overlooking the snowy beach.

"Ooh . . . a pretty end to a hell of a day," Ginny said with considerable feeling.

In the cabin I opened the freezer, hunting for supper. The little Sucrets tin with the shred of bacon winked at me. I opened it, chuckled, and shook my head. I'd have to file it in the evidence room tomorrow—not that it was going to make a lot of difference to the prosecution.

"Let's not waste that sunset," Ginny said. "Grab the peppermint schnapps, and I'll get a couple of glasses."

"Fine idea," I said. "But there's one more thing I've got to do."

224 * Henry Kisor

"See you in the living room," Ginny said.

I picked up the phone and dialed.

"Merry Christmas, Professor Ursuline," I said when he answered. "Can you spare a few minutes? Got a story to tell you."